I   Nicholl Morgan was a classic crime writer of the forties,
    shing Golden Age mystery novels between 1944 and 1947.
    books were originally published by Macdonald & Co., which
    me Little, Brown Book Group. In 2016, *Another Little Christmas*
    er (1947) was published again, over 60 years after it was written.
    rt from her charming crime novels, little else is known about
I   a Nicholl Morgan. If you do have any more information on
t   author, please contact Little, Brown Book Group.

THE
DEATH BOX

LORNA NICHOLL
MORGAN

sphere

SPHERE

First published in Great Britain in 1946 by Macdonald & Co Ltd
This reissue published in 2017 by Sphere

1 3 5 7 9 10 8 6 4 2

A CIP catalogue record for this book
is available from the British Library.

ISBN 978-0-7515-7089-2

Typeset in Spectrum by M Rules
Printed and bound in Great Britain by
Clays, St Ives plc

Papers used by Sphere are from well-managed forests
and other responsible sources.

Sphere
An imprint of
Little, Brown Book Group
Carmelite House
50 Victoria Embankment
London EC4Y 0DZ

An Hachette UK Company
www.hachette.co.uk

www.littlebrown.co.uk

THE
DEATH BOX

Chapter I

The lady in black was really responsible for the whole affair, according to Joe Trayne's story. He was merely standing, one warm summer night, on the corner of Conduit Street, looking towards Hanover Square, and what he was doing there was his own business, as doubtless he would have told anyone bold enough to enquire. He was dressed unobtrusively, and his only claim to distinction lay in the fact that there were very few people about at that hour. Furthermore, he was lost in thought, profound thought concerning his past, his present and the uncertainty of his future.

And then, quite suddenly, there she was, walking rapidly towards him from the direction of the square, a shadowy figure becoming gradually more distinct, until in the light of a nearby lamp he saw her quite clearly, graceful but sombre, fashionable but aloof, attractive and ... yes, she was rather interesting. He stood motionless, watching her impersonally as she approached, expecting her to pass by, and when she stopped, he could think of no reason for it except that she might be about to hail a taxi. But there was no taxi within hailing distance at that moment.

'Pardon me,' she said, and her voice, in the silence of the street, sounded mournful. 'Are you a police officer?'

He eyed her thoughtfully, her serious, piquant face belied by one of those frivolous little hats which mean so little and cost so much, the fluffy fur about her black velvet costume, her fragile shoes, her stockings. All black, but not a dull and dreary black. Rather was there a dash and sparkle and bravery about her clothes and the way she wore them. He hesitated. Then he deliberately prevaricated. He said,

'Not a member of the uniform branch, Madam. But can I help you?'

In point of fact, he was not a member of any branch. He was a man looking for something to do and not quite certain how to set about it. But he was also a man who never let the opportunity for experience knock in vain, and though a weakness for long-lashed eyes and piquant faces and little hats with floating veils might have had something to do with it, he was no less chivalrous than most.

'If you will,' she said. 'I suppose I should have telephoned the station, but I have no telephone, and I had no change to put in the box.'

'You don't need change to dial fire, police or ambulance,' he pointed out, partly to gain time, and partly because he was beginning to suspect that all was not as it should be. For one wearing all the outer trappings of sophistication, she appeared to be remarkably lacking in common knowledge. Unless. . . . But then she did not look that kind of lady.

She frowned. 'How stupid of me. But one doesn't think of these things in an emergency, does one?'

She had begun to walk slowly back the way she had come, and automatically he fell into step beside her.

'If this is an emergency, Madam,' he said, 'I suggest it might be as well for us to hurry.'

'Oh, but there's no hurry. The man is already dead. I just thought it advisable to report the matter as soon as possible.'

He stopped abruptly, and she paused, too, regarding him with some impatience.

'Now let's get this straight,' he said. 'You've a man on your premises, and he's dead . . . by the way, what made you ask if I was a policeman?'

'You're about the right size. And you were obviously planning whom you were going to arrest next. There's usually a plain-clothes man somewhere around that corner. I always know a policeman when I see one.'

'Oh, you do? Well, now, about this dead man . . . '

'Yes. I thought you could see him first, and make notes and so on, and then take him away, or whatever you usually do. I bought a box . . . ' Her voice had become very mournful again. 'I bought it at a sale a few days ago. A big, antique thing it is, very old. I only opened it just now, and there was this dead person lying inside. It was really most unpleasant.'

'Shattering,' Joe agreed, and then recalling his official role, 'but you don't seem to be very upset, Madam, if I may say so.'

'It's not the first dead man I've seen,' she remarked shortly, and turned into a narrow mews, the buildings on either side of which were shrouded in darkness. As they walked, their footsteps echoed hollowly, his slow and steady and, he hoped, powerful with authority, hers lightly tapping as her heels met the cobble stones. She paused before a door inset beside a garage, and by the light of a street lamp he observed that it was number seven.

'In here,' she said, and bringing from her bag a bunch of keys, she opened the door and stepped inside.

He followed as she switched on the light, to reveal a tiny square lobby and a flight of carpeted stairs leading to the regions above. Unhurriedly she began to ascend, and mounting the stairs behind her, he gave himself up to a beautiful dream, wherein they entered a sumptuously furnished apartment, and turning to him with dewy eyes, she put her arms about his neck and whispered, 'You silly boy, did you really think there was a nasty old body?' Whereupon he replied, 'You silly girl, of course not.'

But there the dream faded, for having arrived in the narrow corridor at the top of the stairs, she guided him into a room, again produced light, and said,

'The rest is up to you. I don't think I can bear to look at him any more.'

Joe took a pace or so forward, and glanced round. The room was well, if not sumptuously, furnished as a lounge, in modern style. For that reason alone the attention would have been caught and held by the handsome oak chest, of obvious antiquity, which stood against the curtained windows. It was a massive thing, more than ample in proportions to house the horrible contents the owner claimed for it.

'What made you buy it?' he asked, being no more eager to view a corpse than are most people at that hour of the night. In any case, he was still by no means sure that this was not just a hoax, or an eccentric woman's idea of passing the time.

'I like antiques,' she said. 'I've collected quite a few pieces lately. I'm hoping to furnish a place of my own soon.'

'Isn't this your flat, then?'

'No, I share it with my sister. She's out at the moment, so she doesn't know about . . . this. Aren't you going to open it?'

'I can hardly wait,' he said, and strode across the room. The lid creaked ominously as he raised it and peered inside. The light, filtering from a reading-lamp on the fireside table, was not very brilliant where he stood, but it cast sufficient illumination for him quickly to make up his mind that what he saw he did not like. Within the murky depths of the chest lay the body of a young man, sprawled on one side as if in uneasy slumber. His arms were outflung, as far as possible within the restrictions of that confined space, his right leg drawn up rigidly. His shadowed face appeared livid in patches, the mouth slack, the eyes closed. Joe, bending over, cautiously touched the stiffened fingers, and drew back from the chill contact with death.

A hand gripped his arm, and he spun round, to find that the girl had moved to join him.

'Horrible, isn't it?' she said.

'Not too good.' She had lowered her voice, and instinctively he did the same. 'Ever seen him before?'

'Never, as far as I remember.'

'I shouldn't think you'd have much difficulty about that. Even dead, he's better looking than most of us.' Inconsequently, he was wondering whether the young man's eyes would be as dark as his crisply curling hair. His clothes looked expensive, but rather flashy, and on the little finger of his right hand he wore a gold signet ring.

'Shouldn't you try and identify him?' the girl suggested.

'At a glance,' Joe said, 'I'd put him as a medium successful gangster. Or else a damned good actor. And however he died, it wasn't just a nice, straightforward scene with his relatives at his bedside.' Then seeing her regarding him strangely, he added, 'But that's not my line. I must get assistance.'

Decisively he closed down the lid and turned away. At that moment he did not so much need assistance as a drink. Something potent, something powerful enough to take the atmosphere of death out of his nostrils. Death was unpleasant enough in an appropriate setting, but he had not seriously bargained for it as an end to this adventure. He was all for getting away from it as soon as possible. But the face of the girl, against the darkness of her hair, looked pale and ill. He said,

'Sit down and have a cigarette. No, not here. You've got another room, haven't you?'

'Of course.' Her glance flickered in the direction of the box and back to him. 'But what about that?'

Joe shrugged. 'I'm in no hurry, and he's beyond it. And if I've got to hear more about this, we'd better have some space and air. Let's go.'

'There's only the kitchen,' she said. 'Apart from our bedrooms, and the bathroom.'

'Make it the kitchen,' he decided. 'I could do with a nice glass of ice-cold water.'

But when they had repaired to the tiny kitchen on the other side of the passage, and she actually drew a glass of water and handed it to him in silence, he made a mental note never again to crack a joke with someone who didn't know him. She sat down on one of the plain wooden chairs and accepted the cigarette he offered, and he observed, as he lighted it for her, that she handled it as if it might explode in her face. Not, he concluded, an habitual smoker, which he thought rather odd for a Londoner. Lighting one for himself, he said, 'I'd better have your name,' and brought out his address book and pencil. But she had lifted a warning hand in the attitude of one listening.

'Didn't you hear something?' she whispered.

'Such as what?'

'A scratching sound. It came from in there, I think.' She motioned with her head in the direction of the lounge, and her eyes were fearful.

'Nerves,' he scoffed, and added, with growing impatience, 'Are we going to get on with this investigation or not?'

'Of course. But I can't think of anything else while . . . Oh, *please* go and see. It might be just the cat trying to get in.'

'He'll hear from me if it is,' Joe threatened, and replacing his book and pencil, he went out to make a thorough tour of the apartment, from the front door, on the other side of which the mews lay silent and deserted, to the sitting-room, the bathroom and one bedroom. The other room was locked. There was no sign of a cat, and no sound of scratching. Neither was there any sign of the young lady when he returned to the kitchen. Even her handbag, and the cigarette she had been smoking, had disappeared with her.

He made a systematic inspection of the room, and as far as he could see there was no means of entrance or exit other than the door through which he had just passed. There was only one window, not overlarge, and with a sheer drop of some twenty feet to the ground below. The walls of the kitchen were tiled, the centre of the floor covered by a square of drugget, with the wooden surround stained and polished. There were three cupboards, all of which proved empty save for their rightful contents of food, china, cooking and cleaning utensils.

Conscious of rising irritability, Joe flung the remainder of his cigarette on the ground and stamped it out, then on second thoughts picked it up and hurled it as far as possible through the open window. There was, he decided, only one possible solution. While he had been peering out of the front door in search of a mythical cat, she had retired to the second bedroom and locked herself in. Perhaps, he thought, studying himself in a wall mirror, he was more sinister in appearance than he had imagined. Either that, or he was dealing with a particularly difficult type of mental case.

7

He left the kitchen, satisfied himself that the other rooms were still uninhabited, with the exception of the box and its occupant in the lounge, and hammered furiously upon the door locked against him. This was no time for timid rappings and tappings. Either she wanted his help or she didn't, and in the latter case he would not be sorry to depart. The sound of his fist beating the woodwork echoed away into silence. There was no light showing beneath the door, and nothing to suggest that he was not alone.

'Is anyone in there?' he called, and the foolishness of the query and of the whole situation hit him with sudden force. If she wasn't in there, she must be a figment of his imagination, and he was fast qualifying for a mental home himself. What was he doing here, anyway, he wondered? It was really no business of his that a young man was lying dead in someone else's lounge. Upon an impulse, he turned away and began to descend the stairs.

'She can damned well play Little Miss Muffet on her own,' he said aloud. 'I'm going to get a drink.'

Yet as he stepped out into the mews and closed the front door, his relief at contact with the cool night air was tempered with dissatisfaction. He was not in the habit of leaving anything unfinished.

At the end of the mews he paused long enough to identify it, before rounding the bend, and sighting a taxi, hailed it and drove to the Allsorts, a night club in which he had an interest. That his interest at the moment should be merely financial was also a source of dissatisfaction to him. There had been a time when he had shared his partner's enthusiasm for this very lucrative venture, but though night life was still an intrinsic part of his existence, of late it had palled, and he was oppressed by a feeling of futility. Furthermore, he had formed no positive idea as to what he might do about it.

The problem had again taken uppermost place in his mind as he paid off the taxi outside the Sleigh Street entrance to the Allsorts, off Piccadilly, and went inside to discover Clock, the doorman, exhibiting all the usual signs of a man about to close down after a full night's work. No one quite knew why he should be called Clock, except that he had a round, smooth face and a very bald head, and could guess the time to within a minute either way at any hour of the day or night.

'Just off?' Joe asked, pausing in the carpeted corridor to light a cigarette.

'That's right, Mr Trayne.' Clock grinned widely as he struggled into his coat and clapped a hat down firmly upon his head. Seen thus, he did not look much more than thirty, although he was well past fifty, as he was never tired of telling anyone who would listen. 'Been crowded out this evening. Taken a heap of oof, too, I can tell you.'

This was no news, since there very seldom passed an evening when they were not crowded to suffocation point. And if ever the dismal time did arrive when Clock failed to take plenty of oof from someone, Joe had no illusions that their ingenuous-faced doorman could shortly after be numbered among the missing.

'Good.' Joe grinned back. 'Is Mr Pierce still around?'

'He's inside,' Clock said. 'He told me I could go.'

Joe nodded. 'That's the idea. You pop off and rest your beautiful eyes. We'll see everything's locked up.'

'Thanks, Mr Trayne. Good night. See you tomorrow.'

Joe wished, as he said good night and made his way into the interior, that the doorman and others of his acquaintance were not quite so given to ritual. There was something about that phrase, 'See you tomorrow', used invariably night after night, that irritated him. It gave him the unpleasant feeling of restriction, as if

9

his life had been worked out for him to a stultifying routine, with Clock making certain that he kept to it.

He found his partner, Wallace Pierce, seated at a table on the far side of the dance floor, apparently oblivious to the upturned chairs upon surrounding tables, the lowered lights, the general atmosphere of desolation. He had a bottle of whisky and two glasses in front of him, and he was reading *The Ringside Reporter* with close attention. Nearing sixty, he was a tall, spare man, with grey, closely curling hair, and a face so tired that it gave one the impression he was about to collapse from sheer fatigue. He was well aware of it, and maintained it was good for business, on the theory that people gave one look at his face and felt themselves to be twenty years younger in comparison.

He raised his head as Joe approached, and regarded him over the top of steel-rimmed spectacles.

'I thought you'd be along,' he said, indicating the second glass. 'Been having fun?'

'Loads,' Joe said, drawing up a chair and seating himself. 'My throat's as dry as hell and I've just shaken hands with a dead man. So stimulating.'

He reached for the bottle, poured himself a large measure of whisky, and began to drink. Two waiters, carrying laden trays, crossed the room and disappeared through the service door. Mr Pierce raised an eyebrow, said, 'Oh?' and flicked over a page of his paper. But this blasé acceptance of his statement was no more than Joe expected, for he had never yet seen his partner exhibit much in the way of excitement or emotion of any kind. Energy, loyalty, dogged persistence and business acumen were all part of his make-up, but emotion never entered into any of his dealings or his conversation. He accepted life for the rough and tumble affair he had always known it, and liked it no less for that.

Stubbing out his cigarette, Joe remarked, 'Well, if that's all you've got to say, Wally, we may as well talk of something else. Anyone interesting been in?'

'No one you'd find interesting,' Wally said.

'What makes you think that?'

'I don't think it, I know it. The way you've been acting lately, if I put on Helen of Troy as a cabaret turn, you'd snore right through it.'

'Probably,' Joe agreed, refilling his glass. Wally eyed him speculatively and said, 'You're pretty thirsty, aren't you?'

'I told you, I've never needed a drink more in my life.'

Wally smiled, and when he did that, his wide mouth creased the whole of the left side of his face, causing him to look more tired than ever.

'It's a funny thing, Joe,' he said. 'When anything happens to you, it's news. If it happens to anyone else, it's just a bore.'

'Isn't that true of everyone?'

'Not me. Nothing ever happens to me, thank God. I'm beyond the age. Come on, then, let's have it.'

Joe was silent for a while, staring thoughtfully into the contents of his glass as it caught the light of the single lamp standing between them on the table. He said suddenly,

'I'm thinking of joining the Police Force.'

'Oh?' Wally said. 'Sundays and afternoons?'

'No, full time.'

'Oh,' Wally said again. He brought out a gold case, lighted a cigarette and inhaled with the air of one who smokes from habit rather than for pleasure. 'What do you want, exercise? You look pretty fit to me, though I can't think why. How old are you now?'

'Twenty-nine. Do you mind?'

'Not a bit. It's a damned silly age but we've all got to pass

11

through it. Things have changed, though. When I was thirty, I was all for joining the Foreign Legion. What's her name? Do I know her?'

'Who?'

'The woman in the case. In my experience, when a man wants to join something, there's always a woman at the back of it.'

'There's not in this case. And I don't need exercise, except for my brain.'

'What's wrong with using it around here? You used to like this place.'

'I like it all right now. But I can do this sort of thing on my head. You know that, Wally.'

'Better this sort of thing on your head, than pounding a beat with your feet. Who put you up to it?'

'A woman gave me the idea, but I can't tell you her name, because I don't know it. She took me for a copper.'

'You're lucky. She might have taken you for a couple of quid.'

'I wonder your wit doesn't weigh you down,' Joe said, and turned in his seat as there came from the direction of the back premises a confused sound of men's voices raised in heated argument, and the suggestion of a scuffle. Wally refilled his own glass and yawned.

'Seems like trouble,' he said. 'Now's your chance to get in a little practice on the side of the law. Tell 'em the bar's closed. And if it's someone wanting his money back, he can come again when we've paid our taxes. You never know, there might be a bit over.'

'You're such a leery old cynic,' Joe retorted, getting to his feet, 'you make me feel like a jolly, bouncing schoolboy.'

'Well, bounce, then,' Wally said. 'You're better at coping with these things than I am.'

12

Without further comment, Joe walked leisurely out to the back entrance of the building, in the dimly lighted passage of which he came upon three struggling figures, two of which he recognized as the waiters who had lately been in the throes of clearing up. The third was a young man with sandy hair, very broad shoulders and a vocabulary the strength and range of which caused even Joe no little astonishment. Furthermore, this remarkable young man was winning the fight hands down, in that he had the head of one waiter firmly tucked under his right arm, while with his free hand he vigorously pummelled the other.

Although appreciating it as a fascinating spectacle, it was not a situation that Joe could tolerate. The members of his staff were all hand-picked, highly paid, temperamental and practically irreplaceable. With some difficulty, therefore, and a great deal of determination, he stepped in and extricated the waiters, meta-phorically patted them on the head and sent them off with an adjuration to get themselves a drink and whatever first aid they could find. Then turning to the cause of the trouble, he asked, 'What do you think this is, a gymnasium?'

The young man was leaning against the wall, panting from his exertions and running a hand over his heated brow. Seen thus, he appeared even broader than when in action, although barely of medium height, and his hands and feet were the largest Joe ever remembered seeing on anyone. But there was something very likeable about him, and the way he grinned, somewhat shame-facedly, and said, 'They should not have tried to throw me out.'

'You shouldn't try and get in after hours. What do you want?'

'What d'you think? A drink, of course. I wanted a drink, I still want a drink, and somewhere I'm going to get a drink.'

'I'd say you'd had enough,' Joe said, appraising in a comprehen-sive glance the young man's ruffled hair, his dishevelled lounge suit, with a drooping carnation in the buttonhole, his general air of having made a night of it. He did not look any too wealthy, but his attitude was that of a man with money to spend, and the temporary confidence it inspires. In confirmation, he brought out a couple of bank notes from an inside pocket and waved them in the air.

'I can pay for it,' he said.

'I'm sorry.' Joe shook his head decisively. 'It's gone closing time, and I wouldn't sell a drink to anyone if they offered me the earth.' Then recalling his own earlier need of a stimulant and impatient to get back to it, he added, 'But you can have one on the house, if you like. We've got a bottle going.'

And ignoring the intruder's protest that he always paid his way, Joe grasped him firmly by the arm, and hustled him inside to the table where Wally still sat absorbed in his paper. That imperturbable gentleman glanced up to enquire, 'What have we here?' as if he were being presented with a new form of entertainment.

'A man who needs a drink,' Joe said. 'And if he needs it half as badly as I did, he's welcome.'

'He's welcome in any case. I was getting a bit tired of you and your problems. Sit down, son, and have a go at the bottle. Can't be bothered to find you a glass, and you don't look the fussy type. Am I right?'

'Anything but,' the young man said, and accepted the suggestion rather awkwardly. Replacing the bottle on the table, he asked, 'What are you, Communists?'

Wally leaned back and laughed outright.

'No, idealists. We don't like to see a decent young fellow get tight on anything but the best.'

The blue eyes of their visitor twinkled in response. He remarked, 'You're being a bit hasty, aren't you?'

'I don't think so. What do you say, Joe?'

14

'I'd say he started out with thirty quid in his pocket to hunt up a good time, and he's still looking for it with his last fiver. About twenty-four, I'd say, no near-relatives, works for himself and doesn't make much out of it except when he's in luck. A bit more honest than most people, he's got a sense of humour, and he thinks we're nutty.'

'That's pretty good,' the young man said. 'Except that it was twenty quid, and now I've got three. How do you do it?'

'It's our business,' Wally explained. 'When you run a place like this, you've got to be able to sum people up. No good listening to the tales they tell you. Half the time it's all my eye, and the rest is my aunt's foot. What do you do, exactly? We can't tell that far without going through your pockets.'

'Cars. I run a hire service.'

'You mean *a* car, singular, don't you?'

'That's right. And before you tell me my name, I'll tell *you*. It's Johnny Gaff.'

'Here's luck, Johnny,' Wally said, raising his glass. 'Swig yourself a drink.' And as the young man did so, he added, 'You're wrong about the two of us being nutty. He is, I'm not.'

But Joe was not to be drawn. He had lighted a cigarette and was staring moodily in front of him. Wally went on, 'That's my partner, Joe Trayne. He looks all right, doesn't he? A bit upstage, but that's just his evening kit. In a pyjama suit he's Mother's dream of the boy who couldn't do wrong. Have a good look at him, son, because the next time you see him he'll be taking your number for leaving your barrow on the wrong side of the road. He's aiming to join the police.'

'What for?' Johnny asked, regarding Joe in perplexity. 'If I had a place like this, they'd have to drag me by the hair before I'd join anything.'

'You've got a brain, son. Joe just thinks he has. Are you a good driver?'

Johnny brought out a cigarette from a greasy packet, lighted it, examined his ill-kept fingernails, and said, 'I could drive a tank around a postage stamp and not come unstuck. Why?'

'If you're as good as that, we might put some business your way. Eh, Joe?'

'What's that?' his partner asked, as if coming out of a trance.

'Shake out of it, man,' Wally said impatiently. 'I was just telling Johnny we might get him a few jobs, running people down to the "Nosebag". What do you say?'

Joe shrugged. The 'Nosebag' was somewhat of a thorn in his side. It had originated from a night when, slightly under the influence, he had boasted that he could turn a stable into a restaurant and make it popular. Wally, with his usual eye to business, had subsequently kept him up to it, with the result that they were now the possessors of a small farmhouse on the borders of Hertfordshire, in the converted outhouses of which they ran a thriving supper-dance. The house itself, at present occupied by the manager, his wife and family, had been earmarked by Wally for his own, when he reached retiring age. Exactly what that age would be no one could imagine.

Johnny said eagerly, 'I'd be glad if you could . . . ' and hesitated, looking from one to the other and back again.

'The name's Wally Pierce, if that's what's bothering you,' the older man said. 'And I don't make promises unless I can keep 'em.' He fished in his pocket, brought out a card and pushed it across the table. 'Bring the barrow round in the morning, and I'll have a look at it. If it's not good enough, maybe I'll get you another.'

'It's a nice little job,' Johnny said. 'Nothing wonderful to look at, but it goes. And I don't charge much.'

'That's where you're wrong. People with money and no sense of value don't reckon they've had their whack unless you charge 'em. As for our "Nosebag" lot, you could chop lumps off their bank balances with a hatchet, and they wouldn't notice it. Have a drink. What about you, Joe? Are you going to sit there all night looking as if you'd died?'

'I was thinking of someone who's died,' Joe said.

'Again? Who is it, anyone I know?'

'That kind don't die, they just pickle themselves. I'll tell you about it, but you won't believe me.'

Whereupon he did, leaning with one elbow on the table, his chin resting on his hand. Wally folded up his paper, removed his spectacles, and put them in his pocket. Then he commented,

'So she locked herself in the bedroom. And why shouldn't she, with you on the other side of the door?'

Joe looked at him in disgust. He said, 'But I tell you she *asked* me to go up there with her. She spoke to me first.'

'That was before she saw you in the light.'

'Trust you to overlook the main point, the dead man in the lounge.'

'What was he like?' Johnny asked, leaning forward, eyes alight with interest, as he absently helped himself to another drink.

'Very good-looking, about your age I'd say, black curly hair, fawnish-coloured suit, rather loud. Sort of semi-prosperous gangster type, before the rot's set in.'

'I might know him,' Johnny mused. 'When I drove a cab, I knew a lot of the boys in town.'

'Your chances of improving the acquaintance aren't worth a light, by all accounts,' Wally said, yawning. 'It looks to me as if this young lovely knocked off her boy friend and then tried to pin it on the first mug she could find . . . '

'Meaning me,' Joe finished for him. 'But you're out there, Wally. She wasn't the killing kind.'

'A hell of a policeman you'd make,' Wally scoffed. 'You catch a woman with a corpse on her hands, she tells a damned silly story about having bought it at a sale, and you say she couldn't have done it because she's got a pretty face.'

'She hasn't a pretty face.'

'Well, whatever she's got, it wouldn't cut any ice with the boys who know. And if you don't believe me why don't you get back there and argue it out with them, if they haven't snatched her in already?'

'I will,' Joe said, pushing back his chair and finishing his drink as an afterthought. Wally narrowed his eyes, and made a gesture of protest.

'Now, look,' he began. 'I'm not going back on what I said, but don't do anything hasty. You always were inclined to be impulsive.'

'And why not? I was born on an impulse, I'll probably die on an impulse, so why shouldn't I live the same way?'

'Damned if I know why you've lived so long. Not that I mind you getting ideas, as long as I can turn them into cash and get my cut. But I don't want a cut on any trouble you may run into, and I tell you . . .'

'Tell it to Johnny,' Joe said. 'He looks good for another couple of hours. Happy nights.' Saying which, he pocketed his cigarette lighter, and left them in his usual unhurried way. Wally said quickly,

'Do me a favour, will you, Johnny? Go after him and see he doesn't do anything too daft. If they pinch him, give me a ring in the morning and tell me what bail they want. It won't do him any harm to be locked up for one night. I want to get some sleep.'

Bringing from his pocket a large bunch of keys, he got to his feet, yawning again with an air of abandoned weariness. Johnny also rose, looking dubious.

'But suppose he doesn't want me?' he asked.

Wally patted his shoulder. 'Switch on that young brother smile of yours,' he said. 'It's very fetching. Good night, son, see you tomorrow.'

So far as he was concerned, Johnny was already one of the staff.

Chapter II

There was a suggestion of dawn in the atmosphere as Joe emerged upon the pavement, and stood for a moment, glancing up and down the deserted street. A soft wind had sprung up, cooling the air a little. But to Joe, who had seen dawn as often as sunset, the heralded arrival of one more failed to make any particular impression. He was more interested in the possibility of finding a belated taxi. Seeing none, he lit a cigarette and set off in the direction of Hanover Square. Neither was he specially surprised when, hearing footsteps and glancing over his shoulder, he observed a thick-set figure hurrying after him. He paused long enough to be overtaken, and as the figure came abreast and he recognized Johnny, he remarked, 'I thought it was you. I swear there can't be another pair of feet like that in London.'

'Terrible, aren't they?' the young man agreed, falling into step at his side. 'My old lady always used to say it cost her a fortune to keep me in shoe leather.'

'You live this way?' Joe asked, regarding him sideways in some amusement.

'No, I've got a room down the East End. I reckon that's why I'm not in with the right click.'

'You're coming quite a bit out of your way, aren't you? Or is that force of habit from driving a cab?' Then sensing his embarrassment, Joe laughed and added, 'All right, I won't spoil your fun. He sent you along as a bodyguard, didn't he? And in the dreary light of day you're going to bail me out and return me to Papa, and the incident will be closed. Am I right?'

'Something like that,' Johnny admitted. 'Of course, if you'd rather I hopped off . . . But I'd like to come along. Things have been a bit quiet lately, not like when I used to drive a cab.'

'Please yourself,' Joe said. 'But don't blame me if it doesn't turn out the right way.'

'Not likely. I don't mind a chunk of trouble. I used to see some rum goings-on in the old days.'

'Stick to me and you may see more,' Joe said, and was silent the rest of the way. He felt warmly contented inside now, from drinking whisky in company he liked. In association with people to whom he was indifferent, he could drink continually and feel very little effect from it, but in a congenial atmosphere, a small quantity went a long way.

'This the place?' Johnny queried in a low voice, as they turned into Thunder Mews.

'This is it,' Joe said. 'Number seven. It doesn't look like the scene of the crime, does it?'

The mews was empty and silent, the only moving creature being a cat, black and sleek, which looked at them suspiciously and fled.

'I don't know about that,' Johnny objected. 'A copper I used to know found a man with his throat cut outside a church. How are we going to get in?'

They had paused before number seven, the front and garage doors of which were firmly closed. Above the garage were two casement windows, the left one slightly open. It belonged, Joe judged, to the locked bedroom. The other would be the lounge.

'We'll knock,' he said, and proceeded to do so, at first gently, and then with increasingly violent use of the heavy door-knocker. The noise echoed alarmingly.

'Couldn't you ring?' Johnny whispered. 'They've got a bell up the side here. That row is enough to wake the dead.'

'I hope not,' Joe said, and pressed several times upon the bell set high up to the left-hand side of the door. They heard an electric bell ringing somewhere inside, but apart from that the silence was unbroken.

'That settles it,' Joe pronounced with satisfaction. 'The police haven't moved in yet.'

Johnny, inspecting the lock, remarked, 'Old fashioned bit of work here. I could get it open if I had a pen-knife. But it might take half-an-hour. Chap I used to know showed me how, but he was an expert. He could get on the inside of anything in five minutes.'

'Where is he now?' Joe asked, stepping back to view the windows once more. 'Inside for five years?'

'Something like that. They caught up with him. Shall I have a go?'

'Not with my knife. And it would take too long. I might try that window. It's the room where she locked herself in.'

'But you can't climb into her bedroom, can you? It wouldn't be nice.'

'I don't feel nice. But perhaps you're right. If she's in there, she might start screaming. Why the hell didn't they leave the other window open, on a night like this?'

The cat had returned, creeping stealthily towards them. It eyed them for a moment, then diving for the drainpipe, made its way up quickly but with caution. Arriving on the right-hand window sill, it gently pushed the window with its paw, and squeezing through the narrow aperture, disappeared from view.

'So there was a cat,' Joe said. 'Thanks, puss. Where he can go, so can I.'

'You're a bit bigger than him,' Johnny pointed out, testing the strength of the drainpipe with his large hands. 'Better let me go.'

'With those feet? You'd probably get 'em tangled up and bring the whole house down. Besides, I started this and I'm going to finish it.'

Whereupon he made an agile leap, eased himself on to the first foothold, and began the ascent in the time-honoured fashion of the adventurous schoolboy. Johnny called softly after him, 'What do I say if a copper comes along?'

'Just stand there and ring the bell and by that time I'll be down to answer it.'

'You hope,' Johnny muttered, and watched anxiously as Joe manoeuvred himself on to the sill, and pushing the window wide open, followed the cat's example. If his memory of the room's arrangement were correct, Joe reflected, disentangling himself from the curtains, the box was situated just in front of the window. He had no desire to step on to that ancient relic.

He need not have worried. Cautiously his feet found the floor, and with hands outspread, he fumbled his way through the smothering darkness to the main electric switch which, being turned on, revealed the room exactly as he remembered it, with the exception that the box was missing. He stood looking round, frowning. So far as he could see, there was no place in the room large enough to hide it. The only cupboards were small, and delicately made, presumably for china or odds and ends. He made a careful examination, just to ensure that the dead man himself had not been stowed away somewhere, before going below to admit the impatient Johnny.

'What's up?' the latter asked, in an undertone, as Joe signed to him to keep quiet.

'Just nothing at the moment. No body, no box, nothing.'

'What, nothing?' Johnny echoed, conveying his disappointment in a whisper as they went noiselessly up the stairs and into the room lately occupied by the dead. 'That's rum, isn't it?'

'Don't keep saying that. You're making me thirsty.' Joe had crossed the room and was examining the carpet, in front of the window.

'Would the coppers have taken him away, d'you suppose?'

'And left the place unattended? And carefully removed the marks where the box was? Because that's what someone has done. A thing that weight ought to have left a mark on the carpet just about here.'

'Strewth! What a sleuth!' Johnny said admiringly. 'I'd never have thought of that. Have you looked outside?'

'Not yet. We will, but I've a feeling we won't find much.'

He was right, as far as the kitchen, the bedroom adjacent to it, and the bathroom were concerned. All were unoccupied and in excellent order. Furthermore, this bedroom did not appear to be in use at all. The bed was made, but covered by a silk counterpane, the wardrobe, the single cupboard, the dressing chest, all empty. Joe could not remember, from his previous hurried view of it, whether it had been the same then. In search of the cat, he had given it only a brief glance, before passing on.

'We'll try the other room,' he said. 'And I'll get in there if it's the last thing I do.'

He had purposely left it until last. Somehow he had an uncomfortable feeling about what he might find on the other side of that

24

door. Another body, possibly, lying limply across the bed, but this time the body of a woman. As he grasped the handle, he found that his hands were sweating, and it was with a mixture of emotions that he felt the door give and open easily. He swung it wide, turned on the light, and stepped a couple of paces into the room.

It was equipped in similar fashion to the other, with the difference that this one was very much in use at the present time. There were feminine garments lying about on chairs, the dressing table bore dozens of bottles and jars and all the intricate necessities to a woman's toilet, and in the bed, tucked up snugly beneath blue-tinted sheets, lay a young woman with a vast quantity of blonde hair strewn about the pillow.

She sighed in her sleep, turned, and the light catching her full in the face, she screwed up her eyes and opened them, blinking rapidly. They were curious eyes, light blue and so deep set that the fair lashes fringing them projected spikily. At the moment their expression was intensely hostile. Joe, who had been expecting almost anything, was momentarily thrown off guard. Johnny, shoving his way round from behind, frankly goggled.

The young woman asked sharply, 'Who the hell are you?' and when neither of them offered an immediate reply, she added, 'Well, what are you staring at? You've seen a woman in bed before, haven't you?'

'Surely,' Joe agreed, and it was only later that he wondered whether he had said the right thing. 'I'm looking for a lady with dark hair, probably your sister, and a box with a body in it. Any suggestions?'

He came farther into the room as he spoke, and leaned against the wall. Studying her face, he could see no resemblance to that of the lady in black. This one was not without her share of looks, but she had a flaunting, aggressive quality that marred the first fleeting

25

impression of beauty. Just now she was showing two rows of small sharp teeth in an expression suggestive of a feline animal about to attack, and her eyelids, as she lay blinking, had the slightly puffy look of one disturbed from too short a sleep.

'Mental, just as I thought,' she said. Her voice, drawling and affected, sounded as if it had been carefully planned to irritate as many people as possible. From the doorway, Johnny asked, 'Isn't this the one we're looking for?'

Joe shook his head. 'Not unless she's dyed her hair and changed her face. It's her sister I'm interested in.'

Very deliberately the young woman sat up, showing a glimpse of bare arms and shoulders and a flimsy blue nightgown, before reaching for a bedjacket which she wrapped about her.

'I haven't got a sister,' she said. 'And my only suggestion is that you get out of here before I call the police.'

'What with?' Joe asked. 'Telepathy?'

Her smile, he thought, was one of the most unpleasant expressions he had ever seen on a feminine face, as she said, 'There's a thing called a telephone. They invented it some years ago. But perhaps they didn't tell you about it in the asylum.'

He raised an eyebrow, and glanced about the room.

'Where do you keep it, if it's not too intimate a question?'

For answer, she leaned over and withdrew from beneath the farther side of the bed an instrument, the wires of which had previously been hidden from view.

'You see?' she said, as if explaining something to a half-witted child of four. 'I've only to pick up this receiver and dial, and the police will be here in five minutes to take you away. Not, I imagine, that it would be a new experience for you.'

'Go ahead,' Joe urged her, in the amiable tone that signified he was holding on to his temper with an effort. 'I'd like to see it work.'

His perplexity was the main source of his annoyance, and there seemed to be no logical answer to it. Doubtless the lady in black had some very good reason for locking herself in the bedroom and subsequently for ridding herself of the body and the oak chest. But to replace herself with a blonde appeared to him to be going a little too far. Johnny did not help matters by saying, 'I suppose you couldn't have made a mistake in the flat?'

The blonde flashed him a quick glance from under her lashes, and remarked, 'He's a lot brighter than he looks.' Then replacing the telephone and folding her hands upon the coverlet, she continued in a more reasonable way, 'If you're not both entirely mad, perhaps you'd like to tell me just what you're supposed to be doing? You don't look like ordinary housebreakers, and I don't want to call the police unless I have to.'

'I'd take a bet on that,' Joe said. 'You don't want the police or anyone else round here, or you'd have done something about it before this. For a woman outnumbered by housebreakers and escaped loonies, you're remarkably cool.'

'How do you expect me to act?' she countered. 'As if I'd never been alone with a man in my life?'

'What happened to the last man you were alone with?' Joe hazarded. 'The good-looking one with dark hair? He was in the next room, dead, when I saw him. What did he die of, fright?'

She yawned slightly, behind a delicate hand. 'Sorry I can't answer that one,' she said. 'I like my men alive. And if I knew a good-looking boy with dark hair, he'd be here beside me.'

'I didn't say he was a boy. I didn't even say he was young. But you knew who I meant, didn't you?' Seeing her eyes narrow in suppressed anger, Joe grinned and stepped across to the wardrobe. 'You don't mind if I peep in here? These things fascinate me.'

Saying which, he opened the mirrored door, to reveal a row of

27

feminine apparel, day dresses, evening dresses, suits, coats, on the shelf above a hat or two . . . A hat? *The* hat, the one with the black veil. He was prepared to admit that there might be two like it in London, until he saw below, draped upon a hanger, the identical jacket she had worn, black velvet with the fluffy pieces of fur at the neck and wrists. He paused long enough to observe the label stitched on the inner side of the collar, before closing the door and turning to find the young lady in bed surveying him with the smile that he disliked so much.

'No more bodies?' she asked.

'No.' He stood, hands in pockets, eyeing her steadily. 'As a matter of fact, I'm not very interested in bodies, and I don't care a damn if your black-haired boy friend came to a bad end. He probably deserved it. I don't even care where he is now. All I'm asking you is, what happened to the girl who was here earlier, the one who asked me to help her? She said she shared this place with her sister. Isn't that you?'

The blonde returned his look in silence for a moment. She appeared to be making up her mind about something. On the other hand, she might have been planning a new summer outfit, so blank was her expression. Then she said, 'You may be quite sane for all I know. Some woman may have asked you into a flat in this mews, there are quite a few like that around here, and you may have seen this and that. But it wasn't this flat, because I've been here best part of the evening. I've got friends who can prove it, because they were here, too. I live here alone, and my name is Lysbeth Ritchley. You can check that up in the directory if you like. That's all I've got to say, and you can take it or leave it.'

'I don't want to butt in,' Johnny said, 'but couldn't we leave it? I've a funny sort of feeling I'd like to sleep some time before tomorrow.'

The blonde favoured him with a smile, but now it was softer.

'I don't know who you are,' she said, 'but you've got nice eyes, and you only open your mouth when you've got something worth saying. I like that. Now do you mind taking this woman-chaser out of my flat, and putting him back wherever he came from?'

Joe laughed. 'If you mean me, I'm going, anyway,' he said. 'You're damaging my blood pressure.'

Her eyes surveyed him with sudden interest as he walked to the door. She asked, 'Haven't I seen your face somewhere before tonight? Somewhere around the West End?'

He paused. 'It's just a face. But it goes by the name of Trayne, if that conveys anything to you.'

'It does.' Her smile became three-quarters friendly. 'Why didn't you say so before. You're . . . '

'Don't start telling me who I am,' he cut in. 'I don't like it. What's more, I don't like you. So if you ever fancy your chances of getting into any place I'm even vaguely connected with, you can consider yourself blacklisted.'

The smile vanished. 'I wouldn't be found dead in any place of yours,' she began, and stopped abruptly. Into her eyes had come an expression of almost superstitious fear, quickly suppressed. Joe shrugged, and followed Johnny out of the room, closing the door behind him. As they moved away, there came a rustle of sound from the other side, and the grating of the key as it turned in the lock. There was no other sign of life in the apartment, neither did they speak until they were outside on the cobbled roadway, clearly visible now in the fast-growing light.

Then Joe said, turning to look over his shoulder at the closed door of number seven, 'If that's not the same flat, I ought to be certified.'

'Easy enough to make a mistake,' Johnny said. 'Specially in the dark. And if it wasn't the same, you couldn't blame her for getting shirty, could you? Two of us busting in like that.'

He paused as they turned the corner and gave vent to a peculiar whistle.

'Are you practising to be a Boy Scout?' Joe asked, eyeing him curiously.

'That's for a cab. If any of the boys are around, they'll know. I've got to get home, haven't I?'

'Why not come along to my place? It's nearer than yours, and I feel I owe you breakfast.'

'Well, if it's not too much trouble . . . '

'No trouble at all. And as a special favour, I'll let you cook it.'

'What did I say?' Johnny grinned, as a taxi turned out of the square and came towards them.

'You're certainly a useful man to know,' Joe said. But he was more interested in a long, dark green car pulled up on the other side of the road, the driver of which had just started his engine. The vehicle shot forward, and missing the oncoming taxi by inches, sped rapidly out of sight.

He might be getting fanciful, Joe thought, but it seemed an odd place for a car to be parked at that time in the morning.

Chapter III

'Anything in the press?' Joe asked, pausing in the middle of his shaving operations to glance at Johnny, who sat on the edge of the bath, a copy of *The Daily Review* spread over his knee. They had breakfasted, slept, bathed, and drunk large cups of strong coffee in preparation for the new day. Johnny lit a cigarette and shook his head regretfully. Despite the night's adventures, his face looked fresh and lively in the sunlight streaming in through the open window.

'Not much,' he said. 'Train smash up north, couple of smash-and-grabs down south, two coves pulled in at Hampstead when a cat set off the burglar alarm ... who the hell do they expect to believe that? ... A murder at Hoxton ...'

'What kind of murder?'

'Usual kind, woman found strangled, but you'll have to wait till Sunday for the dirt. There's a bit here about a bloke I used to know ... or are you only interested in murders?'

'Not particularly. I just wanted to see if you could read.'

'And why shouldn't I?' Johnny said, in some indignation. 'I went to a good school.'

'So did I, but I didn't learn much that was any use to me.' Joe finished his toilet, carefully folded the towel and replaced his shaving tackle. Returning his attention to Johnny, he said, 'I wish you wouldn't fling cigarette ends and matches all over the place. My housekeeper will be here any minute. She's stream-lined and super-sensitive, and will probably hit you with a vacuum cleaner.'

'I'm not afraid of a woman,' Johnny said, but he made haste to clear the offending cigarette ends, which he flung out of the window, before following Joe into the bedroom. Here he glanced about him with appreciation, and said, not for the first time since his arrival, 'This is the dandiest dosshouse I've seen for a long time.'

Joe's flat was unusual in that it occupied the ground floor of Hamilton House, a corner building in St Giles' Place, Westminster, and was so situated that while the front door was reached through the general entrance, the kitchen door gave access to a square courtyard, surrounded by a high brick wall. As a private garden, it was not much to boast about, since it was overlooked by the windows of the first and second floors, but it had a certain air of space and isolation, and the beech tree which grew in the centre was Joe's pride and joy. Furthermore, a heavy door inset in the wall formed a separate entrance from Johnsons Passage, the narrow alleyway on that side of the house, and this, too, was a source of satisfaction to Joe, who had an instinctive dislike of habitations with one entrance and exit only. The house was old, but had been modernized during its conversion into three flats, and various improvements had been effected to Joe's portion of it at his insti-gation. It was decorated and furnished throughout in black and white, which some of his friends complained was disconcerting, in that it made them feel as if they were part of a photograph. To which he would reply that if they didn't like it, they could always stay away. Most of them preferred to put up with it.

Johnny had no such criticisms to offer. The bedroom, the lounge, the tiny reception room complete with cocktail bar, all he pronounced as perfect. 'But I'd reckon,' he added, a trifle wistfully, 'that it'd be a bit lonely here sometimes. You know, sort of all air and space.'

'Don't you believe it,' Joe said, putting finishing touches to his toilet. 'Most of the time this place would look like Victoria Station on a Bank Holiday, if I didn't take a firm stand. You get a corner of your own and you'll find out. Better still, why don't you move your traps in here and you'll find out even sooner? You can have the little room, if you swear a solemn oath always to leave a bottle at the bar for me.'

'Better be careful what you're saying,' Johnny warned him. 'I might take you on, if I only half thought you meant it.'

'I do mean it. If you're throwing in your hand with us, you've got to be somewhere on the spot, haven't you? Another thing, you can help me out by keeping at bay all the people I don't want to see.'

'Such as who?' Johnny asked. 'I wouldn't know one from another.'

'Practically everyone. You'll soon get into it.' Joe glanced at his wrist-watch, and observed that the hands indicated ten minutes past twelve. He strolled across to the window, and stood with one hand leaning against the frame, staring out to where the mid-day sun cast shadows in the courtyard. In the bright light of the summer morning, London looked prosaic and singularly unadventurous. The events of the night before had clouded over in his mind with the unreality of a dream. Momentarily he could have persuaded himself that he had merely taken too much liquor aboard, had not Johnny said suddenly at his elbow, 'Anything special out there you're interested in?'

'Where? Outside? No . . . I was just thinking . . . ' Joe turned away and began to pace about the room.

'Not about that piece of black skirt again?' Johnny said. 'I thought we'd settled all that last night. These women!' He glanced expressively at the ceiling.

'What do you know about women?' Joe retorted. 'And I wasn't thinking of her particularly. It was just that there was something odd about her. You'd say I was pretty good at taping people, wouldn't you?'

'I would. Top of the class, I'd say, and more.'

'Well, then, here's one who has me beaten sideways. I can't place her, so I can't get her out of my mind.'

'Do you always have to place everyone?'

'When they involve me in climbing through windows and what have you, yes. Damn it, man, if it had happened to you, wouldn't you feel the same?'

'Depends how she looked,' Johnny said, sitting down on the arm of the nearest chair and running a hand over his forehead, for the morning was unusually warm.

'I told you. She was good-looking, but nothing startling. She was trickily got up, and anyone might have taken her for a girl who knew her way about. But she didn't. The way she talked and acted you'd think she'd spent all her life in the wilds. She had the nerve to accost a complete stranger, and then bolted like a rabbit. She didn't seem to know anything about anything, but she certainly knew how to dress . . . My God! That suit . . . I'd almost forgotten.'

'What about it?' Johnny asked, staring down at his feet as if they fascinated him.

'If that blonde female hadn't the very same suit hanging in her wardrobe, I'll hang myself. But I can check that easily enough. It was made somewhere in Wigmore Street. Geyda or Feyda, some name like that. I saw it on the label. Come on, Johnny, let's have a smash at it.'

'What . . . now?'

'What's wrong with now? Unless you've got a weighty date?'

'I said I'd run round to see Mr Pierce with the barrow,' Johnny said.

'Let it go. Better still, you can drive mine. It's just sitting around in the garage doing nothing at the moment. Here, catch hold.' He brought out a bunch of keys, removed one from the ring and flung it across to Johnny, who caught it in one hand and regarded it dubiously. 'Go and have a look at it while I 'phone Wally. You'll find the garage to the right of the side entrance.'

He strolled across to the bed, sat down and pulled the telephone towards him. Johnny said, 'But I like my little tub, and Mr Pierce said . . . '

'Never mind what he said. You'll like mine better.' Joe dialled a number, and lighted a cigarette while waiting. Johnny got to his feet reluctantly and walked out of the room. Joe said presently, hearing his partner's voice over the wire, 'Hallo, Wal. Top of the morning to you.'

'And the dregs of it to you,' Wally rejoined. 'I'll like you a lot better when you're eighty. Maybe by then you'll be sleeping until a civilized hour.'

'Or forever,' Joe said. 'You ought to thank me for keeping young Johnny away from you. He was planning to come busting round with his car, all full of health and good spirits.'

Wally groaned. 'Don't talk to me about spirits,' he said. 'In fact, don't talk at all for a minute, will you? I want to think.' Joe grinned, and was obligingly silent. He knew from experience that Wally was never at his nimblest until late afternoon, and that only rarely did he rise before lunch. Fortunately, his wife and daughter, with whom he shared a flat at Macclesfield Manor, Mayfair, were also conversant with and agreeable to the peculiarity of his habits, which due to good management in no way interfered with their own. Wally continued at length, 'Have they got private 'phones in jail these days, or was your personality too much for them? The last time I saw you I'd have sworn you were heading for the lock-up.'

Joe laughed. 'Not me. I wish I'd taken a bet on it, but I'd never have had the heart to take the money. No, I didn't turn up any trouble, and I didn't see anyone there, except a blonde in bed.'

'Is that where you are now?'

'No. I'm sitting on my own bed, drinking in the beauty of the morning.'

'Drinking *what*?'

'With a mind like yours, you wouldn't understand. Look, Wally, one more word in your ear and you can go back to your dreams. I've got Johnny on my hands. He kipped here for the night as he lives down east. I've just sent him out to have a look at my car, and if he likes it, and is any good, he can drive it. You know I don't use it much myself, and I've an idea by the way he talks about it that his own is some sort of hell-on-wheels that would be as much use to us as a sore throat. What do you say?'

'You're probably right,' Wally agreed. 'He's a nice lad and I'd like to do something for him. Didn't I say I'd put him on the staff?'

'Something of the sort. But you don't mind if I borrow him occasionally, do you? After all, he's living here . . . '

'Since when?'

'Since just now. He seems to fit in somehow. And anyway, he needs a father's care.'

'He'll need it still more after he's known you a few weeks,'

Wally said. 'But have it your own way. You usually do. Bring him round tonight and we'll work it all out. I'll feel more like coping with the two of you then. When are you being measured for your copper's suit?'

'I'm not. I've decided if I start at all it will have to be at the top. Nothing less than an Assistant Commissioner for me. Cheeroh.' Joe rang off quickly, before Wally had time to say, 'See you tonight.' As he was about to leave, the front door opened and his house-keeper entered. Mrs Bushby was thirty and a widow. She was tall, black-haired and fiery eyed, and dressed as if she were contemplating a motion picture career in the near future. She wasted very little time on words and not a great deal on work. Nevertheless, she contrived to keep Joe's apartment immaculate, his pantry stocked, and his supply of fresh laundry never failed. She gave him a brief smile, observed that the weather could be warmer, but not much, and went out to the kitchen to make herself a cup of tea. He in turn beat a hasty retreat through the front entrance, before she could make any comment upon the crockery they had left piled in the sink.

He found the doors of his garage wide open, and Johnny inspecting the interior of the car with awed admiration.

'Like it?' Joe asked, leaning in the doorway. Johnny straightened himself, his face flushed, a streak of oil across his forehead.

'She's a bit of good,' he admitted, running an experienced eye over the long body. 'Can I really take her out for a run?'

'With me alongside, certainly. And if you get on all right together, she's as good as yours. I never drive myself, if I can avoid it.'

'With a car like this?'

'It's all one to me. I don't like driving.'

Johnny stared at him for a moment or two, unable to express

37

his astonishment at anyone being proof against the attractions of so lovely a toy. But there was something in Joe's expression that stopped him from making any further comment. Instead he manoeuvred himself under the steering wheel and silently accepted the ignition key that Joe held out to him.

'Can you manage?' the latter asked, as the engine came to life and the vehicle eased forward. Skilfully manipulating it into the narrow alleyway outside, Johnny grinned and said he could manage anything. With a critical eye, Joe watched until he was clear, slammed to and locked the garage doors, and climbed in beside him. It was a spacious four-seater, powerful and built for speed. As they turned into St Giles' Place, Joe said, 'We'll try this shop in Wigmore Street. Gresham House I think you'll find it is. About halfway down.'

Johnny nodded. He was enjoying himself too much to indulge in conversation. Neither was his confidence exaggerated, for despite the fact that it was one of the busiest hours of the day for traffic, they swept in and out of main roads and side-turnings smoothly and with extraordinary swiftness. Slowing down as they entered Wigmore Street, Johnny said, 'Tell me where and when.'

'Bit farther along,' Joe said. 'Beyond the lights.' And presently, 'This is it. Can you get in there, do you think?'

'You bet,' Johnny assured him, and they slid to the side of the kerb between a mail van and a gleaming limousine. 'What are you going to do?' he added, staring curiously at the magnificent frontage of 'Feyda', a shop covering the ground floor of Gresham House and dedicated, according to a neat inscription, to the production of Milady's Modes.

'Just going to order my winter woollies,' Joe said. 'You'd better stay here. If the two of us go in, they'll think we've come to lift the till. Shan't be long.'

Saying which, he climbed out and stood for a moment inspecting the shop with care. Then he entered, and the door closed automatically behind him. The interior was a dream of soft carpets and nylon curtains, gilt chairs and ornamental walls, with here and there an isolated exhibit of feminine attire. From an inner recess appeared a young lady of comely aspect, with the fanatical light of the true saleswoman in her eyes. It faded a little as she observed the largeness and masculinity of her prospective customer. She said, 'Monsieur wishes ... ?' and paused, with a slight elevation of one eyebrow.

'Do you make suits?' Joe asked.

'For ladies, yes, Monsieur.'

Her French accent intensified, she regarded him knowingly. He laughed.

'So I gathered. It's a lady's suit I'm enquiring about. A velvet one. Something like this.' He brought out a pencil and a piece of scrap paper, and proceeded to make a rough sketch of the suit he had last seen hanging in Miss Lysbeth Ritchley's wardrobe. It was a good sketch, and he was rather pleased with it. The saleswoman leaned beside him and inspected the finished effort with some surprise.

'You wish a suit like this, Monsieur?'

'Thank you, no. But I believe you made a suit like that for someone, and I'm wondering if you could tell me who you made it for, if it won't disrupt your whole day?'

'I will enquire,' she said, giving him a look full of Continental meaning, and disappeared behind the curtains at the far end. He lit a cigarette and waited, mentally questioning his own sanity in being there. On the face of it, the project seemed peculiarly pointless, for even if he discovered the owner of the suit, what then? It was Wally's fault, he decided. Wally had the knack of bringing out

39

the more obstinate side of his nature. Joe suspected that at times he did it purposely.

He was aroused from his ruminations by the entrance of another woman, older and more dignified, dressed all in black, with grey hair beautifully tended and her face made up with some artistry. In one hand she held Joe's sketch, as she said, 'Monsieur is interested in this suit?'

'Not so much the suit as the owner. I don't know if you can recognize it . . . '

'I recognize it perfectly, Monsieur,' she said, and paused, looking him over carefully and with a certain suspicion. She added, 'Monsieur is, perhaps, from a fashion house?'

'Good God, no!' he said, with force enough to convince anyone. She glanced at the sketch and back at him with a smile.

'Monsieur would make an excellent copyist,' she observed. 'And one must be careful. Our designs, they are all exclusive. This was made for one of our clients, and she would not wish that it should be copied.'

'There's nothing like that about me,' Joe hastened to say. 'The fact that I made a nice job of it just shows I was interested. I still am, but what good is that going to do me, if I can't find out her name?' He leaned upon the showcase again, and smiled into the eyes of Madame, who had taken up a position behind it. 'Imagine that. I meet her, I lose her, and all I have to trace her with is a label on a suit. But what a suit!' He waved his hands in expressive gestures. Madame thawed. Not for nothing had Joe the reputation of getting what he wanted if he wanted it enough.

'Excuse me, Monsieur, I will telephone,' she said. 'Your name, if you please?'

'She won't know it,' he explained. 'Ours was the sort of meeting where names are not exchanged. You understand?'

'Perfectly, Monsieur.' She had a dimple in one cheek that took years off her age. 'One moment, please.' She retired before he could protest, and he stood, hands in pockets, staring out of the window where a single evening dress was on display. This was maddening. For since the lady in velvet had seen fit to fly from him the night before, there was no reason why she should welcome him with open arms this morning. Neither did he particularly wish that she should. It was the mystery of it that intrigued him, and the caustic comments of Wally which urged him on. He took a few steps towards the inner sanctum, and heard Madame's voice speaking too low for him to catch the words. He wondered what the outcome would be were he to step inside and take the receiver from her hand. But while he was toying with the idea, she finished her conversation and came out to him, smiling,

'I may tell you, Monsieur,' she said, with the air of one delivering the goods as ordered, 'that the suit was made for Miss Lysbeth Ritchley of 7, Thunder Mews, W.1. She sends you her very best regards.'

'She does?' Joe said, concealing his annoyance as he lighted a cigarette. 'And did she say anything about her sister?'

Madame looked genuinely puzzled. 'I do not recall that Miss Ritchley has a sister, Monsieur. If so, I have never had the pleasure of meeting her.'

'I'm beginning to wonder about that myself,' Joe said. 'All thanks to you, Madame, and I hope to do the same for you, one day.'

'I am too old for romance, Monsieur,' she said, smiling with a certain sadness as she followed him to the door. 'Ah, but it is good to be young. Is it not so?'

'Too lovely for words,' he agreed, without much enthusiasm,

and walked quickly out and across the sunlit pavement to the car where Johnny still sat awaiting his return with impatience.

'What now?' the latter asked, as Joe climbed in beside him and sat thoughtfully staring at the cigarette between his fingers. 'I've been getting parkers' cramp.'

'Anywhere you like,' Joe said. 'According to everyone but me, there never was a girl who needed any help with any body in any box. So that lets me out and we can go and have lunch. Any suggestions?'

'Maudie's, on the Gray's Inn road,' Johnny said promptly. 'They give you the best lunch in town for half-a-dollar.'

'Sounds terrible. Sure we won't be poisoned?'

'You'll see,' Johnny reassured him. 'The trouble with you is, you don't know your way around outside the West End.' He waited for the stream of traffic to abate and eased the car into the road. 'We'll double down the next turning,' he said, and drove on and round the corner just in time to beat the lights. But as he turned, a girl stepped heedlessly from the pavement to cross the road, her head averted, as oblivious to traffic as if she had been alone in a desert. To avoid her, Johnny was obliged to mount the pavement, swivel round and slam on the brakes almost with one movement. They were thrown right, left and forward as the car screamed to a standstill beside the kerb.

'That was pretty work,' Joe said, recovering. 'Another couple of inches . . . ' He was peering after the girl, who had reached the opposite pavement and was continuing her walk, apparently still unaware of her narrow escape, or of the passers-by who had paused to stare as people will at the sound of brakes suddenly applied. Her back was toward them, and receding at a fair pace, and all they could see of her was a dark head without a hat, a loose tweed coat, and a pair of shapely legs, the feet encased in brogues.

42

'Hang on a minute, Johnny boy,' Joe said. 'I want to talk to that young woman.'

'Give her hell from me,' Johnny urged him. 'She's made me sweat. What does she think she is, a cow in a field?'

But Joe had already leaped out and was sprinting up the road after her. He reached her side within a few minutes, caught her lightly but firmly by the arm, and said, 'I'd know that walk anywhere. But why the disguise?'

She turned quickly and stared up at him. It was the vanished lady in black, but only an observant eye would have recognized her in the strictly country outfit she now sported. Furthermore, she wore very little make-up, and with her uncovered hair hanging loosely about her face, she did not look more than nineteen and was, Joe judged, probably less.

'You?' she said, her voice very low. 'Have you been following me?'

'I haven't, but I'm going to stick right beside you until you tell me one or two things I want to know.'

'I can't,' she said. 'I can't tell you anything. And I mustn't be seen talking to you.'

He laughed, but strengthened his hold upon her arm. 'Is my reputation so bad? We'd better get under cover, then. But what you don't seem to realize is that you were nearly killed just now.'

'Killed?' Her eyes widened in very real fear. 'Oh, no, not that!'

'If you *will* wander about the streets . . . ' he began, and paused, regarding her thoughtfully. It was difficult now to imagine her in that black outfit, impossible any longer to be annoyed with her, she looked so childish, standing there in the sunlight, casting nervous glances about as if expecting attack from an unseen enemy. He found, too, that his original interest in her had disappeared along with the black outfit and the resultant air of sophistication. She might have been someone's young sister up from the country. 'I've got it,' he said. 'You're not a Londoner. You've never been to town before in your life. Am I right?'

'Yes,' she admitted dubiously. 'But I can't stand here talking to you . . .'

'I'm not asking you to. We'll talk in the car.' And placing his trust in Providence not to get him arrested for kidnapping, he propelled her, still protesting, across the road where a bunch of traffic waited for the lights to change, and back to the car, where Johnny sat huddled over the wheel, smoking a cigarette and glowering over his recent misadventure. He glanced up as they approached, and his scowl, as he surveyed the girl, turned to an expression all his own.

'This is the man who saved your life,' Joe said, opening the back door for her. 'Hop in, lady, and we'll get us a little drink and you can thank him nicely.'

She returned Johnny's look, and some of her nervousness departed. 'Thank you,' she said. 'But how . . . I mean who . . . tried to kill me?'

'You nearly killed yourself,' Johnny explained, with graphic gestures. 'There I was, on a sweet little bit of road with nothing in sight, and then there you were, walking right under the wheels as if you were late for a suicide pact.' But he grinned as he said it, his annoyance apparently forgotten.

She gave a deep sigh and passed a hand over her face. 'Is that all? For a moment I thought . . .'

'You thought someone was trying to knock you off,' Joe put in quickly. 'And why you should think that could happen to a kid like you is one of the things I want to know. You needn't look at me as if I had a knife in every pocket, because I'm not going to tear you apart. But you can't come running up asking me to help you one minute and dashing off the next without any explanation. Where's your sense of gratitude? Johnny here and I were up best part of the night trying to sort out your problems. Isn't that right, Johnny?'

'Were we?' Johnny asked, bewildered. And then as some slight comprehension came to him, 'You don't mean to say . . . ?'

'That's exactly what I do mean.'

'But she doesn't look . . . '

'I know she doesn't. That's something else I want to hear about. Let's go and get a drink.'

'I don't drink,' the girl protested.

'You've just had a nasty shock,' Johnny said soothingly. 'Might get a bit of delayed action if you don't have something. You wouldn't like to fall down suddenly in the street, would you? And you all alone, too.'

'No . . . no, I wouldn't like that.' She glanced rapidly to left and right and back to meet Johnny's smiling blue eyes. 'I'll come,' she said. 'But it must be somewhere . . . well, where we won't be seen.'

She climbed into the back of the car, and Joe slammed the door and resumed his former seat, eyeing his driver with new appreciation. It seemed that one look from Johnny and the timid found courage to face unknown odds. He asked, 'Where's a nice, quiet little place outside the West End?'

'Charlie's Crypt,' Johnny said, and tossing away his cigarette end, he started the engine.

Chapter IV

'And now,' Joe said, stretching out his long legs at a comfortable angle beneath the table, 'we'll go right back to where we were last night, and you can tell me your name.'

The scene and general atmosphere were, he felt, exactly right. Situated below ground level, Charlie's Crypt had an air of conspiracy about it, helped out by rough-hewn benches and tables set in alcoves, an ancient floor worn by the tread of many feet, and a long bar running the length of one wall, in front of which were seated a number of customers, none of whom appeared to be interested in anything other than their mid-day refreshment. Nevertheless, the girl sitting opposite Joe and Johnny glanced nervously across at them, and was silent. Joe took a long drink from the pint of beer in front of him, and tried again.

'Let's start from the other end,' he suggested. 'I'm Joe Trayne. That may not mean anything to you, but Johnny Gaff here will vouch for me as an honest, respectable citizen, won't you, Johnny?'

'Every time,' the latter agreed, and added to the girl, 'Have a drink. It'll do you good.'

She reached for the brandy they had ordered for her, added a

46

lot of soda, and sipped it gingerly, replacing it upon the table with a slight expression of distaste.

'But you're not a policeman,' she said, eyeing Joe reproachfully.

'Who said I was, in the first place? You did. You were so positive about it, you almost convinced me. You also nearly convinced me I was crazy. What made you suddenly decide on a game of hide-and-seek?'

She flushed and took a few more sips from her glass. 'I didn't like the look in your eyes,' she submitted at last.

Joe sighed. 'Remind me to get a pair of dark spectacles, Johnny,' he said. 'Right. It was like this, then. You went out to get a policeman, picked on me, decided you'd made the biggest mistake of your life, and thought you'd put it right by playing on my sentimental feeling for cats while you locked yourself in the bedroom.'

'But I didn't,' she said.

'Didn't what?'

'I didn't lock myself in the bedroom. I went through the kitchen floor.'

'Oh, so you went through the kitchen floor. Now why didn't I think of that? Look, Johnny, one of us is barmy, and it's up to you to decide which. Personally, I'm going to have another drink.' He finished his beer, signalled the waiter and ordered a fresh round.

'If you're going to be rude . . . ' the girl began, making movements to rise, but Johnny leaned across and gently urged her back into the seat.

'I bet I can guess your name,' he said.

'Why should you?' she answered sharply, but a slight smile curved her lips, belying the hostility of her tone.

'It'll be a name that suits you,' Johnny said, his expression dreamy. 'Would it be Alice?'

'Of course not.'

'Vera?'

'You're being ridiculous,' she said, and laughing suddenly, she drank the rest of the brandy and soda. 'It's Wendy, as a matter of fact, Wendy Bond.'

'I knew it must be a lovely name,' Johnny commented. 'Isn't that a lovely name, Joe?'

'My God!' Joe exclaimed, and feverishly grasped the fresh mug of beer the waiter had just put before him. Recovering, he paid the waiter, lighted a cigarette, and added, 'If I'm in the way don't hesitate to say so.'

But they appeared to be unaware of him. Wendy was staring into her glass from beneath lowered eyelids, and Johnny was regarding her with the glazed expression of a man whose great moment had arrived.

'I can't believe all that happened to a nice kid like you,' he remarked at length. 'Bodies and picking up strange men and all the rest of it. But it just shows you ... '

'It wasn't my fault,' she interrupted.

'I should say it wasn't. But what are you doing, running round town on your own? You ought to have someone to look after you.'

'I came to London to look for a job,' she said. 'It was so dull living with Mother and Aunt Gwennie in the country. So I came to stay with my sister ... '

'That blonde woman? She can't be your sister. She's not a bit like you. She's ... well, anyway, she said she wasn't, didn't she, Joe?'

The latter nodded, afraid that their source of information would dry up again if he added his voice to the discussion. But she had already taken fright.

'I can't tell you any more,' she said in an undertone. 'I shouldn't have said as much, only you've been so kind and ... I hope you won't think me too silly, but London is such a terrifying city.'

'London's all right,' Johnny assured her. 'You just want to be in with the people who can look after you. We'll do that, don't you worry.'

'But I *am* worried. And I've got to go back home today. Lysbeth said so.'

'That . . . ' Johnny was beginning, when Joe kicked him on the shin, and leaning across the table, enquired gently, 'Then Miss Ritchley *is* your sister?'

'My half-sister. Mother married twice. She says she doesn't know why, because the first time she was unhappy, and the second time it was worse. She says marriage is like toothache, if it goes on long enough you get so used to it you miss it when it's gone. Aunt Gwennie says she's very cynical, but I think it's only because both her husbands died.'

Studying her face, it occurred to Joe that since he had been deceived the previous evening by her pseudo-sophistication, perhaps he was now being deceived into thinking her twice as ingenuous as she really was. Furthermore, he thought that her mother did not sound particularly dull.

'But a half-sister's got no right telling you what to do,' Johnny said. 'We'll soon fix her.'

'Oh, no, you mustn't do anything like that. She said I wasn't to speak to anyone about . . . well, you know what I mean. You see, no one knew I was staying with her, and she said they'd kill me if they found out I knew anything about . . . '

'We know what you mean,' Joe put in quickly. 'Who is "they"?'

'I don't know. I don't really know anything except that I've got to go back to the country. I was just going to get myself some clothes with the money Lysbeth gave me . . . '

'From Madame Feyda?' Joe asked. 'Is that where you were heading when we nearly ran you down?'

'Yes. Lysbeth gets her clothes there. She's very smart.'

'She's too smart,' Johnny said, overlooking the fact that he had only seen Lysbeth in night attire. 'You stick to what suits you.'

'More important, let's stick to the point,' Joe suggested. 'You came to town to get a job. You stayed with Lysbeth and you wanted to look like everyone's idea of a night on the tiles so you borrowed her clothes. Right?'

'Well . . . yes. She said I could, and I thought no one would take any notice of me if I didn't look smart.' She leaned back against the wooden partition, and added, 'But you mustn't keep asking me questions. Don't you see, they'll kill you too, if they think you know as much as I do?'

Joe thought of a suitable reply to that, but refrained from uttering it. Johnny said, 'It's a lot of old bull, and I don't believe a word of it. Who'd want to knock us off, I ask you?'

'Who knocked off the man in the box?' Joe countered. 'I ask *you*?'

'I never saw him, did I? I'm beginning to think it's just something you've cooked up between you.'

For the first time Joe and Wendy exchanged a glance of sympathy. He shrugged his shoulders and went on drinking. She leaned forward and began to speak very quickly in a voice scarcely above a whisper.

'But it's true. They're very desperate people, and if anything happens . . . well, I've warned you. I never met them. I knew that Lysbeth had a lot of friends, but I was only there about ten days, and she was out most of the time. She said I wouldn't be able to live with her always, and I wanted to get my own place, anyway, because we didn't get on very well together. She's lived in town for a long time, and I suppose I seem like a silly kid to her. I think she only let me stay there because Mother would have thought it funny if she didn't. I know now that I was in the way, because of

50

these friends of hers . . . ' Tears had gathered in her eyes, but she blinked them back. Johnny, visibly moved, reached out one of his enormous hands and patted hers. She continued, 'So I started buying one or two little things for a room of my own, and she let me keep them in the garage. Then I thought I'd go to a sale, and I saw that box. I didn't really mean to bid for it, but the auctioneer seemed to be nodding at me and I nodded back, and then I thought it would be fun to have it. No one else wanted it, except a man who was standing near me . . . '

'What sort of man?' Joe asked.

'A funny-looking man.'

'How funny? Tall, short, dark, fair or what?'

'About the same height as me, and dark, I think, but I didn't really notice, I was too excited about the box. Then he moved away, and I didn't see him again until I went to give my name and address and to pay for it.'

'What was he doing then?'

'He was standing just behind me, and as I was leaving he came after me and gave me a card and said could he arrange for it to be delivered for me, the box, I mean. I thought it was rather kind of him, because I was wondering what to do about it, as I'd never bought anything as big as that before.'

'And you gave him the order to clear it, just like that?' Joe asked incredulously.

'Well, what else could I do? I didn't know anyone who'd do it for me, and I thought Lysbeth might be annoyed if I bothered her with it. And he spoke so nicely, and seemed so anxious to help me that I didn't like to refuse.'

'You ought not to talk to strangers,' Johnny said. 'It's always risky.'

'But you're strangers, and I'm talking to you.'

'That's different. We're only trying to help.'

'So was he. And he did. I don't think it was his fault, at all. He said it would take about three days to deliver, and I did think afterwards that perhaps I'd been silly, but on the third day it arrived.'

'Was it locked when you left it at the saleroom?' Joe put in.

'I don't know. There was a key in the lock, but I didn't think to try it or to look inside, so I don't know if the man was in it then, or not.'

'Maybe I'm behind the times,' Joe said. 'But I never heard of anyone auctioning a box with a body in it. Did this removing gink give the name of the firm he was representing, or didn't he bother?'

'Oh, yes. Simpson and Lines. It's on the card.'

She opened her handbag and produced a small card upon which was printed the name of the removers, their address and telephone number in Chelsea, and underneath, printed in ink, REPRESENTATIVE, A.V. GREEN. Joe took it, inspected it with interest, and passed it on to Johnny.

'Anyone could get hold of one of those cards and write any old name on it,' he said. 'We can soon check on it, and I'll bet ten quid to a bent ha'penny that they've never heard of Mr Green. What sort of van did he use?'

'A plain one, drawn by a horse. It was quite ordinary.'

'Too ordinary, I'd say. Simpson and Lines would have had their name on it. Who did he have to help him?'

'Two men. They brought up the box, and put it in the lounge, because Lysbeth was out, and I hadn't the keys to the garage. Then Mr Green asked me to sign a paper, and that *did* have the name on it.'

'He didn't leave you a copy of it?'

'No, he took it away with him.'

'Where were you when you signed it?'

'In the lounge. Then I went into my room to get some money to tip the men, who were downstairs, and then Mr Green came down and they all went away.'

'And the key was in the lock when you went to open it?'

'Yes, but that wasn't until later. I didn't bother about it then. I got dressed and went out for the evening, and when I got back I went in to look at it, and it was locked, but it opened quite easily . . . ' She shuddered, and became silent.

Joe finished his drink and signalled the waiter. 'Now what do you say, Johnny?' he asked, having ordered another round with the air of one who needed it. Johnny ran a hand through his hair and looked from one to the other despairingly.

'I'm going nuts and bolts,' he said, and took a long draught of beer, and followed it by another from the fresh supply the waiter brought them.

Joe laughed. 'That makes three of us. Tell me, Miss Bond, did this Green merchant take any money off you?'

'How do you mean?'

'Well, he didn't make out he was so large-hearted he was doing it for nothing, did he? I shouldn't have thought even you would have taken that.'

'No. I did offer to pay him, but he said the account would be sent in the usual way. But I haven't had it yet.'

'I'm not surprised. How would it look? "To delivering one body . . . "'

'You're pretty sure he knew all about it, then?' Johnny asked.

'What else is there to think? How I see it is this. The box, when Miss Bond bought it, was just a box, put up for sale in the ordinary way. We can easily verify that, too. For some reason this Mr Green wanted it, otherwise he wouldn't have been bidding for it. What did he want it for? To put a body in, obviously, because that's what he appears to have done. But for some reason he decided to let Miss Bond buy the box, and stick the body in it afterwards.'

'What was he doing with a body?' Johnny asked, staring at Joe, fascinated.

'How do I know? Homicidal maniac, probably. Anyway, someone had it, didn't they, and since he brought it along, logically it must have been him.'

'But why should he let her buy the box in the first place? He could have outbid her, couldn't he?'

'Perhaps he's a bit on the near side, and saw a chance to save himself some cash. Or he may have a perverse sense of humour. Whichever it was, he did let her buy it, then he cleared it, stuffed the body in, and delivered it with the help of two of his pals. Or maybe they weren't his pals. What did they look like, Miss Bond? Was there anything odd about them?'

'No, nothing as far as I remember.' She sat with her chin resting on her hand, her face a little flushed, and she seemed to have forgotten her earlier nervousness. Joe pushed a further glass of brandy towards her, but she shook her head, and with an absent gesture he picked it up and drank it himself. She added, 'They were dressed in ordinary working sort of clothes, and they grumbled a lot about the weight of the chest as they brought it upstairs. That's why I thought I'd better tip them, because they were making such a fuss.'

'And well they might,' Joe said. 'But it's odds on they didn't know what was inside it, otherwise they wouldn't have raised the dust about it being so heavy. If Green locked it after he'd got the boy friend socked away, and held on to the key, he could have hired a couple of blokes to deliver it without their being any the wiser, couldn't he?'

'But the key was in the lock when I opened it.'

'He could have put it back, couldn't he, when you left him alone with it while you went to get the money for the men?'

'I suppose he could,' she said dubiously. 'Yes, he might have done that.'

'But why so much flim-flam?' Johnny queried, exasperated. 'If he had a body to get rid of, why not just leave it in a ditch or drop it in the river. Why wish it on you?'

'He didn't . . . it's nothing to do with me,' she protested. And then tears came into her eyes again and this time she did not restrain them. 'It's not fair, the way you keep trapping me into saying things. I mustn't tell you any more. I want to forget all about it.'

'Poor kid,' Johnny said, and stricken with remorse, he moved round to her side of the table and patted her shoulder.

'That's right,' Joe said. 'Let's all have a damned good cry. And while you're telling each other what brutes men are, you don't mind if I have a little talk to myself, do you? I'm just asking myself, what would have happened if you really had picked on a policeman last night? D'you suppose he'd have been dopy enough to slink about looking for cats while you were doing your disappearing trick? Not likely. By now I think you'd be down at headquarters, answering a lot of questions from steely-eyed gentlemen with notebooks, and little Lysbeth likewise, under grave suspicion if not arrest.'

Johnny, who had been ministering to Wendy's tears with his handkerchief, looked up, frowning. 'Did you say something?' he asked.

'No,' Joe said. 'I'm the dumbest thing around here for miles. I think not, neither do I speak. And in just two minutes from now I'm going out to dial Scotland Yard, and tell them they can put me away for as long as they like as an accessory to murder. And you two are coming with me.'

'No ... no,' Wendy said, aghast. '*Please*, Mr Trayne. You don't understand. That's just why Lysbeth sent me away, so that I wouldn't get into trouble. She'd be furious if she knew I was still in London. You don't know her ... '

'Oh yes, we do. We called on her last night. She was alone, and there was no box and no body.'

She stared at him with startled eyes. 'Wasn't there? I mean, did you? Oh, I don't know what I do mean.'

Johnny said, 'The kid's worn out. Can't we go and have lunch, or something?'

'No, we can't. Not until I know the rest of it. And if she won't tell me, then I'm going to finish it off with Lysbeth. I had an idea last night she knew who that dead man was. Now I'm certain.'

'But why should you think that?' Wendy protested. 'I didn't say so.'

'But you said you didn't know him yourself?'

'Of course I didn't know him.'

'All right. So when you found him you rushed straight out to look for a policeman. Perfectly normal reaction, anyone might do the same. But what did Lysbeth do? She gave you money, told you to go back home as quick as you like and to keep your mouth shut no matter what. Then she packs away the evidence of the crime, God knows where, calmly climbs into bed, and when we arrive she says she never had a sister and doesn't know anything about anything. On the face of it, how does that look? It reeks.'

Wendy said unhappily, 'She was only trying to protect me.'

'And incidentally, herself. For some reason she didn't want the police on her premises, and she certainly didn't want them to see

56

that body. My God! Why have I been pinning it all on poor old Green? I'd forgotten Lysbeth. Why shouldn't Green have delivered the box empty in the ordinary way, then while you were out for the evening, Lysbeth knocks off the boy friend and plants him in there, and goes out to get help from these friends of hers?'

'I thought you said he'd been dead for some time?' Johnny queried.

'That's right, he had. That won't do, then. But she might have had the body hidden away somewhere, and the box gave her an idea for getting rid of it.' He glanced at Wendy, and added, 'What did you mean when you said you went through the floor?'

'There's a trap-door in the kitchen. But you're wrong. You're quite wrong. Lysbeth wouldn't . . . '

'Where does it lead to?'

'But Lysbeth couldn't . . . '

'Don't keep telling me what she could or couldn't do. If Green didn't have anything to do with it, then it must have been her or her friends. And you said yourself you thought Green was all right.'

'But I *know* that Lysbeth didn't do it.'

'Do something for me, will you, Johnny?' Joe said. 'Go out and 'phone Simpson and Lines and ask them if they've got a representative called A.V. Green, and did they, or did they not, deliver an antique oak chest to Miss Bond at 7, Thunder Mews yesterday.'

'Where were they supposed to have got it from?' Johnny asked.

'I bought it at a place called Hammonds,' Wendy said. 'I don't know quite where it was, but I think . . . '

'Finlay Street,' Joe submitted. 'And Johnny, you might bring in a mid-day paper with you.'

'Don't I ever get any time off?' Johnny grumbled, getting reluctantly to his feet.

'What are you talking about? You had the whole day off yesterday.'

Johnny paused, resting both hands on the table, eyeing him in astonishment.

'But I wasn't working for you yesterday,' he said. 'I didn't even know you yesterday.'

Joe laughed. 'It's all one in our business. That's the way we work. You'll soon get used to it.'

'Maybe I will and maybe I won't,' Johnny said. 'It might work back on you. It's just possible I might take next year's holiday in advance, as from tomorrow. You never know.'

He moved off and threaded his way past the people who stood and leaned about the room with glasses in their hands. The girl watched him wistfully until he had disappeared through the nearest exit. Joe, on the other hand, saw him go with some relief. The atmosphere of love in bloom had, he felt, been seriously sabotaging his authority.

'Have another drink,' he suggested.

'No, thank you.'

'A cigarette?'

'No, I don't smoke very much.'

'What did you do with the one you were smoking when you disappeared last night?'

'I threw it away.'

'Not in the kitchen. It wasn't there when I came to look for you.'

'No. I threw it down in the garage.'

'You mean you got down there through the trap-door in the kitchen?'

'Yes, it was quite easy. You just lift up that matting they have on the floor, and the trap-door is underneath.'

'What's the idea of that?'

'I don't know. It's just the way it was built, I suppose. Lysbeth said it was very useful when she moved in, because they took some of the furniture in that way when it was awkward to get it up the stairs. They're very narrow, the stairs.'

Joe said thoughtfully, 'What goes up could also go down. They could have taken the chest down to the garage through the trap-door, couldn't they?'

'Who could?'

'Anyone. She must have had someone to help her. Two people, most likely. Men. A woman couldn't shift a thing like that. It took two to bring it in so it must have taken two to get it out. There might have been more, but two certainly. What did she say about me?'

Wendy moved uneasily, and looked away. 'Why should she say anything? She hadn't met you then, had she?'

'But you must have told her you'd brought in a man, thinking he was a policeman. Or did you give her some other explanation for hiding in the garage? You waited there till she came in, didn't you, because the garage was locked, and you hadn't the keys, or so you said, and you wouldn't come back through the trap-door in case I was still around.'

'I think you're horrible,' Wendy said. 'Just horrible.'

'So does Lysbeth, but she put it a bit stronger than that. Why did you go running out looking for a policeman, and tell me you hadn't a telephone, when you could have rung through on the one in her bedroom?'

'But I couldn't. She always keeps her room locked when she's out.'

Joe thought about that, and decided it could be true. When Wendy disappeared, he had not unnaturally assumed that she had locked herself into the bedroom. But that room could have been locked all the time, since there had been no reason for him to try it before.

'When she came back with these friends of hers . . . ' he began, without any particular idea of what he was going to say. But Wendy was so quick to interrupt him that there was no need for him to go any further.

'She didn't. She came in alone.' Then her half-hearted defences went completely, and she continued, twisting her hands together and speaking rapidly as if the torrent of words came as an immense relief to her. 'You mustn't think she had anything to do with it, Mr Trayne. I know she didn't. She was so terribly upset. If you could have seen her. She nearly fainted. And it wasn't as if I hadn't warned her. I told her as soon as she opened the garage . . . '

'She came back in a car?'

'Yes. I wouldn't have known it was her, otherwise. That's why I went down in the garage. I knew she'd have to open it.'

'What sort of car? It wouldn't be a long green one?'

'No . . . no, it's a small white one.'

'And that's the only one she has?'

'Yes. There's only room for one. Why?'

'It doesn't matter. Go on, what did you tell her?'

'Oh, everything. I don't think she believed me at first, but when she'd put the car away she opened the front door with her key and we went upstairs. She said something about me being a crazy kid, and then I showed her the box and she looked inside. That was when I thought she was going to faint. She sort of staggered back and said, "Oh, my God, how awful!" Then she said all kinds of terrible things, and I didn't know what to do, so I ran and got her some brandy.'

Joe thought it would have been nice if she had shown the same consideration for him, but refrained from mentioning it. He merely said, 'What sort of things?'

Wendy glanced at him obliquely. 'Well, things I'd never heard her say before. Swearing. It was horrible. Then when she'd had the brandy she calmed down a little and took me into her room, and made me tell her about it all over again.'

'You did tell her about me, then?'

'Yes. And she said of course you couldn't be a policeman, or you would have been back with reinforcements by that time. But she was quite nice about it and said it was her fault, really, because it was she who'd told me that there was usually a plain-clothes man on that corner, where I saw you. Oh, I know we didn't always get on well together, but she could be very nice sometimes, and you do see she couldn't have killed that man, don't you?'

'No,' Joe said. 'I don't see it at all.'

'But she was so upset. She wouldn't have felt like that if she'd killed him, would she?'

'She might have been upset because you'd poked your nose in, and had confided in a stranger into the bargain.'

'No, it wasn't that. She was cross about it, but she said you weren't likely to come back, and even if you did, she'd be there to see you. And if you told the police, and they came round, there would be no proof that you hadn't imagined it, or mistaken the flat. She said no one knew that I was staying there, not even her friends, so I must go back to the country and not tell anyone what I'd seen. I could stay the night at a hotel, she gave me the address, and everything would be all right.'

'For an innocent woman, she'd got it all remarkably well worked out. What reason did she give, if any, for not 'phoning the police herself and having the body removed in the normal way? That's what you would have done, isn't it?'

'Yes, but I didn't know him. She did, and she said he'd been very silly and got mixed up with some people who were wanted by the police, and he mustn't be found in her flat in case they thought . . . wel . . .'

'What I'm thinking,' Joe suggested.

'I don't know what you're thinking,' Wendy said sulkily. 'That's what I don't like about you. One can't tell what you're thinking.'

'Sorry about that. I'll have to get my face altered, in addition to the spectacles, although I thought you claimed to know what I was thinking last night. So she couldn't have killed him because she knew him? Is that your argument?'

'I didn't mean that. I meant she *cared* for him. She was crying when I went into her room to say goodbye, after I'd packed my things. She was looking at a photograph of him, and crying. I never saw her cry before.'

'Hadn't you seen the photograph before?'

'No, she must have had it put away somewhere.'

'I'm still not convinced. It wouldn't be the first time a woman has killed her lover and cried over him afterwards.'

'But I didn't say there was anything like *that* between them.'

'Where were you born?' Joe asked wearily.

'In a little village just outside Salisbury. Where I live now. But . . .'

'Well, I don't know how they go on in Salisbury, but this is London, and these things do happen, you know.'

'Not in my family,' she said, and he looked up, as relieved to see Johnny returning as he had been to see him go.

'You've been gone a hell of a long time,' Joe said, as Johnny collapsed back into his seat and slapped a newspaper down upon the table.

'I've been waiting while one half of London 'phoned the other

62

half to ask if it's warm enough for 'em,' Johnny said, mopping his heated brow. 'But I finally got through and what do you think?'

'I don't. And if you ever catch me at it again, dot me one, will you?'

'Don't be hasty,' Johnny grinned. 'You'll be buying me a drink in a minute on the strength of this.' He leaned his elbows on the table and went on, 'Simpson and Lines say they don't know anyone called A.V. Green, they can't trace anything about any old chest yesterday or any other day, and they never pick up or deliver anything without a written authorization on Form P.Z. 39, signed by the consigner and countersigned after delivery by the consignee.'

'You can have a drink,' Joe said, waving a hand to the waiter. 'But if you imagine . . . '

Wendy chose that moment to rise a trifle unsteadily to her feet. 'Excuse me,' she said, and making her way across the room, went through a door marked LADIES CLOAKROOM.

Chapter V

'D'you think she's all right?' Johnny asked, looking after her anxiously.

'No,' Joe said. 'I don't think she's very bright, either. We ought to have given her lime juice.'

He ordered two brandies and a lime juice from the waiter who had just found time to attend them. Johnny lit a crumpled cigarette and stared in front of him.

'I think she's wonderful,' he said.

Joe looked at him sharply. 'You're not falling for her by any chance, are you?' he asked.

'I've fallen,' Johnny admitted, and added, 'You don't mind, do you? I mean, you saw her first.'

Joe drew a deep breath, leaned forward and said earnestly, 'Let's level this up here and now. I did see her first, but I'm not going to be responsible for it. Last night was last night, and today is today. What's more, I like you, Johnny, and I wouldn't stand in your way for anything.' He smiled at the waiter as the man put three glasses on the table, paid him, and said, 'You've got one of the nicest faces I've ever seen.' The waiter thanked him, both for the compliment and the size of the tip he had received, and retired, looking inscrutable. 'Here's luck, Johnny,' Joe added, raising his glass. 'I've a feeling you're going to need it.'

'Thanks,' Johnny said, drinking. 'You didn't say anything to upset her, did you?'

Joe shook his head. 'She's one too many for me. I can't make up my mind whether she's acting, or if she was born like that.'

'She's not acting,' Johnny scoffed. 'She's just a thoroughly nice kid. Trouble is, you don't meet 'em often like that these days. But we've got to do something to get her out of this mess.'

'We? You. She's all yours from now on.'

'All right. Me, then. Here, have a look at this.'

He opened the lunch-time edition of *Nightly News* and pushed it across the table, indicating with his forefinger a column headed: *Dead Man in Pool – Surrey Mystery*. Joe read on, frowning, and learned that in the early hours of that morning, local police had been summoned to Coolmeer, Wadham Woods, Surrey, to investigate the story of one Alec Frampton, a gamekeeper who, in the course of his rounds in search of poachers on the estate of his employer, Mr Edgar Leigh, had witnessed movements on the part of two men which had immediately aroused his suspicions. Coming upon them suddenly, he had been in time to see them disposing of some heavy and cumbersome object by throwing it into the pool which, at that point, was approximately eight feet deep. He shouted and ran forward, gun in hand, but they at once made off, and though he gave chase, he was still some distance away when they sprang into a small white car parked in a clearing and drove from the spot. In response to his telephone call, police were very soon on the scene, and discovered the body of a man, fully dressed and partially submerged, caught in a dense thicket of reeds. There were no marks of violence on the body, which had since been identified as that of dark-haired, brown-eyed, twenty-three-year-old Carlo

Betz, known to the police as a one-time racketeer and frequenter of Soho gambling clubs. From medical evidence, it would appear that the body was already dead when disposed of, and a general round-up and questioning of all known associates of Betz was expected.

'Well?' Joe queried.

Johnny gave a surreptitious glance round and lowered his voice. 'Wouldn't you say that was him, the one in the box? This Carlo Betz, I used to know him, well, not personally, but by sight, so to speak. He was just like you said, dark hair, eyes, everything. They could have driven him out and dumped him there, couldn't they?'

'They could, I suppose. It seems a risky thing to do, but if they wanted to shift him in a hurry . . . What about the box?'

'They wouldn't take that along, would they? Stands to reason. The police could trace who bought it in no time, and then where'd they be? She'd have a car, wouldn't she, Wendy's half-and-half sister, I mean? She'd got a garage.'

'Yes, she's got a car,' Joe said. 'A small white one, too. And there's a trap-door in the kitchen leading down into the garage. They could have taken the body down that way, to save the risk of carrying it out through the front door. It looks as if you're getting yourself mixed up with a nice family.'

'I don't care a damn about her family. And anyway, she didn't do it.'

'Who, Wendy?'

'No, the other one. We had a good look round that flat, didn't we, and there wasn't any place big enough to pack a body away. So if she'd knocked off this Carlo she'd have had to keep him in the garage. That being so, why bring him up and stick him in a box, and then take him down again?'

'Fair enough,' Joe agreed. 'But whatever happened, she's going to have a hard time explaining it away when the police catch up with her. The best thing she could do would be to let them have the whole story. What's more, I'm beginning to think that's the best thing *we* could do.'

'And bring that poor, sweet innocent kid into it?' Johnny said. 'No, we've got to think of something better than that.'

'I've only one other suggestion to make, then, and I'm finished for the day. You take that sweet, innocent kid and feed her, then pick up her things wherever she left them, probably at the hotel where she stayed the night, put her on the first train back to Salisbury Plain, and let her spin what yarn she likes to Mum and Auntie Gwennie.'

'Good idea. I'll do that.' Johnny turned in his seat and half rose as Wendy came slowly back to them. She looked pale now, and her smile was somewhat strained. 'You all right?' he asked.

'I don't think brandy agrees with me very well,' she said. 'And I think I'm hungry. It's funny, because this morning I thought I'd never want to eat again.'

'You'll feel fine after you've lunched at Maudie's,' Joe grinned, and got to his feet. 'You can take the car, Johnny. And when you've done what I suggested, you might nip home and collect your traps, look up Wally and fix things with him, then pick me up at the flat.'

'Are you sure you won't be wanting the car?' Johnny looked worried. 'Only we were going . . . well, anyway, what are you going to do?'

'I've got six different appointments in six different directions and I'm skipping the lot. I'm going to snatch some food and some sleep, and if I'm still at it when you get back, mind you come in quietly. Have a key.' He took a spare one from his key ring, tossed it across to Johnny, and added, glancing at the girl, 'What are you planning to do about those bits and pieces you've bought, not to mention that perishing box?'

'Oh, those.' She sighed. 'Well, I'm not sure, yet, but I still want to have a place of my own some time, so Lysbeth said she'd keep them for me. Not the box, of course. I wouldn't want that now, would I? Lysbeth said she'd try and sell it, so I could buy something else. It's a pity, because they said it was a very fine piece, a typical product of its time.'

'Aren't we all?' Joe said. He folded the newspaper, put it in his pocket, and added, with a meaning look at Johnny, 'You won't want this, will you?'

'Are you really going now, Mr Trayne?' Wendy asked.

'Yes. Why?'

'Oh, nothing. Only I just wanted to say . . . well, you've been very kind, really, and I was rather rude to you . . . '

'Don't give it a thought,' he hastened to assure her. 'I'm used to it.'

'And then there's Mr Green,' she went on. 'I don't want to say anything against him, but it *was* all rather peculiar, and what should I do if I see him again?'

'You won't. And if you did, I doubt whether you'd recognize him, would you?'

'Oh, yes, I would, I think. I can't describe him very well but he has a dead sort of face . . . pale and chalky and . . . well, *dead*. I didn't notice it until he came to the flat, but it was the kind of face you don't forget easily.'

'Well, you just try and forget it,' Joe said. 'One dead face in twenty-four hours is enough for anyone. And if you see any more faces like that, run like mad and don't get talking to them. My love to everyone at home, and a very good afternoon to both of you.'

Saying which, he waved a hand and strolled out and up the

stairs into the blazing sunlight. A few yards along the busy street he hailed a taxi and drove home. The prospect of a crowded restaurant was suddenly obnoxious to him. Furthermore, among other accomplishments he had a certain flair for cooking, and since this was one of his housekeeper's early days, when she had what she termed 'a quick rush round', there was no reason why he should not lunch in peace and solitude.

It was a source of astonishment to him that Mrs Bushby could, when she felt like it, accomplish so much in so short a time. The flat was in perfect order when he returned and proceeded to prepare himself a meal, and not until he had eaten, drunk two glasses of iced lager and smoked three cigarettes in the kitchen, did he discover anything amiss.

Retiring to his bedroom, he was roving around, laying out his clothes for the evening, against the possibility of oversleeping, when it occurred to him that the contents of his chest of drawers were not arranged quite in their usual fashion. To anyone of less tidy habits, the disarrangement might have been unnoticeable. Not so to Joe, whose eye for symmetrical detail and unfailing ability to remember where he had put things were matters alternately of wonder and amusement to his friends. Indeed, they had won and lost bets on these special peculiarities of his.

Frowning, he lit a further cigarette and pondered the matter. Mrs Bushby never interfered with his personal possessions, he would have staked his life on it. Cleaning, catering, changing of linen and occasionally cooking she took in her line of duties, but she was not the type of woman to dance attendance upon a man, neither would Joe have wished for such an encroachment upon his independence. On the other hand, apart from himself and Johnny, she was the only person who, to his knowledge, had entered the flat that day.

Carefully he inspected the remainder of the premises, and gained an even more definite impression that someone had been through a similar procedure before him. Yet he had no difficulty in recalling that the front door had been locked, the back door firmly bolted from within, upon his return. The windows were open at the top, and upon the white paint surrounding that of his bedroom which overlooked the courtyard, were certain scratches that he had never observed before. Thoughtfully he ran his finger along them. They might have been made by the shoes of someone climbing through and finding a footplace on the ledge inside. But why should anyone want to do that? he wondered. Certainly he would not put it past some of his friends to make a forcible entry on finding no one at home to receive them, but in that case he would have expected to find the cocktail bar rifled, and at least a note saying that they would be seeing him some time. Alternatively, it could have been the work of a bold burglar, but a singularly mysterious one, since nothing appeared to have been taken.

Puzzled, he was in the act of looking over the suitcases he kept stored away in one of the bedroom cupboards, when his attention was attracted by a piece of light brown paper which had slipped between two of them to the floor. Picking it up, he turned it over to discover, printed on the reverse side, the photograph of a young woman, in profile and gazing downward. It was a head and shoulders study, not a particularly good one, and had, he conjectured, been cut from the brown paper covering of a gramophone record. The display photograph of a recording artist, a singer probably, he thought, and was surprised to find himself wishing that she would turn her head and look at him.

But what was she doing lying between his suitcases? Mrs Bushby was certainly not the woman to carry such a thing around with her. Johnny might, he supposed, but what would he be doing, delving about in cupboards? He took another long look at the young woman's downcast face, her shining dark hair drawn back to a chignon in the nape of her neck, before putting the photograph away in his wallet.

Yawning, and strangely depressed, Joe undressed and retired to bed.

Chapter VI

Johnny returned just after eight-thirty that evening. Joe, having roused himself from slumber, bathed and dressed, was pacing restlessly about the flat, a glass of beer in one hand and a cigarette in the other, when Johnny let himself in, carrying two large battered suitcases, which he set down in the entrance lounge. His face was a shade pinker than usual, his hair ruffled, and he appeared to be out of breath.

'And about time, too,' Joe said. 'Where the hell did you get to?'

'Where you told me,' Johnny hastened to say. He flopped down on to the nearest chair in the reception room, and cast an interested glance at the bar. 'We had lunch, and then . . . well, the kid seemed a bit miserable, so I didn't see it would do any harm going to a flick. Then we came out . . . '

'And as she'd never had tea in a beautiful big cinema lounge, you didn't see any harm in that either. Then what?'

'You ought to be a fortune teller,' Johnny complained. 'Well, then I saw her off at Waterloo, like you said.'

'She really did go?'

'Of course, she did. On the something-to-seven train. She has to get out at Salisbury and take a bus. I hope she'll be all right. She's going to send me a postcard.'

'She'll be all right. For a young woman who doesn't know much about anything, she does very well. She picked a couple of prize mugs to run round her this time, anyway.'

'But she had a heap of luggage.'

'She'll find some other mug to help her with it, I wouldn't be surprised. Where did you pick it up?'

'Croxley Hotel, Marylebone, where she stayed last night. Crumby-looking place it was, too.'

'Well, that's that,' Joe said, relieved. 'Swig yourself a drink and we'll be off. Did you see Wally?'

'That's where I've just come from.' Johnny, nothing loth, seized a pint bottle of beer, filled a glass and fell upon it with the air of a thirsty man. 'We fixed everything up all right, and he said to tell you that he won't be in this evening. He says he's got the totters.'

'Shouldn't drink so much,' Joe said, refilling his glass. 'By the way, you didn't go to the big cupboard in my bedroom, by any chance?'

'Me? What would I want to do that for?'

'That's what I thought. Here, have a look at this.' Joe brought out his wallet, extracted the photograph he had found earlier, and passed it to Johnny, who inspected it in some surprise. 'Ever see that before?'

'Can't say I have. Who is it?'

'God knows. I found it lying between my suitcases. It looked to me when I came in, as if someone had pushed their way in through the bedroom window, so I took a good look round, and that was the only result.'

'That's rum, isn't it?' Johnny remarked, turning the photograph over and back again. 'But it could have been there some time, couldn't it?'

'No, it couldn't, because I had everything out of there the day before yesterday. She's rather nice, isn't she?'

'Is she?' Johnny frowned his doubt upon the point. 'Looks a bit serious to me. You know, as if she'd freeze you up with a look if you said the wrong thing. Wouldn't suit me at all.'

'I'm not offering her to you,' Joe said, taking back the photograph and returning it to his wallet. 'But I think I'll find out who she is just the same. And if I get hold of whichever of her boy friends dropped that picture . . .'

'Couldn't have been a boy friend,' Johnny objected.

'Why not?'

'Because if he was that friendly he'd have a proper photograph, wouldn't he? I mean, if you're stuck on a girl, you don't just cut out pictures that anyone could have, do you?'

'That's true,' Joe agreed. 'And who should know better than you?'

'What are you going to do about it?' Johnny asked. 'You can't just let people climb in and out of windows, can you?'

'On the other hand, there's not much I can do to stop them. They didn't take anything, and I haven't even got any real proof. It's just a feeling . . . and of course, that photograph. I'm wondering whether it was one of Lysbeth's friends. After all, we climbed into her place, so there's no reason why she shouldn't try the same trick on me.'

'Sounds daft to me,' Johnny said. 'But there you are, everything she does sounds crazy. Take last night, for instance, when she got back from wherever she'd been and found Wendy . . .'

'I know,' Joe interrupted. 'Wendy told me. But if you've finished your drink, we'll go. Murder or no murder, I've got work to do.'

He flung a coat round his shoulders, and proceeded to lock all the windows. It seemed a pity, on one of the few warm nights in the year, but he saw no reason why his private apartment should be thrown open as a show place to anyone with sufficient curiosity to break in. True, if they were really determined about it, a lock or two would not stop them, but a closed window was, in his opinion, less encouraging than an open one.

'I got another paper,' Johnny said, as they left the flat by the back way, and climbed into the car parked in Johnsons Passage. 'There's a whole lot more about Betz, and a picture of him. Want to see it?'

Joe declined with thanks. For the moment Betz, his friends and enemies no longer interested him. He had other affairs to think about, and a great many things to do, he discovered upon arrival at the Allsorts. Perhaps on account of the unusual warmth, Wally was not the only one who had decided to stay out that evening, and as a consequence Joe was a very busy man.

Fortunately or unfortunately, according to one's point of view, he could turn his hand to most things, including helping in the kitchen, preparing drinks, checking supplies, throwing out drunks or persuading them to leave, settling an argument between two cabaret dancers, tending the bar, and exchanging badinage with sundry members of the clientele who claimed his attention. It was nearly closing time before he felt justified in retiring to his own office with a plate of cold chicken and salad, a fork and several bottles of beer. Such meals as he took on the premises he was accustomed to eat while standing about in any odd corner that took his fancy, but just now he felt a little solitude to be highly desirable.

Seated on the edge of the desk, he plied his fork, drank his beer, and idly glanced through the newspaper that Johnny had left for him. The latter had proved exceptionally useful during a crowded evening, and had not yet returned from driving home a trio of guests who lived sufficiently far out of town to make transport difficult.

The printed photograph of Betz was not particularly flattering, Joe decided, but the likeness to the young man he had seen in the chest was unmistakable. Even so, he reflected, what difference did it make? In all probability, sooner or later the police would check up on Lysbeth, and if somehow they managed to trace the body back to her flat, she would have some heavy explaining to do. Possibly he would, too, if it came out that he had been on the scene, but the prospect did not worry him overmuch. If Johnny were not so dead set on that ridiculous child Wendy . . . He raised his head as there came a knock at the door, and in answer to his 'Come in', Johnny entered, wearing a light overcoat.

'All right?' Joe queried, pushing aside his plate and lighting a cigarette.

'Yes and no,' Johnny said. 'I dumped 'em and I got back all right, but as I was coming in the back, a rum-looking cove pushed up to me and asked for you.'

'A lot of them do, but they don't usually come in the back. What does he want?'

'He didn't say. He's hanging around outside now. He wouldn't give his name.'

'Maybe he hasn't got one,' Joe said. 'Send him in, and then we'll close down. There's nothing much doing, is there?'

'Nothing much. Just a few odds and ends.'

'Right.' Joe strolled round and sat down on the other side of the desk, as Johnny withdrew and returned a few minutes later with the visitor, whose appearance was certainly not calculated to inspire confidence. He was smallish and slender, with slim wrists and hands and bright brown eyes which glanced quickly this way and that like those of an animal on the defensive. He wore a loose flowing overcoat and a round, dented-in green felt hat closely pulled over his eyes. He stood just inside the door, looking about him, but whether he was admiring the orderliness of the room or merely taking stock of his surroundings would have been difficult to say.

Joe said, 'All right, Johnny,' and the latter, with a grimace at the stranger's back, went out again, shutting the door but not, Joe imagined, moving very far away from it. With another lingering glance round, the newcomer advanced, leaned both hands upon the desk, and enquired, 'Name of Trayne?'

Joe, examining him with some curiosity from the other side, said, 'That's right. What can I do for you?'

'Name of Dight,' the man said, and sat down, from which vantage point he proceeded to appraise Joe with the same attention he had previously given to the room. While appreciating his economy of speech, there was something in his manner that Joe found vaguely irritating. To be affable at that hour of the morning was always somewhat of an effort, and on this occasion he saw no reason why he should attempt it. He therefore crushed out his cigarette and lighted another without offering the box standing at his elbow. The lack of courtesy did not appear to worry his visitor, who promptly brought out a cigarette from a gold case, lighted it, and returned case and lighter to his pocket, before continuing, 'Joe Trayne . . . and you run this place. That right?'

Joe nodded, wondering why he could never be identified as himself, without his background.

'You know Miss Ritchley?' the man asked, as if he were not very much interested one way or the other. Equally disinterested, but his mind watchful, Joe countered,

'Any particular one? I don't know if you've noticed it, but quite a few people live in these parts.'

The man who called himself Dight brought out a notebook, consulted it, and said, 'Lysbeth Ritchley, 7, Thunder Mews, W.1. Said you'd give her a reference.'

'She did?' Joe's stare was frankly incredulous. 'What would she do that for?'

'You know her, don't you?'

'I know a lot of people, but some of them wouldn't get past the first ditch for a reference. What is it for, a job?'

'Something like that. She sings, doesn't she?'

'Not when she sees me,' Joe said. 'If you want her, Mr Dight, to sing or anything else, you're welcome, as far as I'm concerned. I met the lady once, and that's enough for me. Not that it would stop me giving anyone a reference if I felt like it. But I don't and that's final. What's more I'm going to ring through and tell her so.'

He pulled the telephone toward him and reached for the directory lying nearby, at the same time keeping a thoughtful eye upon Dight, who neither moved nor changed his expression. Having found the number, he dialled, and they waited in silence, while Joe listened in to the monotonous ringing tone, and Dight, finishing his cigarette and ignoring the ashtray, flung down the smoking end and crushed it with his heel on the carpet, much to Joe's annoyance. Replacing the receiver, he said, 'The little lady appears to be out. What happens now?'

'Nothing,' Dight said, and was about to rise, when Johnny knocked on the door and entered, and came across to Joe, carrying a slip of paper in one hand.

'Excuse me, Mr Trayne,' he said, and Joe looked up in surprise at the deference in his tone. But Johnny's face was a mask of servility and anxiety to do the right thing as he continued, 'There's a gentleman just leaving who says he's run short of cash, and would you sign the bill until next time?'

Joe took it from him, saw a jumble of meaningless figures, and was about to ask what Johnny was playing at, when he caught the hint of a smile in the latter's eyes, and looked at the bill again. Beneath the figures, in a scrawl that he took to be Johnny's handwriting, he read: 'Anything I can do? J.' He thought for a few seconds, then bringing out his fountain pen, he wrote: 'Follow Dight', and signed his name with a flourish.

'I'll do it this once,' he said. 'But he'd better not try that trick too often. I don't trust him.' Handing back the bill, he added, 'Show Mr Dight out, will you, Johnny? I don't think we've anything else to say to each other.'

'I'll show myself out,' Dight said, rising, as Johnny departed. 'Where would Miss Ritchley be, if she's not at home? D'you know?'

'Sorry to be so unhelpful,' Joe said. 'But this isn't an enquiry office.' He walked to the door, which Johnny had left partly open in making his exit, and flung it wide. Dight, with a last glance round, went out, and Joe followed closely. There was no sign of Johnny in the passage. Probably he had gone to bring the car round. Joe hoped so. He had a strong desire to find out who Dight was and what exactly he had come for. The reference story was a fake, if ever he had heard one. He would have preferred personally to follow Dight, but someone had to close down, and though the clientele had departed there was still much to do.

The band was packing up, but as they passed through, Joe observed Bon Casey, the pianist, still sitting at the piano, a cigarette drooping from one corner of his mouth while he idly ran his hands over the keys. Joe smiled slightly. Although he had been playing best part of the evening, Bon would sit like that for hours if someone did not drag him off the stool and take him home.

Still following upon Dight's heels, they had almost reached the back exit when the latter stopped abruptly, half turned and then remained motionless, as if paralysed, one hand pressed against the wall. From the inner room drifted the sound of Bon's playing, a very individual version of some theme which Joe found vaguely familiar, but could not immediately place. He asked, 'Anything wrong?' and instinctively put out a hand and caught Dight's arm.

The latter muttered, 'Who's that playing?' Under the artificial light, sweat showed on his forehead. It was a warm night, but until now he had seemed pretty cool.

'Casey, the pianist,' Joe said. 'Who else would it be?'

'I ... don't know.' With an obvious and tremendous effort, Dight pulled himself together, shook off Joe's hand with an impatient movement, and added, 'Sorry. Not feeling well. The heat, I expect.' Saying which, he went quickly out and disappeared into the darkness of the early morning. Joe followed, and stood within the doorway, peering left and right. He was in time to see the hurrying figure of Dight round the bend on the other side of the road, and then another figure about the size of Johnny emerge from the shadows and move off in pursuit, at a discreet distance. Slowly Joe retraced his steps and returned to find Bon Casey being gently persuaded by the rest of the band to make tracks for home. Joe leaned one elbow on top of the piano and ran through the pile of music lying there.

'What was that you were playing just now, Bon?' he asked. 'Just after I walked through.'

'Didn't you recognize it?' Bon grinned, pushed back his curly black hair, and finished the drink with which he had been toying for the last half hour. '*Lament for the Dead*. Vivesco's masterpiece. I was jazzing it up a bit. Straight, it goes like this.'

'Oh, God, you're not going through it again?' the drummer

groaned, and turned away to collect his own things as Bon flopped down upon the stool and recommenced his playing.

'Yes, I've got it now,' Joe said. 'But it's not what you'd call a popular piece, exactly?'

'Not exactly. Highbrow. Needs pepping up a bit. Like this.' He proceeded to illustrate with many weird variations of his own. 'Good, isn't it? But they wouldn't appreciate it, not the gang you get here.'

'No, I doubt whether they would.' Except, perhaps, Mr Dight, Joe thought. It had appeared to make a deep impression upon him. Yet he did not look the kind of man to take an interest in classical music. 'Thanks, Bon. That was grand. But you'd better pack up now. The boys want to go home.'

The pianist struck a few chords and reluctantly got to his feet. 'Okay, Joe. But one of these days I'm going to sock something like this at 'em, and they're going to like it.'

Joe nodded absently, and strolled away. Most of the staff had gone now, but it took him some considerable time to get everything clear, and he was thinking longingly of a last drink, a cigarette and bed, when he went the final round of locking up, and emerged into Sleigh Street, where he was lucky enough to pick up a passing taxi.

As he got out his keys the other end and entered Hamilton House, he wondered whether Johnny would have arrived before him. Then as he reached his own front door, he stopped thinking about Johnny, and stood staring at sight of Wendy Bond seated on the floor. Her back was propped against the door, her eyes were closed. She appeared to be asleep.

Chapter VII

With a quickening of the heart, Joe bent down and gently touched Wendy on the shoulder. To his relief, she opened her eyes with a start, and stared back at him.

'And what,' he said, with a baleful glance, 'do you think you're doing here?'

She lifted both hands to massage her temples, shook her head several times in a dazed way, and said, 'I must have fallen asleep. I'm waiting for Johnny.'

'Oh, you are? Did he tell you to come here?'

'No . . . no, of course not. He only gave me his address to write to. But I just had to see him, so I came along. I'd no idea he'd be out so late. But I'm glad you've come. We can wait together now. I was getting frightened, being alone.'

'I'm not waiting for anyone,' Joe said. 'I'm going to bed as fast as I can get there.'

'Oh . . .' She rose and eyed him doubtfully as he inserted his key in the lock. 'Do you live here, too?'

'Yes. D'you mind?'

'Of course not. Only . . . well, is it all right for me to come in and wait?'

Joe looked down at her with some bitterness. 'I'd like to leave you just where you are,' he said. 'But my upbringing won't let me. Come in.' He switched on the light, stood aside for her to enter, and closed the door. Then very deliberately he walked across to the bar, poured himself a large rum and lime, and opened the door of the lounge. 'In here,' he said, switching on further illumination. 'Take off your coat, sit down, and tell me, before I do something desperate, *why aren't you in Salisbury*?' On second thoughts, he picked up the rum bottle and took it with him, as she sidled into the lounge, looked cautiously about her, and sat down on the arm of a chair.

'I'll keep my coat on, if you don't mind,' she said.

'By all means. It's a hot night, this room is like an oven, but if you want to stifle, go ahead and stifle. It's all one to me.'

'Why do you keep the windows closed then?' she asked, watching him curiously as he strolled round opening them.

'Because I'm terrified of burglars. But suppose, instead of asking *me* questions, you answer mine?'

'I can't talk to you,' she said, her face setting in the childishly obstinate fashion he was beginning to know and to dislike intensely. 'You're so horrid and unsympathetic. You make everything I say sound silly. I want to see Johnny.'

Joe drank his rum, refilled the glass, dropped down into the nearest chair, and regarded her in exasperation. He wanted to rid himself of the restrictions of his evening clothes, to lie down on his bed in cool pyjamas, or better still, without, and to let his mind drift until it found solace in slumber. The presence of Wendy was stultifying enough, but there was no point even in seeking the comfort of a dressing-gown and slippers, while he was still uncertain where Johnny was and whether he might have to institute a one-man search party. Mentally he cursed the impulse that had

83

caused him to send Johnny on such an errand. At the moment he did not care who Dight was or what was the reason of his visit.

'Well, if you feel like that about it,' he said at last, 'we'll talk of something else. How was the country looking, or didn't you get as far as that?'

'I got out at Basingstoke,' she said.

'Is that an evening paper?' he asked, indicating the bundle of news sheets she was clutching with her handbag. 'You might pass it over. Since we're turning this into a waiting-room, we may as well have the atmosphere right.'

Silently she handed them to him. There was a lunch-time edition of *Nightly News* and three other evening papers. They all carried the story of Carlo Betz. There were further details which Joe had not previously seen, and in particular he noted that the police were on the track of the white car driven away by the two men who dumped the body, and that Betz, who had served a short prison sentence some time back for forgery, had been known to his fellow convicts as 'The Artist', because of his gift for caricature.

Joe lit a cigarette, drank some more, and turned to the sports pages, in an effort to switch his mind to other things. Wendy asked, as he was refilling his glass, 'Aren't you ever afraid of getting drunk?'

'No, but sometimes I'm afraid of staying sober, and this is one of them.' He looked up with relief as there came the sound of a key in the lock of the front door. He called, 'That you, Johnny?'

'Me once more,' Johnny said, coming in with a grin which faded at sight of Wendy. Joe laughed, and said, 'This isn't how it looks. Little Wendy has returned like a homing pigeon, and it's you she's waiting for. Hog yourself a drink while she tells you whatever it is she can't tell me. I'm going to give me a change of

84

clothes.' Saying which, he rose and went into the bedroom, shut the door, and breathed several deep sighs. Then he removed his clothes, took a cold shower, donned pyjamas, dressing-gown and slippers, lay down on the bed and smoked three cigarettes, while dozing happily.

'Sorry to bust in ...' Johnny's voice said, and he looked up to see the young man peering at him round the door.

'Bust away,' Joe said. 'This is just anyone's flat. Some come in through the door and others prefer the window. What is it now?'

'Wendy's in trouble.' Johnny looked worried as he came across and flopped down on the edge of the bed. 'That sister of hers has disappeared.'

'Good. Got any more news like that?'

'The box has gone, too.'

'Better and better. And why shouldn't they disappear? She's probably sent herself away in it somewhere, C.O.D. To fox the police. And I don't blame her, as far as that side of it goes.'

'This isn't funny,' Johnny said. 'It was like this, see. I put Wendy on the train all right, as I said. I purposely didn't give her a paper to read, because I reckoned you didn't want me to, and I thought the same. But feeling nice and matey, some dimwit has to go and pass her one, and she sees all that stuff about Betz. So she gets out at the next stop, because she figures her sweet sister is in a bigger hell of a mess than she thought ...'

'Why?' Joe asked, watching him dreamily through half-closed eyelids. 'She hadn't much to go on.'

'There was a picture in the paper she saw. It was a later one, see. So she felt she couldn't very well go back home without knowing what was going to happen to her sister.'

'But it was her sister who was so keen on her leaving, wasn't it?'

'That's right. Maybe it suited her plans, but it didn't suit Wendy, not when she realized that the police were in on it. They don't hit it off together much, but Wendy sort of admires her, you know how kids are.'

'Thank God I don't,' Joe said. 'What then?'

'Well, after she'd messed about changing trains and so on, it was round about nine. She puts her traps in the luggage dump, and goes round to her sister's flat, but it was all locked up and no sister. So she gets herself some grub at a café and hangs about a bit, and then back she goes to the flat, and what do you think?'

'There was a wolf sitting up in Lysbeth's bed wearing a natty nightshirt,' Joe suggested.

Johnny eyed him in some anxiety. 'You wouldn't be tight, would you?' he asked.

'No. And if anyone else accuses me of being tight, I'm going to get tight, and then you'll all know about it. I'm just one very tired and bored individual, who needs a lot of sleep.'

'We can't go to sleep and leave the kid parked in a chair,' Johnny pointed out.

'I realize that. All right, go on and tell me the best and the worst. She got back to the flat, and then what?'

'Well, she rang and rang and didn't get any answer, so she tried the garage doors, and this time she found they weren't locked, so she went inside, thinking to see her sister there, just come back. But again no sister, no car and no box.'

'Lysbeth said she was going to get rid of it, didn't she? That's probably where she's gone.'

'Wendy thought of that. She's a pretty bright kid, when you get to know her. She's got guts, too. Because although she was pretty scared by then, she went up through the trap-door to have a look round the flat, just in case. But all she found was your name and number written on the telephone pad.'

'*My* name?' Joe cut in. 'Who the hell did that?'

'Her sister, she reckons, because it was her writing.'

'But I only saw the woman once in my life. And first she scrawls my name all over the place and then starts chucking it around as a reference. Unless Dight was lying, which was quite likely. Did you find out anything about him, by the way?'

'Not much. I've an idea he expected someone to tail him, because he nipped along, all crafty, and suddenly dived into a barrow he had hidden away round the corner. So I dived into mine, I mean yours, and went after. He didn't half lead me a dance, too. But anyone'd have to be pretty slick to drop me off once I'm on, and with a barrow like yours it was kids' stuff.'

'What sort of a car was his?' Joe asked.

'Two-seater Spick, dark blue, fairly new and fast, but not fast enough. We finished up in Maida Vale, ordinary sort of house, a lot of steps up to it, and a basement, that sort of thing. I've got the address. I parked the barrow round the corner and hung about a bit, just to give Little Willie a chance to settle down. Then I whisked back and took another look. There was a name on the door. Mendoza.'

'And the address?' Joe asked.

Johnny brought from his pocket a slip of paper, and Joe read: Mendoza, 13, Cleeve Rise, Maida Vale. He put it down on the bed-side table, and said, 'It all means less than nothing to me.'

'You haven't heard the rest of it,' Johnny said. 'I'm thinking that Wendy saw this Dight merchant tonight, and another one, who might be this Mendoza.'

Joe sat up slowly and ran a hand over his forehead. 'That young woman digs up more trouble in one evening than anyone else I've ever heard of,' he complained. 'Why doesn't she go home?'

'She's missed the last train. And you can't make her catch the first one down in the morning, because she's too jittery to go home now.'

'Her name ought to be Windy,' Joe said. 'Why d'you think she saw Dight, and where?'

'At her sister's place. She went back to the garage, see, after she'd found there wasn't anyone upstairs. Then she had another poke round, and on the wall someone had written: "We shall need it again". Well, that put the wind up her properly . . . '

'Why? It might have been there for years.'

'No. It was written up big and fresh in chalk. She said she never saw it before, and she wouldn't have seen it then if she hadn't thought to switch on all the lights. The first thing she thinks is that someone has nabbed Lysbeth and the box and is going to stick one in the other, if you see what I mean. So she whisks out to come and find me.'

'You needn't look so damned smug about it,' Joe said. 'For all you know someone is planning to dump that blasted box and Lysbeth on our doorstep at this moment.'

'That's just where we've got to get clever,' Johnny urged. 'How I see it is that we can't go to the police and tell them Lysbeth has gone. For one thing, she may have skipped out for her own reasons. For another, it means dragging Wendy into it, and it's all too airy-fairy anyhow. But this Dight merchant is in it somewhere, I'll bet anything. Because as Wendy legged it up the mews, a little barrow came bowling along and stopped outside No. 7. She dived under cover and watched, and two men got out, and one of 'em, from what she said about him, sounds like Dight to me. The other was a big, fat sort of cove. And what do they do but open up the front door with a key and go inside, and that's that.'

'Did she leave the garage doors open or shut?'

'Shut, but of course they weren't locked because she hasn't got a key. She used to have a front door key, but she gave that back to Lysbeth when she was packing up.'

'Had they been forced?'

'She said not. They work on a padlock, see, and someone had just left it stuck through.'

Joe lit a cigarette and lay back again. 'Could have been Lysbeth,' he said. 'Women do that kind of thing. Or these other two. If they've got a key to the front door, why shouldn't they have one to the garage? Say they're friends of hers, say they were the two who ran her boy friend's body out and dumped it in the pond, wouldn't they be likely to take the box off her hands, too?'

'And what would they be doing, chalking things on the wall?' Johnny asked.

'That may not have anything to do with it. As for Lysbeth, I think it highly probable she's looking after her future by walking off and leaving everything to sort itself out.'

'This Dight, then. Why did he come and see you? I didn't like the look of him. I thought he was up to something. I still reckon so.'

'That was odd,' Joe agreed. 'He said Lysbeth had given my name as a reference. For what, he didn't say. A job of some kind. It sounded barmy to me, but if that really was Dight popping into her place with a key, then the whole thing reeks. If you're that friendly with someone you don't ask them for references.' He was silent for a moment or two, then added, 'That note on her telephone pad about me. Wendy left it there, I suppose?'

'No, she tore it off and stuck it in her bag. She thought it might be a good thing to do.'

'She's got a little sense,' Joe admitted. 'Now the question is, what are we going to do with her, if she won't go home? She can't stay here. I'm not giving up my bed to anyone.'

'She couldn't in any case,' Johnny said. 'With two men alone – I ask you.'

Joe laughed. 'If you feel like that about her, you'd better tuck her away somewhere nice and safe. She wants a job, doesn't she?'

'That was the idea. But I still say London's not the right place for her.'

'Good.' Joe got up and strolled to the door. 'D'you think she'll faint if she sees a man in a dressing-gown?'

'Not if I'm right behind you,' Johnny said, as he rose and followed Joe into the lounge where Wendy, still wrapped in her old tweed coat, lay back in an armchair, her eyes closed. She opened them as they entered. She looked, Joe thought, as if she had been crying. Smiling, he sat down opposite.

'How do you feel now?' he asked. 'Better?'

'Yes, a little, thank you.' Her glance went past him to Johnny, and back again. 'Has Johnny told you . . . ?' Joe nodded. 'Then you do see, don't you . . . ?'

'That you can't go back to Mum with all this on your mind. Yes, I see that. Well, just leave it to Johnny and me and we'll work it out for you. But meanwhile, you've got to have a job. Right. Know anything about horses?'

'I've always been able to ride, well, as long as I can remember, if that's what you mean. But . . . '

'That's just what I do mean. I can imagine you galloping all over Salisbury Plain. No, don't get alarmed. I'm not going to ask you to do a Dick Turpin tonight. But we've got a riding school attached to our place in Hertford, and you can give them a hand there, if you like. That'll keep you out of mischief for a bit, anyway. Johnny, do you feel like doing some more driving?'

'Makes no difference to me,' Johnny said. 'As long as Wendy's all right.'

'Fine. Then you can run her out to the "Nosebag", and pick up her luggage and send it down later. I'll give you a couple of letters to the people there, and they'll look after her. MacNeil is the riding master. He looks a tough nut, but he's a sentimentalist at heart.'

Suddenly businesslike, Joe rose and went to the writing bureau, wrote two letters, sealed and addressed them and handed them to Johnny. Then he got out a road map, and gave explicit directions as to the quickest route, after which he made coffee and sandwiches to speed his departing guests.

'You're sure it's all right?' Johnny asked, as Joe saw them to the door. 'I mean, it isn't everyone who likes people busting in on them all hours.'

'I put up with it,' Joe grinned. 'So why shouldn't they? In any case, they never sleep much before breakfast. I'd give them a ring through to say you're on your way, only I've a fellow feeling for night operators.'

'You're very kind,' Wendy said, shaking her head in a puzzled way. 'I can't understand you at all. Why aren't you always the same?'

He patted her shoulder. 'It's a matter of mood. Just now I feel like a nice, fatherly type. By the way, have you still got that sheet you tore off your sister's telephone pad, the one with my name on it?'

'Somewhere,' she said, rummaging in her handbag. 'Why? Do you want it?'

'Thanks.' He took it from her, glanced at it and thrust it into the pocket of his dressing-gown. 'Are you sure that's your sister's writing?'

'Oh, yes. I'm certain about that. Although I can't think . . . '

'Don't you try. We'll do all the thinking for you.'

'But I feel rather mean,' she said, tears gathering in her eyes again. 'Going off like this, while Lysbeth . . . '

'You couldn't do any good staying in town, could you? Now you run along and don't read too many newspapers. We'll keep you posted with all the latest. And Johnny . . . ' He took the young man by the arm and added, in an aside, 'If you see anyone on the road who seems to be going your way, I should give them the slip, if I were you.'

'Trust me,' Johnny said, and with his arm about Wendy's shoulders, they departed.

Closing the front door, Joe found to his surprise that he was no longer particularly tired. He collected the cups and saucers, washed and put them away, and lighting a cigarette, he lay down on the divan in the lounge and gave himself up to a little serious thinking.

Chapter VIII

The fine weather broke the following day. Joe, strolling along Bond Street just after eleven in the morning, glanced at the pall of fast-gathering storm clouds, and congratulated himself on having donned a light raincoat. The air was stifling with an unpleasant humidity in it. Johnny had telephoned earlier to say he had snatched a few hours' sleep at the 'Nosebag', and would be back about mid-day. Wendy, he said, was perfectly all right.

Joe was not very much concerned about that. He had other things to think of. The press that morning had come out with a statement that the police were anxious to interview Lysbeth Ritchley, who was not at her home when they called to interrogate her regarding her association with Carlo Betz, to whom the newspapers now referred as 'Dead Artist-Gangster'.

Outside Oakey's Music Shop Joe paused and took a long survey of the records, sheet music and advertisement displays in the window. There were several photographs of recording artists, but the one in which he was interested was not among them. He entered, walked through the musical instrument and theatre ticket sections, and up the stairs at the back to the record department, where sundry music lovers were vying with each other for the attention of three lady assistants.

Joe selected the youngest, leaned upon her end of the counter and smiled. He had been smiling for several minutes before she noticed him, and he was obliged to go on smiling for some time after that ere she approached and asked his requirements, whereupon he brought out the photograph he had been carrying in his wallet, pushed it across to her, and said, 'Forgive me for troubling you with such a question at such a time on such a day, but do you know who this is?'

She picked it up, pursed her lips, frowned and put it down again. 'I do,' she said. 'But I can't place her ... Half a minute.' She turned away and began to search through a row of records on the shelf behind. A slim, pale young man standing beside Joe reached for the photograph, glanced at it and smiled with a hint of patronage.

'Melda Linklater,' he said.

'Thanks.' Joe took the photograph from him and replaced it in his wallet. 'What does she do for a living?'

The young man raised an eyebrow. 'I said, Linklater,' he repeated, and proceeded to spell it. 'The concert pianist, you know.'

Joe grinned. 'I didn't know. We move, I think, in different circles. But thanks just the same.'

The young man was about to say something, but the assistant returned just then and placed upon the counter a record, the cover of which bore a photograph identical with that in Joe's possession. Beneath it was printed the caption: 'Melda Linklater, who records exclusively for Excellaphone.' She announced with triumph, 'Here she is.'

'That's right,' Joe said. 'Is this a recording of hers?'

'No. We have thousands of those covers. But I can get you one. Which would you like?'

'I don't know. Anything'll do.'

The slim young man, with a scornful glance, moved away. The assistant rapidly turned the leaves of a catalogue, and indicated a list with her pencil. 'Any of those?' she asked. Casting a rapid survey up and down the page, Joe's attention was caught and held by one line ... *Lament for the Dead* ... *(Vivesco)*.

'I'd like that, if you have it,' he said. She took a note of the number, turned again to the shelves and came back presently with the record, for which he paid and thanked her. Tucking it under his arm, he left the department. Outside in the theatre ticket section he paused to light a cigarette, and from a display notice three names in bold type seemed fairly to leap at him: *Titanic Hall ... The Imperial Symphony Orchestra with Melda Linklater.* He moved in for a closer view, and carefully read through details of three concerts. One had taken place a fortnight ago, the second would be given that afternoon at two-thirty, and the third a fortnight hence.

Upon impulse, Joe strolled to the counter, waited his turn among the throng of amusement seekers, and enquired whether there were any available seats for the afternoon's concert at the Titanic. A very aloof young woman told him that she doubted it, but she would make certain. She kept him waiting ten minutes, before returning to say that he was fortunate. A box had been cancelled, and she inferred that he could take it or leave it. He decided to take it, paid for it and walked out to find the atmosphere even more oppressive, the darkening sky illuminated by intermittent flashes of lightning.

Taxis being in great demand, he walked to the nearest empty telephone box, and put through a call to his flat, from where he was answered by Mrs Bushby, who stated that she was alone, and about to leave. Never having heard of Johnny, it took him some time to explain the identity of his guest, but eventually he elicited from her a promise to leave a message asking Johnny to meet him in the vestibule of the Titanic Hall at two o'clock.

Emerging, he succeeded in commandeering an empty taxi and drove to Cleeve Rise, Maida Vale, at the top of which he dismissed the vehicle, and walked slowly down in search of No. 13. It was a somewhat dreary neighbourhood, the houses on either side of the road tall, monotonously alike and exuding a vague atmosphere of decay. No. 13 was similar to the rest, three storeys high, eight stone steps leading up to the front door, a basement with an area surrounded in iron railings, the iron door to which was padlocked. At the windows, the curtains were mostly drawn, and frankly dirty.

Joe, feeling depressed at sight of it all, walked up the steps and rang the bell, above which a card bore the name of Mendoza. As he half expected there was no reply. He spent approximately fifteen minutes alternately ringing the bell, knocking, staring at the windows and glancing up and down the street which, probably due to the impending storm, was almost deserted. He brought out all his keys and systematically tried them in the lock, but without result.

A window on the second floor, he observed, was partially open. Not very helpful, but sufficient to inspire a speculative glance in that direction. From merely feeling that a personal interview with Messrs Dight and Mendoza might prove interesting, he had developed a passionate desire to gain entrance to the house with or without permission. Thunder rolled in the distance, came nearer, and finished with a terrific clap overhead. Two cars passed along the street, a woman with a dog, and then a window-cleaner, going as fast as his loaded cart would allow him. Moved to action by this last welcome sight, Joe ran down the steps and hailed him. The window-cleaner drew into the side of the road, and eyed him enquiringly.

'Have you got a ladder you can lend me?' Joe asked. 'Like a damned fool I've left my keys inside, and my wife'll give me hell if she comes back and finds me sitting on the doorstep in the middle of a thunderstorm. Luckily I've left my bedroom window open.'

The eyes of the window-cleaner followed his glance, but his gaze was dubious. 'Don't know if I've got one long enough, chum,' he said.

Joe looked suitably despondent. 'A pity,' he remarked. 'It'd be worth a quid to me to get inside within the next ten minutes.'

The face of the window-cleaner became a shade more hopeful. 'Might try an extending one,' he suggested. 'Let's have a go.' Whereupon he took down the longest ladder of his collection, carried it across the pavement and fixed it to his satisfaction, with the top portion within easy scaling distance of the open window. 'There you are,' he said. 'How's that?'

'Fine, thanks,' Joe assured him, handing over a pound note which his accomplice hastily pocketed. 'It just shows you that housebreaking isn't as hard as it sounds.'

'It does and all,' the window-cleaner grinned, and held the ladder while Joe cautiously ascended, slid up the bottom half of the window, and climbed through.

'Thanks very much,' he called down, and an errand boy, who had been loitering on the other side of the road, picked up his basket and went on, satisfied that the fun was over. The window-cleaner nodded to Joe, replaced his ladder and continued on his way, just as the first heavy drops of rain began to fall. Joe watched him go, then closed down the window and took a quick survey of his surroundings. There was no need for more, since the room was quite empty, the floor bare. He inspected the interior of two cupboards and discovered nothing but space.

He went out on to the landing, and into two other rooms and a toilet, all empty and neglected. The floor above was identical, except that from the top landing a short flight of stairs led to an attic, the door of which was padlocked. He could, he supposed, do something about that, given time, but glancing at his wrist-watch, he decided that time was not on his side. He went below, and found that from the first floor to the ground the house was furnished, and that with a certain style and comfort.

The first floor boasted three bedrooms, a bathroom and toilet, and below a large office, a sitting-room, a kitchen opened off the passage, where the stairs continued down to the basement. But here he was again brought to a standstill by a padlocked door. The atmosphere in this part of the house was that of a place well used. There was nothing remarkable about it, but the contents of the office proved not uninteresting.

In the centre of the carpeted floor stood a massive desk, the drawers of which were locked, barred and bolted to all but the most sophisticated of cracksmen. But a small bureau by the window yielded better results. The top drawer was open, and in it Joe discovered miscellaneous correspondence addressed to Gilbert Mendoza, Esq. It was not very illuminating, consisting chiefly of bills, paid and unpaid, but sandwiched carelessly between two of them was a slip of paper, obviously torn from a telephone pad, for it was headed: *Telephone Memoranda*. The sheet was blank of ordinary writing, but bore an imprint as if a sharp pencil had been used upon the previous sheet immediately over it. Holding it sideways, Joe could read quite easily his own name and telephone number.

He brought out the original slip which, according to Wendy, Lysbeth had written, and compared the two, one beneath the other. They fitted exactly. It seemed that Johnny's surmise was right, he thought, and Mendoza must have been one of the two men Wendy had seen entering Lysbeth's flat the previous night. He placed both pieces of paper in his wallet, took out a pencil and scrawled across the blotting pad upon the desk, 'I should like to see you some time . . . Joe Trayne.'

Making a final tour of the room, he was intrigued at sight of a large, flat oblong parcel propped against the wall to one side of the empty fireplace. It took him some time to undo the string, which was tightly tied, but he had it unwrapped at last, and brought to light a modern painting in oils in a plain wooden frame. It was a study in blues and greens of a woman seated at a piano, with light filtering on to the keys across one shoulder. She was in profile, and whether the piano suggested the idea he could not be sure, but she looked to him extraordinarily like Melda Linklater. At the base, a single name was boldly signed: 'Solby'. He studied the picture for a few moments longer, before re-wrapping it and returning it to its place by the wall. Then he left the office and walked quietly out of the front door, shutting it behind him.

Torrential rain now beat upon the pavement, and thunder and lightning continued to add a theatrical touch to the scene. He turned up the collar of his coat, beneath which he held the gramophone record for greater protection, and walked as far as the main thoroughfare, where he entered the nearest saloon bar and refreshed himself with a couple of drinks and lunch at the snack counter. Then finding a disengaged taxi at a rank nearby, he drove to the Titanic Hall, Mayfair, to find a vast throng in the vestibule and no sign of Johnny. He consigned his waterproof and the record to the care of the cloakroom attendant and returned in time to see Johnny charging up the steps.

'What's the idea?' the latter asked, staring about him in some bewilderment.

'We're going to hear a concert,' Joe said. 'Get rid of that coat, and come on. It starts at two-thirty.'

'Not me,' Johnny protested. 'Saturday afternoons I go to the dogs.'

'In this weather?'

'In any weather. I wouldn't know what to do at a concert.'

'All you've got to do is to sit still and keep quiet. I've taken a box, and I've got to fill it up with someone besides me. Don't you want to improve your mind?'

'No,' Johnny said, but sensing that the prospects of immediate escape were slight, he parted reluctantly with his coat, and followed Joe and an attendant into the precincts of a box from where, he declared, he could only see the stage by crossing his eyes.

'You don't have to see,' Joe remarked, studying the programme. 'You're supposed to listen.'

'To what?'

'To Melda Linklater, the young lady whose photograph I found in my flat.'

'Is she here?'

'She will be. She's the soloist. I bought a record of hers today. We'll make a music lover of you yet.'

'Not if it means sitting in a dump like this,' Johnny said with a shudder. 'It gives me the creeps.'

There was some truth in his contention. The Titanic Hall was old and large and very draughty, and even fully illuminated the gloom caused by its loftiness was intense. Below, in the auditorium, the audience was slowly filtering in. Viewing them idly, Joe asked, 'How's Wendy?'

'Fine. That MacNeil seems to be a right sort of cove, too. He said he'd look after her, if she looked after his horses. Funny that, isn't it? She gets on a treat with horses.'

'It doesn't surprise me in the least,' Joe said.

'And that manager cove, what's-his-name . . . '

'Toni?'

'Yes, Toni. He seems all right, too. His wife has given her a nice little room, so everything's lovely.'

'I'm just hoping,' Joe said, 'that Wally is going to take this the right way. I didn't think to ring through and tell him about it. Still, we'll be seeing him tonight, I wouldn't be surprised.'

The orchestra was entering, amid applause, the audience settling seriously into position. The hall was fairly crowded, and all the boxes taken with the exception of the one immediately opposite their own. Johnny, casting melancholy glances in all directions, brought out a cigarette and was about to light it, when Joe caught his arm, and said, 'Can't you read? They've got about a thousand notices saying "No Smoking".'

Johnny looked at the nearest one, replaced his cigarette and groaned. 'Crumby lot,' he muttered. 'Don't they ever have any fun?'

He was about to enlarge upon the theme when the audience, as one man and woman, rose to the strains of the National Anthem, and Joe jerked him to his feet, in which position he stood, staring down at the floor. Brightening visibly at the finish, he remarked, 'Well, that's a bit of luck,' and made decisive movements towards the exit.

'Where d'you think you're going?' Joe asked in an undertone.

'Out. It's all over, isn't it? They just played "God Save the King".'

'It's just starting,' Joe said. 'And if you don't sit down and shut up . . . '

Many crushing glances were turned in their direction as Johnny subsided, temporarily suppressed, and the programme began. But within a very short time he was leaning over to tug at Joe's sleeve and to whisper, 'What about this woman of yours? I don't see her.'

'She's not on until after the interval,' Joe whispered back. 'This is a symphony.'

'Is that what it is? I thought they'd just dropped in to practise.'

'Someone's going to drop you over the side in a minute,' Joe said. 'And I wouldn't be surprised if it's me.'

Whereupon he shut his eyes and refused to be drawn into further conversation. So far, he was not having a particularly good time himself, but for the sake of an idea and the people who had come to listen he was prepared to suffer in silence. Not so Johnny, who, halfway through the performance, went to sleep and snored gently but with a rhythm irritating to anyone within hearing distance. As the symphony came to an end, he awoke in time to join in the applause, adding a cheer or so for good measure.

'Sorry,' he said, catching Joe's eye, 'I was dreaming we were at a cup tie final.'

'You'd better go back home and finish your dream off there,' Joe said. The curtain had come down for the interval, and they stepped out into the corridor and lighted cigarettes.

'Not now,' Johnny demurred, leaning against the wall and inhaling with obvious pleasure. 'Not just as the fun's starting. Didn't you see that man staring at us through some of those whatsit glasses?'

'Opera glasses? I didn't see him. Where was he?'

'Just opposite.'

'But the box opposite us was empty. I noticed it particularly.'

'Well, he must have come in after, because there he was, just before I dropped off.'

'What did he look like?' Joe asked, slowly pacing the carpeted floor.

'That's just it. He'd tucked himself craftily behind a curtain so I couldn't really see him at all. Only his hands, and the glasses. But he was interested in us, all right.'

'He probably had designs on you,' Joe said. 'Why didn't you mention it at the time?'

'You told me to shut up, didn't you? So I shut up.'

'And if you'd seen the ceiling about to cave in, I suppose you wouldn't have mentioned that, either? Come on, let's go and take a look at him now. If there's one thing I can't stand, it's people staring at me through opera glasses. We'll have to move fast, though. There's not a lot of time.'

They moved very fast indeed, so fast that several people, returning to their seats from the opposite direction, eyed them with some distaste. Arrived on the other side of the house, they investigated the box in question, only to find it empty. Stepping back into the corridor, they encountered an attendant who, upon enquiry, said that as far as she could remember, the box had been occupied by a gentleman.

'Could you tell me what he looked like?' Joe asked. 'I was expecting to meet a friend here, and I seem to have missed him.' She wrinkled her brow in thought. 'An elderly gentleman, I think, sir. And he wore dark spectacles. I remember that now. But he should be back any minute. That's the second bell going.'

She went on her way, and they lit a further cigarette apiece and waited. Nothing sensational occurred. A few loiterers passed, en route for their seats, and the distant strains of a piano concerto told them that the second part of the programme had started. The box to which their backs were turned remained unclaimed.

'I'm sick of this,' Joe said, dropping his cigarette end into a wall ashtray. 'Let's get back. And if you spot anyone else playing tricks, you might let me know.'

They returned the way they had come, entered their box and sat down with the minimum amount of noise. The audience, dimly seen, was as silent as an audience can possibly be, the orchestra was in full strength, and centre stage sat Melda Linklater, dressed in black, a spray of orchids in her dark hair, looking very young and rather fragile against the size of the piano she was playing. Joe watched her, fascinated. From his vantage point, the view of her reminded him sharply of the blue-green portrait of a pianist he had seen in Mendoza's office. Directly or indirectly, he felt certain she had inspired the painting of it. He did not pay much attention to the music, but became lost in thought, until a sharp dig in the ribs from Johnny caused him to turn his head impatiently.

'He's back again,' Johnny whispered, and glancing across to the box opposite and adjusting his eyes to the gloom after the brightness of the stage lighting, Joe could dimly discern the figure of a man, seated well back and half-hidden by an overshadowing curtain. He stared until his eyes ached, but the man remained motionless, giving no clue to his possible identity.

'To hell with him,' he said in an undertone to Johnny, and with a shrug of the shoulders returned his attention to the stage. Once or twice during the remainder of the concert his eyes were irresistibly drawn back to the man who sat so still he might have been a statue, but when, at the end, with the lights on and the hall echoing to tumultuous applause, Joe looked again, he had disappeared.

'What do we do now?' Johnny asked, as they made their way out once more into the corridor.

'I'll tell you what *you* can do,' Joe said. 'Get down to the box office and find out when that box was taken and who by, if you can. Then get the car and meet me round by the stage door. I shan't be long.'

Without waiting for a reply, he went off to the cloakroom, collected his coat and gramophone record, found a conveniently quiet spot, and tearing a sheet from his address book, he brought out his fountain pen and wrote: 'I don't want your autograph, and I hardly know a thing about music. But may I see you? Very urgent.' He signed it, sealed it into an envelope he had stowed away in an odd pocket, and addressed it to Melda Linklater. Then seeking out an attendant, he tipped her generously and asked her to deliver it for him.

'Will there by any reply?' she asked, eyeing the note with some curiosity.

'I hope so,' he said. 'Anyway, I'll wait here and perhaps you'll come and tell me the best or the worst.'

She went away, and he took a seat in the vestibule and lit a cigarette. Within a few minutes Johnny came elbowing his way through the thinning crowd from the direction of the cloakroom, and stopped short at sight of him.

'Thought we were supposed to meet at the stage door,' he said.

Joe grinned. 'So we are, but all in good time. Did you have any luck?'

'No.' Johnny looked a trifle despondent as he struggled into his coat. 'It was booked by someone here a couple of days ago, but they don't know who.'

'Well, that's something to know. Whoever it was, he was only sitting opposite us by chance, because it never occurred to me to come here until this morning.'

'What are we waiting for now?' Johnny asked, flopping down beside him.

'You needn't wait,' Joe said. 'You'd better run yourself home and catch up with some sleep. You look half dead. I'll pick up a taxi when I want one.' Seeing the attendant returning, he added,

'I'll give you a ring later. But if Wally comes through in the meantime, tell him I'll be at the Allsorts at the usual time, and I hope to see him. And Johnny, don't 'phone Wendy more than a couple of times or Toni will start getting shirty.'

'I never meant to do any such thing,' Johnny said, but he looked rather pink about the ears as he walked away. The attendant, reaching Joe's side just then, said, 'Will you come this way, sir?' and he followed her backstage, which was twice as gloomy and formidable as the rest of the theatre, with long cold passages echoing to the slightest whisper or footfall.

Once he had the distinct impression of someone following them, and turned to investigate, but in the dim lighting he could see nothing to confirm his suspicion. He was still a trifle on edge when the attendant knocked upon the door of Melda Linklater's room, and opened it to admit him. He entered, to find her standing in the centre, a long fur cape about her shoulders, a lighted cigarette in one hand. He observed, as the door shut behind him, that she looked more mature than when he had seen her upon the stage. Her manner was assured, yet somehow conveyed the suggestion that she did not consider herself particularly important.

'How do you do, Mr Trayne?' she said gravely, but her eyes twinkled as if at some secret joke. He took the hand she extended to him, a soft and delicate hand, yet with a supple strength about it. He said, 'It's very nice of you to see me. I expected to find you crowded out with admirers.'

She smiled. 'I was, but I sent them away.' She withdrew her hand and sat down with her back to the dressing-table. 'I'm very curious to know what is so urgent and important and why you have to see me about it?'

'Now I see you,' he said, 'it doesn't seem so very important.'

He put down his coat and gramophone record on a nearby chair, lit a cigarette, and went on, 'But why so curious? It can't be very unusual for people to try and crash in on you?'

'It's all too usual,' she sighed. 'But not anyone like you.'

'How do you mean? You don't know me.'

'I do, by sight. I was dining one night at the Granchester, and you were there with a party. Someone pointed you out to me. They said you'd been running night clubs since you were fourteen.'

Joe laughed. 'Exaggeration is a vice with some people,' he said.

'But you admitted yourself that you're not interested in music.'

'I didn't say that,' he cut in quickly. 'I don't understand it, but I'll have a smash at anything that takes my fancy. I'm off to a flying start already with one of your records.' He picked it up and passed it to her, and a little frown drew together her dark brows as she inspected the label.

'It's not a very popular one,' she observed at length, and there was a fleeting expression of sadness in her eyes as she handed it back to him.

'No?' He replaced it, turned back to her, and asked, 'Will you have dinner with me?'

'When and why?' She was staring straight ahead of her as if lost in not very happy thoughts.

'Tonight and because I want you to,' he said. 'I think you and I could find a lot to talk about. But not here. As a young friend of mine would say, this place gives me the creeps.' He walked suddenly to the door, opened it, glanced left and right, closed it and returned to find her standing and watching him in frank curiosity.

'Who did you expect to see out there?' she asked.

'Anyone or no one. It was just a feeling, don't give it a thought. But you haven't answered my question.'

'Conversation is a little difficult, with you popping in and out.' She was smiling again. 'But it's no, I'm afraid. I've promised to dine with some relatives and I can't put them off. I doubt whether I would, in any case. I don't go out very much. I prefer to rest at home.'

'Do you need so much rest, then?'

'In order to keep fit, yes. I get tired very easily.' She passed a hand over her forehead and added, 'I'm tired now.'

'I'm sorry. And to prove it I'll take you home.' He collected his possessions and moved to open the door for her. 'How do you go, car or taxi?'

She appeared to hesitate, then she said, 'Taxi, please,' picked up a large, flat bag, switched off the wall-light and accompanied him without further comment.

Rain was still falling when they stepped out from the stage entrance, a fine steady rain that struck chill after the morning's warmth. Joe found a taxi without much difficulty, and they drove in silence to Welling House, the small block in Welbeck Street where Miss Linklater lived. She sat in her corner of the vehicle, her hands folded in her lap, her eyes closed, and he studied her face with interest. In conversation she was animated, and radiated an undercurrent of sympathy that would, he felt, put almost anyone at their ease. But in repose she seemed to withdraw into a world of her own, the depths of which the average person would find difficult to penetrate. Joe, at that precise moment, did not propose to try. But as they drew up at their destination and he was about to open the door, she came out of her reverie and said, 'Would you care for a drink? There's plenty of time before I have to dress for dinner.'

'Thank you,' he said. 'Just now I could care for a drink very passionately.'

He alighted, paid off the driver, helped her out and they made a dash through the rain and into the lobby, where she said apologetically, 'My flat is three flights up and the lift isn't working. Do you mind very much?'

'Not a bit.'

'I do,' she said. 'I hate walking.' And in illustration of her statement she paused at the top of each flight of stairs to draw breath and to say many uncomplimentary things regarding lifts that ceased to function. On the third floor she brought out her keys and admitted him to an apartment of four rooms opening from a spacious hallway. The lounge was gaily furnished and curtained, yet with an atmosphere faintly Victorian, aided, perhaps, by the grand piano which was its dominant feature.

'Help yourself to a drink,' she said, waving a hand in the direction of the sideboard. 'I'll join you in a moment.' Whereupon she withdrew. But Joe, despite a thirst to rival that of a shipwrecked mariner, did not immediately follow her instructions. He had wandered over to the fireplace, and was staring up at the picture hanging above, a picture too modern to fit in with its surroundings. It was a study in oils, ranging from blue to purple, of Melda Linklater, reclining in a chair, her gaze pensive and rather wistful. It was signed: 'Solby'.

Chapter IX

Armed with a glass of rum and lime and a cigarette, Joe had retreated to an armchair by the time Miss Linklater returned. She entered with a soft rustling of the long black taffeta house dress she wore, and in silence she walked to the sideboard and poured herself a glass of white wine, which she placed on a small table beside the divan. Then she lay down and stared thoughtfully at the ceiling. Joe, who had been idly watching her movements, asked, 'Do you always act as if you were alone?'

'Not as a rule,' she answered, without turning her head. 'But I can with you.'

'Good.' Automatically his glance had returned to the portrait above the mantelpiece. 'This fellow Solby, he seems to be pretty popular, doesn't he?'

'Does he?' She did not sound very interested. 'Genius will out, you know. But it's not always popular.'

'Is he a genius?'

'He's generally considered one. But can't you see for yourself?'

'Frankly, no. I'm no better with painting than I am with music. But you . . . what do you think about it?'

'He was a genius,' she said, and leaning over, she sipped her wine and stared across at him as if he were not there.

'Was?' he repeated, returning her look, and for some reason not resenting it.

'Yes, he's dead now. He died about ten years ago.'

'As long as that? No wonder these pictures aren't a lot like you. I thought it was me not knowing anything about painting. But obviously you were only a kid.'

'I wasn't very old,' she admitted. 'But what do you mean by *these* pictures? Where have you seen the others? You don't, I imagine, spend hours wandering round the galleries.'

'Only one other,' he said. 'A fellow named Mendoza has it. A portrait of you, in blue and green, sitting at a piano. D'you know him?'

'Mendoza?' She sat up slowly, and stared down into the contents of her glass. 'I once knew a man of that name. Gilbert Mendoza. I knew him in Paris, or rather, Solby knew him. I only saw them together a few times.'

'And Dight?' Joe prompted. 'Do you know him, too?'

She frowned, and drank a little. 'I don't know. Solby knew a lot of people. So did Mendoza. But is he in London? Mendoza, I mean?'

'He's got a place at Maida Vale. I was there this morning. That was when I saw your picture. What do you know about him, if anything?'

'Nothing very much. He loaned Solby money, and took a lot of his pictures as a kind of security. He must have made a fortune since. Solby wasn't well known at the time, in fact, he wasn't known at all. He's only become famous since he died. That's unfair, isn't it? But life is unfair.'

'Most,' Joe agreed, in an undertone calculated not to disturb her train of thought. 'And what were you doing about that time?'

'I was studying music in Paris. Solby gave me that picture. It's the only one I have.' She moved restlessly, replaced her glass upon the table and added, 'But can't we talk of something else? You didn't come to the concert because you saw a picture of me at Mendoza's?'

'No. I came because I found a photograph of you in my bedroom.'

'Really?' For the first time she looked interested. 'How was that?'

'I don't know, and I'd like to find out. It's not very important, I suppose, but I'm not keen on mysteries.'

'I am,' she said. 'When they're to do with me. What kind of photograph was it?' He brought it out and showed it to her, and she viewed it in disgust. 'Oh, that old thing, I know I'm not a breathtaking beauty, but that's terrible. Why should anyone go to the trouble of cutting it out, I wonder?'

'One of your admirers, I imagine. I found it in my place just after someone had broken in. Any suggestions?'

She laughed. 'None, I'm afraid. I don't know any housebreakers personally. But if one of them likes to cut out my photographs, I can't stop him, can I? Did he get away with the family jewels?'

'He didn't take anything, if it was a he.'

'And that's all you came to see me about?'

'More or less. I also wanted to find out what sort of a person you are.'

'And have you?'

He regarded her critically, as he replaced the photograph in his notecase. 'About twenty-six, I'd say, but older than that in the head, super-sensitive but practical, unusually broad-minded, and you forgive faults in other people that you wouldn't tolerate in yourself. You're fond of seclusion, comfort, good food and drink and you don't like anything that takes a lot of physical exertion. You also get bored very easily, except where your work is concerned, and you're inclined to be neurotic.'

'Almost exact,' she said, smiling. 'Only I happen to be twenty-seven, and I'm so neurotic I count my eyelashes every morning to see if I've lost any.'

'If you were as bad as that you wouldn't know it,' he retorted. 'What's more, you'd be only too glad to talk about yourself, instead of cagily shutting your thoughts away, and looking at me as if we were living on different planets. That's right, isn't it?'

'I'm so sorry, I wasn't listening.' She finished her drink, rose to her feet, and added, 'I was thinking about you.'

'Oh? And what were you thinking about me?'

'Well, you were so good at reading my character, I was trying to work out yours. You must be thirty-five, I should think. You've done a lot of different things. You make money without particularly meaning to. You've had a great deal of success with women, but it hasn't gone to your head. And once you start a thing, you follow it to the end even if it doesn't seem very practical. How's that for a beginning?'

'Too good,' he admitted grudgingly. 'I wouldn't have started this if I'd thought you were going to beat me at my own game. And I don't like having five years snatched out of my life, just like that. I'm not thirty yet.'

'Really? You're a big boy for your age, aren't you?'

He got up and went across to her. 'It's time someone did something about you,' he said, and putting a hand beneath her chin he gently kissed her. She eyed him with a strange expression for a moment, then disengaged herself and moved towards the door, saying, 'It's also time I dressed for dinner.'

'I know, I know.' Smiling, he picked up his coat and followed.

'You haven't much time and I'd better leave. All right, dress for dinner. And I hope your evening's a dead loss and your relatives bore you to desperation.'

Pausing at the door, she queried, 'You think I'd be better off dining with you?'

'I know it. But I shan't ask you again . . . not until next time. And then you're going to tell me the story of your life.'

'You'd probably sleep through it,' she said, her eyes twinkling. 'Can you find your way out?'

'And back, I wouldn't be surprised.' Whereupon he waved a hand and departed. But he had hardly reached the stairs before she came running after him, carrying his gramophone record.

'I'm hurt you could forget it,' she said. 'Or did you leave it as an excuse for calling again?'

'Hardly.' He took it from her. 'I couldn't hatch up anything as old-world as that if I tried. When I want to call, I call.'

'And when I'm not at home, I'm not at home,' she said, and he heard her laugh as she retreated into the flat and closed the door.

The rain had ceased when he stepped out into Welbeck Street, and the moist air was pleasant to the nostrils. He walked as far as the nearest telephone box and put through a call to his apartment. Johnny answered, in a voice drowsy with sleep.

'Time to turn out,' Joe said. 'We've got work to do.'

'Oh, is that you?' The sound of a vast yawn drifted over the wire. 'How's everything?'

'Pretty nice. Listen, Johnny, where do all the arty people go to drink these days?'

'What sort of arty people?'

'Any of 'em . . . painters, writers, critics and all the hangers-on. Berets and sandals and velvet pants with patches on. You know the sort of thing.'

'Well ... there's a heap of places I know of, but I'd say "The Happy Man" is about what you mean. It's a pub, just back of Cambridge Circus. They get a real gang there. You'll see 'em going in and out. You can't miss it.'

'I don't intend to,' Joe said. 'I'll see you there in half an hour. Bring the car and we'll go straight to work. Did Wally ring?'

'He did. Said he'd be along tonight.'

'Good. I'll be lining up a drink for you. Don't stop to comb your hair, and you'll look just right.'

He rang off, ruffled his own hair with both hands, hung his coat about his shoulders at a rakish angle, lit a cigarette and strolled to Cambridge Circus, where he located 'The Happy Man' without much effort. The saloon bar was thronged with as motley a collection of people as one could hope to see anywhere. Joe edged his way to the bar and leaned upon it. Around him, voices and glasses were raised, and the smoke from countless cigarettes added to the thickness of the atmosphere.

Two harassed barmen bobbed hither and thither in fervent attempts to keep pace with it all. Men and women, young, old and middle-aged were telling anyone who cared to listen of their artistic achievements, past, present and future, and those of their friends and relatives. Others, forming a group of their own, were deploring the fact that anyone should try and achieve anything at all in what they termed 'This decadent age'. Joe, achieving the improbable by obtaining two large rums and lime from one of the barmen, held firmly to his coveted place beside the bar, thereby proving the ability of the fittest to survive. Johnny came in just then, and charged through the crowd with the ease of long experience.

'We get into some rum places,' he said, arriving, red in the face, at Joe's side. 'What does all this add up to?'

'I'll tell you,' Joe said, handing him his drink, and proceeded to give a précis of his movements to date, omitting certain details in connection with Melda Linklater.

'So what are we doing here?' Johnny asked at length, wrinkling his brow. Joe peered into the face of the nearest barman, ordered another couple of drinks and turned back again. 'I want to find out something about this Solby,' he said. 'The picture galleries and other sources of information being closed, this seems as good a jumping-off place as any.' Raising his voice to a pitch well above those around him, he added, 'Personally, I think Solby reeks.'

The effect was instantaneous and electric. Several faces, belligerent with the stimuli of alcohol and superior knowledge, were thrust close to his, and voices demanded that he should take back his categorical statement or enlarge upon it. Then without waiting for him to do either, they went on to expound their own views upon the subject, from which he gathered that Solby was at once a genius of the highest degree, and a charlatan of the lowest order, according to one's school of thought.

'Have a drink,' Joe said, to no one in particular, whereupon fifteen people took advantage of the offer, including Johnny, who had been pushed out of his original position, and was leaning at the other end of the bar, reading an evening newspaper. A young woman in a bright yellow sweater and red velvet trousers raised her face from a tankard of beer and observed, 'It's all a lot of ballyhoo. No one would ever have *heard* of Solby if he hadn't jumped in the Seine.'

'Why don't you jump in the Thames yourself and see what it does for you?' someone advised her.

A man laughed loudly. He leaned, shoulder to shoulder with Joe, pressed against the bar by sheer weight of the forces behind

116

him. Catching Joe's eye, he said, 'Sorry if I'm crowding you, but there's not much I can do about it.' He received a pint of beer from the barman, paid for it, and drank thirstily.

Joe said, 'It's all right. I wouldn't keep a man from his drink.' He was about to return his attention to the girl in the yellow jersey, when the man said, 'If you're interested in Solby, perhaps I can help you. I knew him in Paris. Not very well, but then who ever does know an artist well? Not half the people who make out they do.'

Joe turned and looked him squarely in the face. He was shorter than Joe, but with a big frame, all bone and muscle, emphasized by a short-sleeved, dark blue shirt and grey flannel slacks. His grey hair was abundant, but cut short in contrast with some of those around him, his eyes smiled through horn-rimmed spectacles, and there was about his lined and sunburned face an air of careless good humour.

'Have a drink,' Joe said.

The man laughed again. 'No, thanks. Cadging drinks isn't in my line. I'm dying on my feet here, anyway. Surely there's some corner of this pestilential place where one can breathe?'

He made a determined movement through the crowd, and picking up his glass, Joe followed. They emerged beside the entrance, near which they leaned against the wall, eyeing each other appraisingly.

'I'm Eric Sanderson,' the man said, taking a long pull at his beer. 'I know who you are . . . Joe Trayne.'

'That's very nice.' Joe paused in the operation of lighting a cigarette, staring at the flame of his lighter before putting it out and returning it to his pocket. 'It's odd the number of people who know me these days. They seem to know what I'm going to do next, some of them, too.'

Sanderson smiled. 'I don't claim to know anything like that. I just like to be *au fait* with what's going on in my own line. I'm a private investigator from Paris.'

'And what would you be investigating, Mr Sanderson, if I'm not speaking out of my turn?'

'The death of Bernard Solby,' Sanderson said.

'They certainly move fast in Paris,' Joe observed. 'According to my information, it's only ten years since he died. That is, if we're talking about the same man.'

'The very same. Solby, the painter. The man who jumped in the Seine because he was up to his neck in debt and couldn't stand it any longer. At least, that was the story at the time. But since he's been discovered as one of the finest painters of the modern school, the question has arisen, did he or didn't he?'

'How's that?' Joe asked. 'If they fished him out of the Seine . . . '

'They didn't. They found his clothes, but they never recovered his body. The French police had their hands pretty full when it happened, and I suppose they didn't worry too much over the death of one obscure English painter.'

'And who's worrying about it now?'

'Chiefly his brother, Charles. Since Solby's pictures jumped into the limelight, there are some who say it was just a trick, a kind of publicity racket. His brother wants to put a stop to all that.'

Joe finished his drink, placed the empty glass upon a ledge, folded his arms and said, 'You're investigating the death of Solby, so you leave the banks of the Seine and come all the way over here to sample the beer in a London pub. Why?'

'I have my reasons. But I wouldn't be very good at my job if I told them to you, just like that.'

'Why are you interested in me, anyway? I wouldn't be wanted for murder or anything, would I?'

Sanderson smiled again. 'I'm interested in you because you're interested in Solby,' he said.

'I see. We've reached the stage where you'll tell me if I'll tell you. Is that it?'

'Something like that,' the other admitted, and as Joe's glance strayed toward his empty glass, he added, 'Have this one on me.'

'No, thanks. It's so long since anyone stood me a drink it would only embarrass me. Come along to my place, and we'll talk this thing over.'

'The Allsorts?' Sanderson asked, and when Joe nodded, 'Sorry to seem such a know-all, but I have to keep my ear to the ground. It's my business.'

'I'm seriously thinking of changing mine,' Joe said. Raising his voice, he shouted above the medley of sound, 'Hey, Johnny! Are you going to prop up that counter all night?'

Johnny started, gulped down his drink, folded his newspaper and fought his way across to where they stood. 'I wondered where you'd got to,' he said.

Joe noticed, as he introduced the young man to Sanderson, that the latter did not appear to pay much attention. Probably, he thought, because he had earlier observed the two of them together.

'I'll be glad of a change of atmosphere,' Sanderson remarked, when they stepped into the comparative quietness of the street. 'That place is bedlam. I used to indulge in the arty life myself a bit, but a little of it goes a long way. And it didn't pay off well enough for me.'

They reached the side turning where Johnny had parked the car, and climbed in. 'The Allsorts?' Johnny queried over his shoulder, as Joe settled down beside Sanderson at the back.

'That's the idea, boy. But there's no need to break our necks. It's hours to opening time.'

Johnny grinned and nodded. Nevertheless, they reached their destination at a speed which caused Joe to alight outside the Allsorts with some relief. There were times when Johnny, for all his skill at the wheel, was a trifle nerve-racking.

'You may need her again presently,' he said, pausing with one foot on the running board as Johnny was about to head for the garage.

'Suits me.' Johnny pawed the wheel tenderly. 'I'll just run her round and check her over.'

'Right. But don't be all evening about it. Saturday night here is no rest cure.'

He stood back and watched the car glide away before bringing out his keys and opening up the premises.

'Interesting,' Sanderson said, following him in. 'I like seeing behind the scenes in this sort of place.'

'Do you?' Joe did not sound enthusiastic. 'It's just so much bread-and-butter to me.' Opening the door of his office and switching on the light, he added, 'Take a seat and a drink.' He was, he found, still clutching his gramophone record along with the coat which he had not troubled to put on since it had ceased raining. He placed both upon a chair, unlocked a cupboard, and brought out a bottle of rum and one of lime and two glasses. 'Straight or with?' he asked, sitting down on the edge of the desk.

'With, please,' Sanderson said, seating himself in a chair opposite. 'I can't drink like I could in my youth.'

'You're not so old,' Joe remarked, pouring out the drinks and pushing one glass across to him. 'Or are you?'

'Quite old enough.' Sanderson picked up his glass and eyed it with pleasure. '*Salut!*'

'Same to you,' Joe said, drinking. Sanderson reached over, inspected the label of the gramophone record and carefully replaced it.

'Are you a Linklater fan?' he asked.

'Vaguely speaking. Are you?'

'Not particularly. I believe she's a fine pianist though. Not bad-looking, either, or she used to be. Solby painted her a few times, but that's a good many years ago.'

'How old was Solby then?'

'Twenty-five, or thereabouts.'

'You said you knew him, didn't you? What was he like to look at?'

'Quite good-looking, dark, some people even called him hand-some.' Sanderson shrugged his shoulders. 'But that's neither here nor there. I'm investigating facts. And I'm prepared to give you a few, in exchange for any information you care to give me. I can't tell you a lot, because it wouldn't be in the interests of my client, and I don't suppose you'll be over-chatty, or you're not the man I take you for. But for one reason and another we're both interested in the same man, and I'd like to know, for a start, what your reason is? I've told you mine.'

Joe slid off the desk, sat down in his chair facing Sanderson, his expression blank.

'Where d'you live, when you're at home?' he asked.

Sanderson brought out a notecase, extracted a card and pushed it across the desk. Joe read: *Eric Sanderson, 78, Avenue des Chattes, Paris.* He stared at it for a long time in silence. Then he said, 'I haven't really anything you'd call a reason. That's fact number one, and you can believe it or not, just as you like. But I don't mind telling you how I got into one of the most damned silly mix-ups of all time.'

Whereupon he did, omitting many details which he thought irrelevant or better kept to himself. Thus expurgated, the account did not, he felt, add up to much. A dead man in a box, two men of doubtful character disposing of the body, a girl who seemed to be frightened of everything, her sister disappeared, the box gone, some writing on a wall, a man named Dight calling to see him, an interloper in his apartment . . . He did not mention the photograph he had found there, nor his subsequent meeting with Miss Linklater, and his unorthodox entry into the house of Mendoza he considered nobody's business but his own.

'What happened to the first girl?' Sanderson asked. 'The one to whom they originally delivered the box?'

'Gone down to the country,' Joe submitted, promptly and without the slightest hint of evasion. 'And I hope it's the last I see of her for a long time.'

He lit a cigarette and passed the box across to Sanderson, who took one and surveyed it dreamily for a while. Then lighting it, he said, 'From what you've told me, and of course you haven't told me everything, it looks to me as if you've started something that will be difficult to finish. My advice to you is to chuck it.' He leaned one elbow on the desk, his expression serious. 'I mean it. This fellow Mendoza, you haven't met him?'

'No, but I intend to.'

'Well, don't. He's a nasty type. Know anything about him?'

'Not a thing. Except that Solby owed him money and gave him pictures as security.'

'Who told you that?'

Joe laughed. 'I, too, like to keep my ear to the ground when it's not against the crack of a door,' he said.

'Well, you're right. Fortunately, Mendoza didn't get the lot. Charles Solby had most of them. He's sold some to private collectors and galleries and so on.'

'What does he do for a living?' Joe asked. 'Besides selling his brother's pictures?'

'He was a psychiatrist. He's retired now.'

'You're sure he didn't give his brother a helping hand into the Seine?'

Sanderson smiled in the slow way he had. 'You're not the first person to suggest that. But it's hardly sense, is it? In the first place, he couldn't guess that his brother's work was going to be a financial asset, and secondly, he wouldn't employ me to look into it if he'd been the cause of his brother's death, would he?'

'I suppose not.' Joe frowned. 'What exactly have you got against Mendoza?'

'Nothing, yet. But Charles Solby has reason to believe that his brother was murdered, and not by being pushed into the Seine.'

'You think Mendoza did it?'

'I don't think anything. But Carlo Betz, who knew him, came to a nasty end, didn't he? I'm glad you told me about that box. It's interesting.'

'It's hell,' Joe said. 'It's getting on my nerves. I've got the feeling it's going to pop up somewhere any minute.'

'Why don't you take my advice, then, and stick to your own business? You don't stand to gain anything by it, so all you've got to do . . . '

'I'm not made that way.' Joe raised his head as there came a knock at the door and Johnny entered. He was still carrying the evening paper, which he slapped down in front of Joe with the remark, 'Thought you might like to see this.' Joe glanced at it and saw, scrawled along the top margin in Johnny's writing: 'Anything I can do?'

Before he could speak, Sanderson said, 'I may as well tell you I can read upside down.' And blandly eyeing Johnny's flushed face, he went on, 'The best thing you can do, young man, is to keep your eye on Mr Trayne and try and stop him from making a perfect bloody fool of himself.'

123

Johnny stood looking helplessly from him to Joe and back again. Joe laughed. 'All right, Johnny,' he said. 'Thanks for trying to help. Has Wally turned up yet?'

'Just arrived,' Johnny submitted.

'Well, go and give him a hand. And you'd better clean yourself up a bit. You look a mess.' Johnny shot a baleful glance at Sanderson and went out, shutting the door with a bang. Rising, Joe added, 'I've got to get changed myself. But have another drink if you want one.'

'No, thanks.' Sanderson crushed out his cigarette in the ashtray and got up, yawning slightly. 'I'm pushing off. I don't want to be in your way. Where d'you live, in case I want to get in touch with you some time?'

'Don't you know that?' Joe looked profoundly surprised. 'I thought you might have been the merchant who climbed through my window.'

'Sorry, you're on the wrong track. I'm too old for that sort of thing.' He took the card that Joe gave him, looked at it, and put it away in his notecase. He continued, earnestly, but with a twinkle of amusement in his eyes, 'Look, Trayne, if you must play amateur detectives, why don't you play in line with me? I only warned you off Mendoza for your own good, but since he sent Dight to see you, it might be as well for you to keep tapes on him. I'm staying in Handel Street, No. 29. I've got a room there. Ridgemont 8697.' He wrote it out in block letters on a slip of paper, which he left upon the desk. 'If you catch up with anything interesting, I'd be very grateful if you'd give me a ring. It can't do you any harm to have my help and I'm not going to pretend I'm above accepting yours. I get information where and when I can. So far I don't think what you've told me has anything to do with Solby, it's more likely some other game of Mendoza's. He's crooked through and through.'

'I'll think about it,' Joe said, seeing him to the door. Sanderson smiled, shook hands, and departed. Wally, coming from the opposite direction, turned to look after him before joining Joe in the office.

'Who was that?' he asked. 'Friend of yours?'

'Sort of.' Joe picked up the slip of paper from the desk and put it in his notecase. 'Feeling better, Wally?'

'I was, until I saw you.' Wally leaned against the desk, his lined face expressive of concern. 'What's got into you, boy? Hair all over the place, a suit that looks as if it had been dry-cleaned with you inside it . . . '

'I was just about to change,' Joe said.

'Well, go ahead and change. You're not getting coy, are you?'

'I wouldn't be surprised.' From a built-in cupboard Joe produced a spare evening suit which he kept handy for such occasions. 'What with some of the people I've been running around with . . . wait till I tell you about little Wendy.'

Wally poured himself a glass of rum, drank it and lighted a cigarette. His face was inscrutable as he watched Joe make his toilet, and listened to his account of the addition of Wendy Bond to the 'Nosebag' personnel.

'Sounds a half-witted scheme to me,' he said at last. 'But then so do most of the things you're doing lately. You'd better keep an eye on that young woman or you'll find she's landed you in a mess. My God! What it is to be under thirty! Tell you what. Some friends of mine want to go out there this evening. I'll get Johnny to run them along and he can see how things are shaping.' He opened the office door and yelled at the top of his voice, 'Johnny! Come here a minute, will you?'

Johnny entered, his face shining from the cleansing he had given it, his hair brushed as smooth as it would lie. Joe, fixing his tie in front of the wall mirror, grinned and said, 'Now we're both nice clean boys again, and Father's got a job for you, Johnny.'

'If you were a few inches shorter, I'd swipe you one,' Wally said. 'Come outside, boy, and I'll tell you what I want you to do.'

Johnny, turning to follow him, cannoned into the chair whereon lay the gramophone record that Joe had left there. Promptly it slid to the floor and lay shattered in several pieces.

'Sorry,' he said, regarding it in dismay. 'I didn't see it there.'

'A bull in a china shop would look like a ballet dancer compared with you,' Joe grumbled, walking round to pick up the pieces, which he consigned to the waste paper basket.

'It was a blasted silly place to leave it,' Wally said. 'Come on, son, before he bursts into tears.' They went out, and closing the door behind them, Wally went on, 'Tell me, frankly, what's your impression of Joe?'

'How do you mean?' Johnny asked, as they paced slowly down the passage.

'Well, between friends and no question of it going any farther, d'you think he's all there?'

Johnny looked surprised. 'He seems all right to me,' he said. 'As all right as anyone is. I mean, everyone's a bit cracked in some way, aren't they?'

'I suppose so. I hadn't thought of that. Which way d'you think it takes Joe?'

'Well . . . this not wanting to drive, with a car like he's got. That's cracked, isn't it?'

'Not really,' Wally demurred, with a slight shake of the head. 'It was this way. His mother and girl friend were killed in a car smash. Joe was driving. It wasn't his fault, the other driver was tight and came head on. But you see what I mean?'

'I see,' Johnny said thoughtfully. 'That being the case, I'd say he's not so daffy as most of us.'

'You're probably right. It's just that he's been acting kind of queerly lately. But we're wasting time, son. Let's get on with the business.'

In his office, Joe, happily unaware of their comments, was dialling Melda Linklater's telephone number. He heard her voice over the wire presently, low and rather sleepy.

'Hallo,' he said. 'Had a nice time?'

There was a long pause, before she said, 'Would that be the intrepid Mr Trayne?'

'It would. I just thought I'd 'phone through and ask after you and your aunties, or whoever it was you were dining with.'

'That was kind of you. They were uncles. I was telling them about you, as a matter of fact. You know how it is with relatives. One has to amuse them with something.'

'And were they amused?'

'They appeared to be. But they were probably being polite. Where are you speaking from?'

'The Allsorts. I'm just going to work.'

'And I'm going to sleep. Good night, Mr Trayne.'

'Good night,' he said. 'I'll probably 'phone you again tomorrow.'

He heard her laugh as he hung up the receiver. Turning away, his glance encountered the newspaper that Johnny had brought in. He opened it, and discovered a paragraph marked in pencil. The headline ran: *Dead Gangster – Abandoned Car Clue*. He read on and learned that the police had found abandoned on the Great West Road a small white car answering to the description given of the one used by the two men who had disposed of the body of Carlo Betz. Ownership of the car had been traced to Lysbeth Ritchley, the missing girl whom the police were still anxious to question.

'Oh, hell!' Joe said, just as Wally looked in to remark, 'Are you planning to sit around here all evening? We're going to be busy.

There's the devil of a gang just arrived and the McLaughlins are coming tonight.'

'And the Campbells, too, I wouldn't be surprised.' Reluctantly Joe left the solitude of his office to plunge into one more hectic evening. Neither did he think any more of his personal affairs until just after two, when he was snatching a meal in the kitchen, and Wally came to say that he was wanted on the telephone.

'Who is it?' Joe asked, putting down his plate and lighting a cigarette.

'A female,' Wally said. 'She didn't give her name, but she sounds in a bit of a sweat. I hope it's not your little horsy girl got into trouble again.'

'So do I.' Hastily Joe returned to his office, shut the door, picked up the telephone receiver and said, 'Hallo . . . ' He did not immediately recognize the agitated voice of the woman who answered, 'Is that Joe Trayne?' He admitted his identity and she went on, 'I was afraid you'd be gone. I know it sounds crazy, but could you come round here right away?'

'I could,' he said. 'If I knew who and where you are.' And then, as vague recognition came to him, 'It wouldn't be . . . ?'

'It would.' The voice of Melda Linklater was still tremulous, but she managed the ghost of a laugh. 'It's so silly, but I woke up suddenly . . . and there was someone in my room.'

'Did you see who it was?' Joe asked quickly.

'No . . . it was just a feeling. And when I switched on the light, there was no one here. But . . . Oh, God! . . . I'm terrified!'

'Hallo,' he said, as her voice trailed away into silence. 'Melda! Are you still there?'

'Yes . . . ' She sounded as if she were a very long distance away.

'I'll be with you in ten minutes,' he said. Whereupon he slammed down the receiver, seized his coat and a bottle of brandy from the cupboard and charged out of the room at a speed which caused Wally, who was emerging from the bar, to stare in amazement.

'Where the hell are you going?' he wanted to know.

'Just got a call from my aunt,' Joe told him. 'Very urgent.'

Wally narrowed his eyes. 'I didn't know you had an aunt,' he said.

'Neither did I. And neither did she. But she just found out, and she needs brandy. The McLaughlins are all yours, Wally. See you tomorrow.'

Saying which, he strode out through the back way, yelled for a taxi, climbed in and told the driver he could name his own price if he reached Welbeck Street in seven minutes. The driver managed it in six, and they were pulling up at a fine speed outside Welling House when Joe observed a man come quickly out of the house next door. It was only a brief glimpse before the man turned and walked off down the street, but in those few minutes Joe had the impression of a pale, expressionless face that looked curiously dead.

Leaping out, he was in time to see the man climbing into a long car, which almost immediately sped away. He was not near enough to see the colour of it, but it could have been dark green. He would have liked to follow, but a taxi was not the best vehicle in which to attempt it, and Melda Linklater awaited him. He paid the driver, went quickly into the illuminated entrance of Welling House, where no porter was in evidence and the lift was still not working. He took the stairs at a run and arrived on the third floor breathless. The front door of Melda Linklater's flat stood open and stepping in, he almost stumbled over her where she lay face downwards in the carpeted hallway.

Chapter X

It took three doses of brandy and what seemed to Joe a very long time to bring Melda back to her senses. Congratulating himself on his foresight in providing a stimulant which he had earlier noticed was missing from her own wine and spirits department, he sat beside the lounge divan to which he had carried her, and watched her in some anxiety as she opened her eyes and stared at him in a dazed kind of way. She wore a long white satin nightgown and a black lace négligée over it. Her hair hung loose and tumbled about her shoulders, the deadly pallor of her face gave to it the remoteness of an idol, and it flashed across his mind that an artist might well find pleasure in painting her.

Her voice sounded curiously distant when she said, 'Have you been here long?'

He smiled. 'Long enough to think you'd passed out forever. How do you feel?'

'Terrible.' She waved aside the brandy he offered. 'No more of that, please. I want to think.'

She closed her eyes and was silent for a while, until he said, 'Do you mind letting me into what you're thinking? I'm not psychic, you know, and I'm still waiting to hear what happened.'

'Of course.' She opened her eyes to look at him again, her brows drawn together. 'I was having a nightmare, I can't remember what it was all about, but it was horrible . . . and then I came to myself and I felt there was someone in the room, standing quite close to me, and it was more horrible still. The curtains were drawn and it was very dark, so I couldn't see anything. I wanted to scream, but I couldn't. Then I felt a draught, as if the door had been opened and shut, and I switched on the light above my bed.'

'And no one was there?' he prompted.

'No one. I suppose I should have gone out to investigate, but somehow I felt paralysed. I managed to lock the bedroom door and window, and then I telephoned you.'

He eyed her searchingly and asked, 'Why did you pick on me?'

'I don't know.' A faint colour came into her face, and she went on, 'Yes, I do. You're the sort of person one can telephone in the middle of the night, and the only one I know who isn't likely to be in bed.' She smiled faintly. 'After all, I did listen to your story of someone getting through your window, so there's no reason why you shouldn't listen to mine.'

'Fair enough,' he agreed. 'And you think that's how they got in, through the window?'

'It's quite likely. I've been sleeping with the french windows open as it has been so warm, and the front door was bolted.'

'Then what was it doing open, with you lying just inside, ready for me to step on you?'

'Was I?' She looked blank for a moment. 'Oh, yes, I remember. I heard a terrific noise coming up the stairs which I thought must be you, and I ran out to open the front door. Then I suppose I fainted.'

'Are you often taken like that? Or was it just me coming up the stairs that did it?'

'You *are* absurd.' Her smile and voice were more natural now. 'I may not be an Amazon in strength, but I'm certainly not in the habit of fainting. It must have been the reaction.'

'Probably.' He rose and walked across to pull back the curtains. The french windows were closed but not fastened. He opened them and looked out on to a narrow verandah. 'Do you always leave these unlocked at night?' he asked over his shoulder.

'No.' She raised herself on one elbow. 'I'm pretty certain I locked them.'

He came back into the room, produced an electric torch from the pocket of the coat he had left there, and went out again. The night was dark and damp, with a hint of returning thunder in the atmosphere. The verandah gleamed wet from its recent washing by the rain. It ran between the lounge and the bedroom next door, the french windows of which he found to be locked from the inside, as she had said. Leaning over the iron railing that side, he flashed the light in the direction of the house to the left, the one from which he had seen the man emerging. It was designed in similar fashion, with just such a verandah, and between the adjoining buildings ran a narrow parapet. An agile person might, he thought, climb from one verandah to the other without too much risk.

The house next door was in complete darkness, the windows appeared to be uncurtained, but the white frames looked newly painted. To the right of Welling House was a hotel, which he had noticed earlier in the day. It had no verandahs, and short of leaping like a kangaroo, access from that direction would have been impossible.

Returning to the lounge, he asked, 'What goes on in the house next door?'

Melda looked surprised. 'Nothing, except workmen tramping

in and out all day, painters and so on. It's being reconstructed, I believe.'

He glanced thoughtfully round the room. 'Have you missed anything, or weren't you feeling strong enough to look?'

She sighed. 'I did think of that, while I was waiting for you. But I haven't much here of value. A little jewellery in the bedroom, and that's still there. I didn't come into this room until you brought me in. But I shouldn't think ...' She got to her feet uncertainly and began to walk about the room, opening drawers, frowning. Turning to him she said, 'Nothing appears to have been taken. Do you think I could possibly have imagined it?'

'Do *you*?'

'I don't know.' She clasped a hand to her forehead and closed her eyes for a moment. 'It's all still there ... the horror of it. And when I switched on the light and found no one in the room it was almost worse than if there had been. I thought if I didn't speak to someone I should go mad. I'd never felt like that before. I don't mind being alone as a rule. I live alone and I spend a lot of my time alone.'

'There's such a thing as being too much alone,' he said. The room was only dimly lighted by a pedestal lamp alongside the piano. Idly flashing the beam of his torch across the carpet, he observed that his feet were leaving damp traces wherever he moved. There was the suggestion of other footmarks in line with the window. He surveyed them with interest. 'Have you had any other visitors here this evening?' he asked.

'No. I went out as soon as I was dressed, and came back alone at about ten, I should think.'

'May I take a look at the rest of the place?'

'Of course, if you think it will do any good. May I have some brandy? I feel stronger now, but not quite strong enough.'

'Help yourself. I brought it for you,' he said, and went out and into the bedroom, a spacious apartment which seemed, in its furnishing, to have slipped back in time even farther than the lounge. The bed was a draped four-poster, the rest of the furniture beautifully preserved but resolutely antique, and even the curtains and carpet contrived to look like the background to an eighteenth-century painting.

As he had expected, the thick pile of the carpet was damply marked in places, and by the window he discovered a distinctly muddy footprint, the position of which confirmed the theory of someone having entered that way. Trying his own foot against it, Joe was surprised at its size. Whoever had made it must have extraordinarily large feet, unless he had worn overshoes, which was not unlikely. The remainder of the room yielded no clue to the identity of the intruder, and the kitchen and bathroom on the other side of the passage looked normal enough, their only point of interest being that access to them through their respective windows would have been impracticable for anything but a fly.

'I think you're right,' Joe said, returning to the lounge. 'He came in through the window, went out through the bedroom door, came in here and out through this window, and back into the house next door via the verandah.'

'Well it's something to know you don't think I'm losing my mind,' Melda said. 'Should I tell the police?' She was seated on the divan, a cigarette in one hand and a small glass of brandy in the other.

'Do you want to?'

'No. It sounds silly, to say that a man walked in through one window and out of the other, without taking anything. It would have been different if I'd seen him. In that case, I'd have 'phoned them immediately, I daresay, without bothering you. How do you know it *was* a man, by the way?'

'Either that, or a woman with the largest feet in the world, to judge by the marks on the carpet,' Joe said. 'In any case, women don't usually spend their nights climbing in and out of third-floor windows.' He lit a cigarette, leaned his back against the piano, and asked, 'Do you know any man with a deathly pale sort of face, dark hair, and not very tall?'

She regarded him in perplexity. 'I shouldn't think so. I don't know many men ... But surely you can't have guessed all that from a few marks on the carpet?'

'No. It was just an idea. Know anyone with a long, dark green car, a tourer?'

She thought for a moment, sipped a little from her glass and said, 'I'm sorry, no. But what has all this to do with me?'

'God knows,' Joe said, and began to turn over the sheets of music on top of the piano.

Melda remarked, 'I feel I should apologize for interrupting your evening. In retrospect, it all seems rather stupid.'

'Don't let it worry you. I shouldn't have dashed over here if I hadn't wanted to. Or are you giving me a gentle hint to go?'

'I don't give gentle hints,' she retorted. 'If I wanted you to leave, I should tell you.'

'Good. Then we know how we stand.' He was silent for a while, inspecting a musical score he had just uncovered. He read the title: *Lament for the Dead* and the bold handwriting beneath: 'For when it is finished ... Solby.' Joe said, 'I wonder what he meant by that?'

'What?'

He strolled across and handed the sheet to her, and she took it and looked at it with studied indifference. 'Oh, that. He meant when his life was finished. He had an idea he wouldn't live to be very old. In some ways he was rather morbid.'

'He committed suicide, didn't he?'

'So they say.' She leaned back, placing the music and her glass upon the table beside her. 'Aren't you going to have a drink?'

'No, thanks. I'm not in a drinking mood.' He crushed out his cigarette in the ashtray and stood looking down at her broodingly. 'You don't think he took a leap into the Seine?'

'It's a subject I prefer not to discuss.'

'That's a pity.' He sat down beside her. 'It's a subject in which I'm particularly interested just now.'

She said, staring up at the ceiling, 'You like your own way, don't you?'

'Not specially. But I'm used to getting it. I find it's no good hanging about wondering what other people want, because they very seldom make up their minds. So I nip in quickly while they're still dithering. It's the only way to get anything done.'

'And do you always know what you want?'

'Not always. But I'd rather take any kind of action than none at all. Why is it that when I start talking about you, somehow you always twist the conversation back to me?'

'We weren't talking about me.'

'That's right. We were talking about Solby. It's quite possible, then, that he's still alive?'

She sat up suddenly, and her eyes sparkled anger. 'Once and for all, let me assure you that he's dead, definitely dead. And it's customary to leave the dead in peace.'

'When they *are* dead. But have you any proof of it, in this case?'

'I don't need proof. If he were alive, I should know.'

She lay back again, and he said softly, 'I'm sorry. I didn't realize . . .'

'I think you did. Do you suppose you're the only person who has ever asked me questions about him? When some bright critic first discovered him, it was sickening. Such a romantic story, the

136

young painter cut off in his prime. Did he do it because of his debts, or was it the fault of the girl he was in love with? Or perhaps he just sneaked off, leaving everyone to think him dead. There was no limit to their theories. Rows and rows of curious eyes, and I told them nothing to satisfy their curiosity, and never will.'

'In that case,' he said, 'we'll talk of something else. Did you ever meet a man named Eric Sanderson in Paris?' He took out the card that Sanderson had given him and handed it to her.

'I seem to remember the name.' She looked at it for a while, and passed it back to him, adding, 'I don't know about the address, but there was a man named Sanderson who used to hang around the cafés. He was interested in criminology, I believe.'

'You haven't seen him lately, by any chance?'

'Not by any chance. I avoid anyone I even vaguely knew in Paris.'

'Well, don't be surprised if he turns up to see you one of these days. It was he who really got me interested in Solby.'

'But why on earth . . . ? They're not suggesting now that he did anything *criminal*, are they?'

'No. But there's a theory going round that he was murdered. And there's no need to look at me like that. It's his brother's idea, not mine. Did you know his brother?'

'I knew he had an elder brother, but I never met him. He took his degree in medicine, but practised as a psychiatrist. And I should think he must have analysed himself into a state of lunacy, if that's the story he's putting about.'

'On the contrary, he seems to have retired.'

'I'm not surprised. I heard that he took to drugs, after his brother died.' She was silent for a long time, looking away from him. Then slowly she got to her feet, picked up the musical score from the table and walked over to the piano. Opening it, she sat down and began to play. Joe watched her for a few moments,

137

before reaching for a glass and pouring himself some brandy. He might not be in a drinking mood, but *Lament for the Dead* was not doing his nervous system any good. Strolling across to the piano, he remarked, 'No wonder that's not very popular. My record of it got broken, and I can't say I'm sorry.'

She smiled a little, but her eyes had a far-away expression. 'It was Solby's favourite piece,' she said. 'I was playing it earlier. The association of ideas, I suppose . . . your buying a record of it. You've never known what it is to be afraid of anything, have you?'

'I'm not afraid to die, if that's what you mean.'

'Neither was he. But he had a terrible fear of being buried. It worries me even now not to know what happened to him. That's one of the reasons why I don't like talking about it. He used to stare into the Seine sometimes and say that would be a better place to lie than under the earth. He was a little mad, I think, by most people's standards. Obsessed, at any rate. And then there were his debts . . . He was more desperate than I knew, although he loved me at the time. We needed each other, we gave each other confidence. I think he would always have needed me. But I've grown up since. I don't need him now, but I'm fond of his memory.'

'Ten years is a long time,' Joe said.

'A very long time. Long enough to forget anything, if one were allowed to.' She stopped playing and regarded him gravely. 'You don't think he was murdered, do you?'

'How should I know? You just dismissed the idea as ridiculous.'

'So it seemed, on the face of it. But now I'm not so sure. He knew a number of peculiar people, and it happened so suddenly. I was away in the country for a few days. I was to meet him in Paris when I returned. He never kept that appointment and I never saw him again. No letter, no message of any kind.' She passed a hand over her forehead, and added, half to herself, 'If he was murdered, perhaps the same person might want to murder me.'

'Now *you're* being morbid,' Joe said, largely because the suggestion echoed an earlier thought of his own. 'Who'd want to murder you?'

'Who'd murder Solby? Who'd murder anyone, you might say, until it happens. It's probably nerves, but I've had an odd feeling lately, as if I were being watched. Nothing one could pick on, just something fanciful. And then tonight . . . ' She shivered.

'You've been reading too many newspapers,' he chided. 'You'd better get some sleep. You'll feel all right in the morning.'

She got up and looked at him uncertainly. 'I don't think I can sleep,' she said. 'I'm on edge tonight, and I'm afraid of being alone again.'

With a smile in his eyes he remarked, 'What would you like me to do? Entertain you with a little light conversation? Or do you prefer cards?'

'I'm not very keen on cards. I always lose. And I'm being neurotic, and extremely selfish.'

'Don't give it a thought. One night's sleep doesn't make any difference to me. And if you're worrying about someone waiting for me with a lighted candle in the window, you're wrong again. I, too, live alone, except for Johnny, and I'll bet he's tucked up and snoring by now.'

'Who's Johnny?'

'Johnny Gaff. A lad I picked up at the Allsorts some nights back. He's been appointed chief bodyguard by my partner, who seems to think I need a nurse.'

'Do they know you're here?'

'No one knows I'm here, except you and I.' In saying which he was happily unaware of his mistake.

139

She sighed. 'Well, if you don't mind . . . I feel safe with you.'

'I shouldn't be too sure about that. You know you attract me, don't you? Or did you think I go around kissing every woman I meet?'

'More or less.'

'Make it rather less than more, and you'll be somewhere near it.'

'But you've never been in love?'

'I have . . . once.' He turned away and began to drum with his fingers upon the piano.

'What happened?'

'She died,' he said. Mechanically he brought out his cigarette case and stared at it as if it were strange to him. Offering it to her, he queried, 'Why did you ask that?'

'There's a desperate look at the back of your eyes sometimes.' She selected a cigarette and added, 'Thanks.'

'And do you always study the back of people's eyes?' he asked, supplying her with a light.

'No. I'm not sufficiently interested as a rule.'

He lit his own cigarette, took her by the arm, and said, 'Come and sit down. If you're all that interested, and you won't talk about yourself, I may as well bore you with the story of *my* life.'

Chapter XI

The quietness of a wet Sunday afternoon pervaded Welbeck Street when Joe emerged from Welling House and stood for a moment, regarding his surroundings with a speculative eye. Rain fell in a chilling drizzle, and he was again pleased with his foresight in having held on to his waterproof. Over an evening suit it was not, perhaps, the most correct garb, but the point failed to worry him.

What did worry him was the problem of Melda Linklater. He had left her packing a suitcase preparatory to catching a train for Bognor, where her people resided. She had, she said, been promising to visit them for some weeks past and now seemed to be as good a time as any. Joe was in complete agreement with her, for although in sober daylight she was inclined to attribute her earlier fear to the need of a change and rest, he had other ideas on the subject. He had told her he would call or telephone round about seven, and see her to the station. Meanwhile, there were several things he wanted to investigate.

First, the house next door. The front of it, like the back, had been newly painted, and everywhere there was evidence of work in progress. The front door was partly open, and Joe, with the air of a sightseer, stepped inside. The interior was almost identical with that of Welling House, except that here the walls were stripped, the floors and staircase bare, with the doors of rooms standing wide open to allow the paint to dry. There being nothing below to excite his interest, he mounted to the third floor, selected the apartment situated parallel with that of Melda, and found it desolate and empty, save for a painter's overall in one corner and a ladder in another. Here the french windows were open, the paint upon them still tacky, and one smeared as if by a dirty hand. The painters would be annoyed about that, Joe thought, and his own hands being none too clean from contact with the banisters below, he was careful to avoid the doors as he stepped on to the verandah.

By day, the climb from there to the corresponding verandah of Melda's flat looked more risky, but certainly not impossible. At that moment, Melda herself leaned out from her own window, and sighted him with a start of surprise.

'What do you think you're doing?' she called across to him.

'Just taking a look round,' he said. 'I'm a prospective purchaser, if anyone wants to know.'

'You're not thinking of opening a palace of entertainment next door to me, I hope? Because I like to get some sleep occasionally.'

'In Welbeck Street?' He laughed. 'I know my limitations.'

'As long as you do,' she said. 'I'm going to rest now. I'm tired.'

'Good idea, and I think I'll do the same. See you later.'

He waved a hand and retreated, in case she should feel disposed to question him further. He had no particular wish to advertise his presence there to the world in general. Finding there was nothing more to be gleaned, he left the house then, sought for and found a taxi, and drove to Cleeve Rise, Maida Vale, alighting outside No. 13. No beating about the bush this time, no climbing through windows if he could avoid it. Most people were at home on a wet Sunday afternoon, so why not Mendoza?

But apparently Mendoza did not conform with the habits of the majority, for repeated knocking and ringing failed to bring anyone to the front door. Furthermore, the windows were all closed and, Joe guessed, firmly fastened. Frowning, he went down the steps and it was only then he observed that the chain attached to the padlock of the iron gate to the basement had been severed in two. This, he thought, was too good an opportunity to miss. Swinging open the gates, he ran lightly down the stone stairs and tried the door below. It yielded to his touch, having been obviously and rather clumsily forced from the outside.

He entered, to discover a stone passage and two large rooms opening left and right, both devoid of furnishing and smelling of mould, with the walls damply peeling. Stored here were several wooden crates, alongside reams of packing materials, the floors strewn with nails and other odds and ends of an innocuous character. The third room, situated at the back, had once been a kitchen boasting a dirty sink and an old and rusting gas stove. It was only dimly lit by a grating, and for a moment Joe had difficulty in making out the contents. At one end a short flight of steps led up to a door, opening, he surmised, on to the rest of the premises.

He was making his way across to it when he almost fell over a massive object standing against the wall, which he had hitherto overlooked in the semi-darkness. Cursing softly, he brought out his torch, switched it on and confirmed his worst suspicions. There it was, solid, ancient, its carving scratched in places, the box which he had last seen in the flat of Lysbeth Ritchley. It was unlocked, he observed, and there was no reason why he should not open it. Nevertheless, he hesitated long enough to light a cigarette, before approaching and raising the lid.

The same creaking sound, the same atmosphere of death,

causing his inside to contract a little. The body of Lysbeth Ritchley lay within. Her eyes were open and seemed to stare back at him with an expression between horror and accusation. She was clad in the black velvet suit he had not long ago seen hanging in her wardrobe, her fair hair hung lankly about her face, and though there were no obvious marks upon her skin, Joe had the impression that, unlike Carlo Betz, she had not died without a struggle.

He drew back and gently closed the lid. So much for Lysbeth. And the same might soon be said of Mendoza, or his guess was very wide of the mark. And Melda? He stared at the box, appalled by a mental vision of how she might look lying in there . . . The cigarette had burned almost down to his fingers when he was brought back to reality by the sounds of a car drawing up outside the house, brakes applied, the bang of a door. He walked quickly through to the front of the basement but from the angle of the windows there the steps leading up to the house blocked his view. If he once left that way he might not get back so easily, and this was something that had to be settled right away.

He retreated to the kitchen, ascended the steps, and tried the door at the top. It was locked from the outside and padlocked, if his impression of his last visit were correct. He stood there for a moment listening. Vague sounds reached him from the passage beyond, and putting his ear against the door, he heard footsteps approach, pause, and a man's voice say, 'You may as well pack it up so you can get it off tomorrow.'

Another, which sounded not unlike that of the terse Mr Dight, agreed, 'Could do.' There came the rattle of a chain, and the sound of a key being inserted in the lock. Slipping his torch back into his pocket, Joe went down the steps and flattened himself against the wall, his muscles tense. The door half opened, and he caught the glimpse of a man's cumbersome form, before the first voice said, 'Half a minute, though. You'll want the other, the one in the office.' He heard them move away, and their remarks became unintelligible.

In a couple of bounds he was up the steps again, through the doorway and into the main passage. There he paused, thinking. Dight, and almost certainly Mendoza, just returned from some business known, probably, only to themselves. But did they, in turn, know about the box and its contents in the basement? The point was open to doubt. Even the most hardened individual did not, as a rule, leave anything like that about with the door open. On the other hand, they must have been in too much of a hurry or too concerned with some other affair to notice that someone had forced an entry.

Silently he moved along the passage and paused outside the office, the door of which was closed. Muffled sounds came from within but no one was speaking. He took a firm grip upon the handle and turned it gently. He had opened the door about a couple of inches when something hit him a violent blow on the back of the head, so violent that he could have sworn the house was falling in. Then he ceased to think as unconsciousness engulfed him.

It seemed to him that days and weeks must have passed when he opened his eyes again. There was a numb feeling at the base of his skull, shot here and there with little stabbing pains. He put up a hand and cautiously touched his head. By the feel of it there should, he thought, be a pool of blood soaking the carpeted floor on which he lay. There proved to be none. Partly reassured and partly disappointed he sat up, shook his head several times, and registered the facts that he was alone in Mendoza's office, the time, according to the clock on the mantelpiece, was nearly six, and he was very thirsty.

Steadying himself against the desk, he got to his feet and said many unconventional things. At that moment the door opened and a man entered briskly. By the size of him, Joe judged that he was the one whose silhouette had earlier appeared for a brief moment in the doorway leading to the basement. Large, fleshy, with dark curly hair and bold features, he was, Joe judged, well over forty but fighting a determined battle against the encroaching years. His lounge suit looked expensive, and he had the air of a man long accustomed to comfort. Leaning against the desk and eyeing him warily, Joe said, 'Name of Trayne. I take it you're Mendoza?'

There was, he thought, something to be said for economy of speech, particularly when the brain was feeling far below form. The man smiled, and nodded.

'Gilbert Mendoza is the name.' His voice was deep and rather throaty. 'But I'm surprised you can remember yours, young fellow, after the whack you took. Must have a head like iron.' Giving Joe a wide berth, he walked round to the other side of the desk, sat down, and continued, 'Now suppose you tell me what you were doing breaking into my house?'

Joe, who had swivelled round to face him, sat down on the edge of the desk, brought out a cigarette, lighted it, and inhaled for several seconds in silence. Then he said, 'You've got a perishing nerve. Suppose I ask you what you and your pal were doing, bashing me over the head with a crowbar, or whatever it was?'

Mendoza went on smiling. 'You're wrong, Mr Trayne. I came in and found you going through the drawers of my desk. With great presence of mind, I quickly pulled the rug from under your feet, and you fell and crashed your head against the fender. I'm afraid the blow has upset your memory a little.'

'Is that your story?' Joe asked. 'In case I feel like calling on the police?'

'That's my story. And it's a very good one. I believe I read it somewhere. It's not the first time you've broken in here. I've still got the little note you left me yesterday. I can't think what you want to see me about, but breaking and entering is a serious business and I advise you to try the more lawful method of knocking and enquiring, in future.'

Joe sat and stared at him. Mendoza appeared to be remarkably unruffled, and his hands, as he selected a cigarette from a gold case, were quite steady. A cool customer, and one whose wits had become sharpened over the years through pitting them against those of would-be adversaries. Not a man to be easily tricked, cajoled or threatened into any kind of admission whatsoever. Joe said, 'I ought to bust you one, but in my present state I couldn't do full justice to it. Have you taken a look at your basement lately?'

'I have. And I was most annoyed at the way you'd broken into it.'

'The way *I* did?' Joe paused, massaging the back of his head. Impossible that Mendoza could have gone down there without seeing the box, not unless he were half blind, and the brightness of his eyes suggested that he had very good sight indeed. Or was this just part of some carefully worked out plan of wholesale murder, to rid himself of associates who for some reason he wanted out of the way? Casually he put the question, 'What are you planning to do with the old oak chest down there? Putting it up for sale?'

'I don't quite follow you,' Mendoza said, smoking complacently.

'Then suppose you follow me below and I'll show you what I mean. Or better still, I'll follow you. I should hate to be knocked out twice in one day.'

'I'm afraid I haven't the time or inclination to show you over the house, Mr Trayne, although you seem to have made yourself pretty free of it lately. But I don't think you can have found much in the basement to interest you. A few packing materials, and so on. We use it for packing pictures. That's my business, as I expect you've made it yours to find out. Buying and selling pictures.'

'More especially Solby's. That was a nice one of Melda Linklater you had here yesterday. I was thinking of making you an offer for it.'

'Too late and, I daresay, too expensive. That picture would have fetched a good bit of anyone's money. But it was already sold to a collector who knows how to appreciate it financially as well as artistically. Now if it was a picture you were interested in, why didn't you telephone or call in the ordinary way? No need to break in like a common thief, unless you intended to steal it.'

'I'll tell you why I broke in presently,' Joe said. 'Just now I'm interested in Lysbeth Ritchley. I wouldn't give her a reference, but I do think she should have an official inquest.' Mendoza dropped the ash of his cigarette into a large bronze tray, and clasped his hands on the desk in front of him. 'I suggest,' he said, 'that you go round to the nearest hospital and get them to treat you for concussion.'

Joe glowered at him. The pains had gone from his head now, leaving only a feeling of extreme irritability. 'Now don't you start giving me that no-box-and-no-body story, or I'm going to get violent,' he said.

'I was afraid of that. I took the liberty a little earlier of 'phoning your partner, Mr Pierce. I explained the situation to him, how I'd found you apparently burgling my house and had, vulgarly speaking, put you out for the count. I said to him that I didn't want to call the police if I could help it and what did he advise? He said he was glad I'd told him, as you'd been acting very queerly, and would I put you in a taxi and send you home? So if you're feeling strong enough, Mr Trayne, perhaps you'll go?'

'And perhaps I won't.' Joe leaned across the desk, suddenly

affable. 'That's another nice story, Mendoza, or rather a new angle to an old wangle. You may have fooled Wally that I'm crackers, but he's always thought that, so it doesn't help you much. Now suppose we go back to the beginning. You're not going to deny that your little friend Dight came to see me a couple of nights back, to ask if I'd give Lysbeth Ritchley a reference?'

'I certainly don't deny it,' Mendoza said. 'Why should I? It was Dight who identified you here, after you'd taken that unlucky fall.'

'I'll be identifying him with a black eye, I wouldn't be surprised,' Joe said. 'And then all his troubles will be over. He said you were thinking of giving her a job. Is that right?'

'That's right.'

'Doing what?'

'Well, if you insist upon knowing all my business, I was thinking of opening a little place like yours. Miss Ritchley sings . . . '

'She doesn't any longer,' Joe interrupted. 'And if you want my advice, you'd be just a bit too fussy to run a place like the Allsorts. In our business, you have to be careful, but you don't want to overdo it.'

'How do you mean?'

'I mean that if I were friendly enough to pop into a young woman's flat with a front door key in the middle of the night, I shouldn't bother asking her for references. Silly of me, but that's how I'm made.'

Mendoza raised his bushy eyebrows. 'That's a nasty allegation to make against a young lady who isn't here to defend herself,' he said.

Joe shrugged. 'I don't think it would have bothered Miss Ritchley, and she's beyond caring now. But I'll tell you what I do think. You and Dight knew her pretty well. You both went along there on Friday night, let yourselves in with a key, but you didn't

149

find her there. What you did find was this.' He brought out his wallet, extracted the duplicate telephone memorandum bearing the imprint of his name and telephone number, and pushed it across the desk. 'You tore that off Miss Ritchley's telephone pad, and you sent Dight round to see me with a lot of old so-and-so about a reference to try and find out how well I knew her. That's right, isn't it?'

Smiling sardonically, Mendoza queried, 'And if it were, why should I go to that trouble?'

'Since she was lying dead in your basement when I stepped in, it looks as if you were checking on anyone who might know her well enough to kick up a stink if she disappeared.'

'It could only look like that to anyone with a diseased mind. If Miss Ritchley has disappeared, then no doubt she'll turn up somewhere sooner or later. Young women usually do. But to satisfy your morbid obsession, I'm quite prepared to accompany you downstairs, and then perhaps you'll leave quietly.'

'No.' Mendoza had half risen from his chair, but sank back again with an air of resignation. Joe went on, 'If you say she's not downstairs now, I believe you. It's not the first time you've shifted a body in a hurry, is it? And personally I don't think it'll be the last.'

Mendoza laughed. 'You're full of theories, aren't you? And by the way you talk, anyone might think we were undertakers.'

'You could show them a few points,' Joe said. 'How to do the job without any fuss or bother. And now I'll tell you another of my theories, and this is the best of the lot. If you aren't responsible for the death of Lysbeth Ritchley then someone's got it in for you and everyone working with you. Why they've taken a shine to shoving the bodies of your friends into a box, I don't know. An offshoot of homicidal mania, I daresay. But it looks to me as if you might be the next one to finish up in the same way.'

Mendoza's dark face had flushed to a mottled red. He crushed out his cigarette and eyed Joe malevolently.

'Take care you don't come to a quick end yourself,' he said.

Joe smiled. 'Quick or slow, it doesn't worry me. But it's worrying you, Mendoza, because you're fond of your life and you've a lot of enemies. It could be Solby's brother . . . '

'What the hell do you know about it?' Mendoza's pseudo-friendly manner was turning to one of concentrated fury.

'Quite a bit. Someone left the body of Carlo Betz in a box at Lysbeth Ritchley's flat. If it was nothing to do with you, then it was a mean practical joke on the part of whoever murdered him. And now Lysbeth. The joke has gone a step farther, and this time it's very much on you. Stop me if you've heard this one before, but it looks to me as if this joker plans to deliver the body of each victim to the home of his next intended, which in this case would be either you or Dight. Unless, of course, there's anyone else around that I don't know about.'

Mendoza was sweating. His hands, no longer steady, were moving restlessly about the desk, picking things up and putting them down again. He glared at Joe from under lowering brows, and seemed to have difficulty in speaking.

'That'll be all from you,' he said at last. 'I've listened to enough of your babbling. I've been pretty patient up to now, but if you don't get out of my house and stay out, I'm going to call the police.'

'I don't think you will.' Joe slid off the desk and sat down in the chair facing him. 'I don't doubt you could tell them a plausible yarn, or you wouldn't have gone off and left me here this afternoon while you ditched Lysbeth's body. You must have done the job thoroughly, too, or you wouldn't be so sure of yourself. But just the same you'd rather keep the law out of it.'

'As far as that goes, you're right,' Mendoza said. He had recovered himself a little. 'I was brought up in a hard school, and I like to settle things my own way. Like this.' His right hand had dropped below the desk, and now reappeared holding a small automatic. He handled it with the air of one accustomed to lethal weapons.

'What's the idea of that?' Joe asked.

'What does it look like but a threat, Mr Trayne?'

'It looks damned silly to me. D'you know how to use it?'

'I do. And I shall, if you're not out of this house within five minutes.'

'You must want to get rid of me pretty badly.'

'You can be a very irritating man.'

'I'm doing my best. Well, what are you waiting for?'

'I'm waiting for you to go.'

'I'm not going.'

'Five minutes, Mr Trayne.'

'You said that half a minute ago. But why wait so long? Why don't you go ahead and shoot, if you've got the nerve?'

'I don't want to take your life unless it's necessary. Otherwise, it will be a pleasure. And I've the perfect explanation. You broke into my house, attacked me, and I shot you in self-defence.'

Joe smiled. 'You might get away with it, too, although it's a bit thin in places. But do you really think I care whether I die now or in forty years' time? We've all got to go one day, and being shot is probably as good a way as any. Go on, have your fun. I expect I shall love it.'

He lighted a cigarette and leaned back comfortably in his chair. For the space of another half minute, the older man stared at him, his expression alert and speculative. Then he lowered the revolver and very deliberately put it away in the middle drawer of the desk.

'Do you know,' he said, 'I think I believe you?'

'Why shouldn't you?'

Mendoza had begun to smile again. 'Because of all things men fear death the most. Many a time they've tried to bluff me, but I always know. As for you . . . well, I can only say you're an unusual character.'

'Fascinating is the word.' Joe grinned. 'But that's no reason not to shoot me.'

'On the contrary. A man who isn't afraid to die could be very useful to me.'

'I've a horror of being useful,' Joe said.

'But you'd like to make some money, say, five hundred pounds?'

'Frankly, no. I should hate to make five hundred pounds.'

'You've so much already?'

'Enough to make five hundred repulsive if it came from you.'

Mendoza said slowly, 'In a pleasant way, you can be very insulting.'

Joe laughed. 'With a hide like yours, it shouldn't worry you. What did you want me to do for that handsome gift? Knock some-one off, or go home and forget I ever saw you?'

'You're not giving me credit for much intelligence,' Mendoza retorted. 'If you were that type, you'd be back in the morning asking for more.' He got to his feet, and with his hands behind his back, began pacing about the room. Joe eyed his movements guardedly. 'No, as I see it, Trayne, you're a man with gifts of obser-vation, shrewdness and a lot of common sense. For some reason I don't know, you've got mixed up in affairs that don't concern you, or didn't, until lately. And you're determined to stick. I don't like you, but I'd rather have you on my side than against me. Who is Wendy?'

He shot the question out as he came to a standstill by the desk. Joe returned his interrogating look with a blank stare. 'I love a guessing game,' he said. 'What is it, animal, vegetable or mineral?'

Mendoza's eyes glinted with something that might have been admiration. 'I should have known you wouldn't be tripped up as easily as that. You ought to go far, if someone doesn't bring your career to a sudden end.'

'Be reasonable,' Joe protested. 'How many women do you suppose I meet in one year? Too many to remember all their faces, let alone their names. And you ask me who Wendy is.'

Mendoza thrust his hands into his pockets and was silent for a while, staring down at the carpet. Then as if he had reached a decision, he withdrew one hand, in which he held a crumpled sheet of notepaper. 'Maybe I'm being a fool,' he said. 'I do slip up sometimes. But you don't get anywhere without taking chances. And I've gone so far, I may as well go a bit farther.' Saying which, he dropped the sheet of paper on the desk in front of Joe, went round to the other side, and resumed his seat.

Joe smoothed out the paper, which had once been pale blue and was of the cheap, ruled variety, and read with interest a few lines of typewriting: 'I must see you at once. Will you meet me at the "Bottle and Tankard" tonight at ten o'clock? It's a big hotel on the Portsmouth road just outside Esher. You can't miss it. I'll be waiting outside. It's terribly important.' The note was signed 'Wendy', in ink and in large, childish handwriting. There was no address or date, but it was headed 'Friday'. Joe looked up from his perusal and met Mendoza's enquiring gaze. He shrugged his shoulders.

'What's it all about and why show it to me?' he asked indifferently.

Watching him closely, Mendoza said, 'I just wondered what you'd make of it.'

'All anyone could make of it. Someone named Wendy wanted to meet someone else outside a pub on a Friday night at ten o'clock. As you've got the message, I suppose it was sent to you.'

'You suppose wrong. I found it in Lysbeth Ritchley's right shoe, and I imagine she put it there for safety. All right, I know what you're going to say. Well, suppose I admit that I did find her here, lying in that box in my basement, after you and I had had our little disagreement earlier this afternoon? She's not there now, and neither is that infernal box, so you can't make anything out of it. I don't think you would, in any case. That was one of the things I was banking on when Dight and I went out and left you here. The story that you could tell to anyone would sound like so much gibberish.'

'You were taking a long chance,' Joe said. 'Everyone knows that Miss Ritchley has disappeared, and the police are looking for her. And since you knew her . . . '

'You're the only one who knows that, and I don't suppose you've told half London. You're not the blabbing kind.'

'That's very flattering.' It would, Joe thought, be indiscreet to mention that Johnny also knew. Johnny had been in enough trouble lately, without incurring the possibility of more. As for Wendy . . . 'Got anything to drink around here?' he asked. 'My throat feels like a gravel pit.'

'Why didn't you say so before?' With the air of the perfect host, Mendoza went to a cupboard and brought out a bottle of whisky, half full, and one glass. 'I don't drink much myself, but I keep this for emergencies.'

'Haven't you got a fresh bottle?' Joe said. 'I'm not keen on it once it's been opened.'

'Afraid of being poisoned?' Mendoza smiled.

'I'm not afraid of anything. I'm just rather fussy about my drink, being in the business.'

'As you like. I'll have to go to the kitchen for it.' Mendoza walked to the door, but turned to say over his shoulder, 'Don't bother to go through the drawers of my desk. I've made certain there's nothing in them to interest you.'

'I won't,' Joe promised, and the moment Mendoza closed the door behind him, he brought out his wallet, sought for and found the case containing a club membership card, and ripped a piece of mica from the front of it. With this placed over the typewritten note upon the desk, he traced the signature, 'Wendy', with his fountain pen. He was sitting back in his chair, smoking a further cigarette, when Mendoza returned with a fresh bottle of whisky and a corkscrew, which he slapped down with the remark, 'You wouldn't get better drink than that anywhere.'

'And certainly not such interesting company,' Joe said. 'But it's the least you can do, after knocking me for six.' He opened the bottle, poured himself a glass of whisky and drank deeply. Picking up the typewritten note, Mendoza remarked, 'So you don't know who Wendy is?'

'No. Do you?'

'If I did, I should be having a little chat with her, instead of wasting my time on you.'

'How do you know it's a female? Could be a man using a woman's name as a pseudonym. Or whoever murdered Miss Ritchley may have put the note in her shoe sheerly as a blind. It looks a pretty amateurish effort to me, that "Meet me at the crossroads" stuff.'

Mendoza flushed and banged down his fist upon the desk in an abrupt return to anger.

'Blast you and your theories!' he exploded. 'I've a good mind to take a chance and knock you off just to get you out of my way. D'you think I'm such an imbecile that I haven't gone into all that? Lysbeth Ritchley went out somewhere last Friday night. We know that because, as you so cleverly pointed out, she wasn't there when Dight and I turned up to see her. The garage was empty, too, so it's my belief she drove out to meet whoever wrote that note. And it was someone she knew and hadn't any reason to doubt, since she'd just lost Carlo and wouldn't be taking any chances. But the plain fact is we didn't see her again until she turned up dead in the basement.'

'Gang warfare?' Joe queried gently. 'That's what the Press is suggesting.'

'Gang warfare be damned, man! They'd make a splurge out of someone swatting a fly. I don't run a gang. Mine is a straightforward, respectable business, and don't you forget it. But you were right when you said I'd got a lot of enemies. Bound to have, when you're as successful as I am. And it's my belief that some lunatic among them is out to ruin me.'

Joe helped himself to another drink and asked, 'Did you have any bother with the police over Carlo?'

'No bother at all, because I didn't know him. He was Lysbeth's friend, not mine.'

Joe met his steady gaze and smiled. Evidently Mendoza believed that the best way to tell a convincing lie was to stare the hearer straight in the eyes. He remarked, 'So when Lysbeth rang through and said the body of her boy friend had been delivered to her in a plain van, and what should she do, you bundled over there post haste to take it away, all out of pure friendship. The age of chivalry is certainly back with a bounce.'

'If you like to twist facts . . . ' Mendoza began, but Joe cut him short.

'I've listened to a lot of old bull from you,' he said. 'And now you can listen to me for a change. Say what you like, Mendoza, you're scared. You'd like to go to the police and get their help like any ordinary citizen. But you can't, any more than you could when Carlo died. Carlo was known as a bad boy, and you didn't want to be associated with him. Neither did Lysbeth. So you and Dight lost no time in shoving him out of sight. But you were in too much of a hurry and you didn't shove him far enough. Now Lysbeth's dead, and you don't want to be linked up with her either, because she might lead back to Carlo, and once the police start delving about anything could happen. So she's gone, too. But suppose that box turns up again, who's going to be inside it?'

Controlling his voice with difficulty, Mendoza said, 'It won't turn up. I've taken care of that. I'm a match for any half-wit who thinks he can scare me, and that goes for you, too.' He leaned back, with a ghastly attempt at a smile. 'We got it out of here, didn't we? And in broad daylight. That takes some nerve, doesn't it? And in case you're racking that so-called brain or yours to think how we did it, I'll tell you. We wrapped it in sacking, roped it round, labelled it "Pictures, with care", and drove it away on a trailer at the back of the car. That'll give you some idea of the kind of man I am.'

'Pretty smart. And where did you drive to? Not the same place as you parked Carlo, I'll bet.'

'That was a mistake. There wasn't much time to think, and no one is infallible. But I take care not to make the same mistake twice. And I'm certainly not making the very obvious one of telling you more than I think you may usefully know.'

'Well, this'll give you some idea of the kind of man *I* am,' Joe said. 'I take it, since you can't go to the police, you offered me that five hundred quid to get to the bottom of this business, to find out who is trying to get you on the run? Am I right?'

'Something of the kind,' Mendoza admitted. 'But of course there'd be more in it for you if . . .'

'I don't want your money,' Joe interrupted. 'But I'll take on the job just the same. I'm in it anyway, and as you put it, I'm determined to stick. But if, in the process, you land up in jail, don't blame me.'

He got up and moved towards the door. Mendoza was gripping the arms of his chair, breathing thickly.

'What are you going to do?' he asked.

Joe paused to look back. 'A number of things. But first I'm going to have a smash at finding Wendy. See you later, if you don't get screwed down in the meantime.'

As he descended the steps of the house, he heard the front door being locked and two bolts shot into position. Mendoza seemed to be in pretty bad shape.

Chapter XII

Joe walked as far as the main thoroughfare, entered the first empty telephone box, and put through a call to Melda Linklater's flat. He heard the instrument ring for half a minute the other end, before her voice drowsily answered him. He said, 'Joe Trayne here. Did you fall asleep waiting for me?'

'I've been asleep all the afternoon,' she said. 'You just woke me.'

'Sorry about that. But haven't you got a train to catch?'

'I don't think I will, after all. That's a dreary journey, and they're not expecting me. I think I'll give a party instead. I feel so much better.'

'You change your mind pretty quickly, don't you?'

She laughed. 'Put it down to the artistic temperament. You ought to be glad I feel like entertaining. I don't very often.'

'I think I'd be a lot gladder if you were tucked comfortably away with Ma and Pa for a bit.'

'What's the matter, Joe?' she asked, a touch of anxiety in her voice. 'You sound odd. Didn't you sleep this afternoon?'

He grinned into the transmitter. 'On the contrary, I slept a treat. Went off like a log and didn't wake up until six. But listen, Melda. There are things happening in this city that I don't like, and certain people I don't want to get mixed up in them. You're one.'

She was silent for a while. Then she said, 'I'm sorry. But I really don't want to take that journey tonight. And I can't imagine anyone breaking into my place with a party going on. Safety in numbers, you know.'

'What sort of numbers and what sort of people?'

'Oh, just a few.' She reeled off half a dozen names which he knew vaguely in connection with the worlds of theatre and music. 'And of course, you,' she added. 'If you're not too busy digging skeletons out of cupboards, to drop in for a drink.'

'I'm never too busy for that. What time is all this taking place?'

'About nine, I should think. But come along whenever you like. If I know my friends, they'll be here until the early hours of the morning.'

'Good,' Joe said. 'Keep 'em there at any cost, even if they drink you dry. I'll bring relief supplies along later. And until they arrive, keep the door and windows locked and don't open up to anyone unless you're sure it's one of your pals.'

'Are you trying to make me nervous?' she demanded.

'No. I just want to go on seeing you, that's all. And with unknown quantities performing acrobatics, you can't be too careful. You'll do that for me, won't you?'

'I believe I'd do quite a lot for you,' she said, and hung up before he could answer. He lit a cigarette, and put through a further call to his own apartment. Johnny's voice came across the wire with a stream of questions as soon as he announced his identity.

'What happened to you last night, Joe? Where've you been all day? Where are you now? Wally's been nagging me something awful . . . '

'Never mind Wally,' Joe cut in. 'If he's getting to want a

161

day-and-night account of my movements, he'll have to find himself a new partner. How did you find Wendy?'

'Oh, she's all right, but worried sick. It seems she 'phoned her mother, just to let her know where and how she was, and the old lady's in a stew over Lysbeth disappearing.'

'What time did you get back last night?' Joe asked.

'Latish, I waited around a couple of hours for you, then I turned in.'

'Well, now, look, Johnny. Will you run out to the "Nosebag" and bring Wendy back to the flat right away? I want to talk to her, and it can't wait.'

'I don't mind,' Johnny said. 'But how will she feel about it?'

'Don't worry about that. Just get her. Tell her anything you like, but don't let me down over this. It's important.'

'All right,' Johnny promised. 'Half a minute, message for you from that Sanderson we were out with last night. He rang about an hour ago, said would you go round to his place, 29, Handel Street, Room 11. I didn't have much truck with him, but he said it's urgent.'

'Thanks,' Joe said. 'I'll go round there, and I'll probably be back at the flat before you are. But if I'm not, wait for me.'

'What'll I do if Wally rings again?' Johnny asked. 'He sounded wild last time. Said you'd been picked up for housebreaking, or something, and would I see you had a hot drink and got to bed soon as you came home.'

'He ought to have been a mother,' Joe snorted. 'Tell him that I'm in bed writing poetry and don't want to be disturbed.'

He rang off. The air in the telephone box had become thick with cigarette smoke, and his head felt numb again. He stepped out, took several deep breaths and walked briskly to the nearest saloon bar, where he entered and sat for a while, drinking and thinking.

It was nearly eight when he emerged, and there being a dearth of taxis at that moment, he went by Underground as far as Tottenham Court Road, from where he walked the short distance to Handel Street. No. 29 was an old but well-preserved house, four storeys high, with clean curtains at the windows. The front door stood open, and a mixed smell of furniture polish and potted ferns greeted him as he entered. Apart from a tabby cat sitting on the stairs immediately facing him, there was no sign of life, and discovering that the doors on the ground floor were numbered one to four, he mounted the stairway, pausing to stroke the head of the cat in passing. The latter appeared singularly unmoved.

Room 11 proved to be on the third floor, and Joe's knock upon the door echoed loudly through the quiet house. There came muffled sounds from within, and after a brief interval, the door opened and Sanderson stood there, wearing a long blue woollen dressing-gown. He smiled, but his eyes behind the spectacles looked tired.

'Come in,' he said. 'I hoped you might be along, but I doubted it. I was just taking a bath.'

'Go ahead, I'm in no hurry.' Joe entered, closing the door behind him, and the warmth of the room after the comparative coldness of the damp streets felt to him as if he had thrust his head into a lighted gas oven. The high windows were closed, an electric radiator was burning at full power, and clouds of steam filtered in from the open doorway of the adjacent bathroom. 'What are you trying to do?' he asked. 'Hatch out eggs, or something?'

'Sorry.' Sanderson moved leisurely across to open the window a chink at the top. 'The fact is, I feel like hell today. I had a cold coming on last night, and took large doses of whisky to smother it, and now I've got the cold plus a hangover. Sit down and I'll get you a drink.'

163

'Thanks.' Joe removed his coat, took possession of one of the two comfortable armchairs, lit a cigarette and glanced about him with frank curiosity. It was a service apartment like any other, but looked as if it had not seen much service during that day at least. Sanderson's clothes were lying about in all directions, there were magazines on the floor and the ashtrays were filled to overflowing. Sanderson himself was still standing by the window, staring fixedly down over the net curtain. 'Anything wrong?' Joe asked. 'Apart from the cold and hangover?'

'Eh?' Sanderson turned with a start, and his smile was rather strained. 'Well, yes and no. I expect you're wondering why I asked you to come here.'

'I've given up wondering. I just ride with the tide. How about that drink?'

'Yes, of course.' He produced two clean glasses from the cocktail cabinet, half filled them with whisky, put one of them on the table beside Joe and added soda to his own. 'You're not looking too good yourself. What sort of a night did *you* have?'

'Very sober, for a Saturday. But hadn't you better finish your bath?'

'I will, if you really don't mind waiting. I'm beginning to feel a bit shivery.'

'In this heat? You must be nearly dead.'

Sanderson looked at him a trifle oddly, as he remarked, 'I don't feel far off it,' and went into the bathroom. The door closed, and Joe heard the splash of water as a tap was turned on. Rising quickly, he walked to the window and peered down over the top of the curtain. The room overlooked Handel Street. There were not many people about, and those who passed mostly carried umbrellas, for it had begun to rain again. One man in particular caught his attention, standing on the kerb opposite. His hands were thrust deep into his raincoat pockets, a trilby hat was pulled

164

down over his eyes, and from his vantage point Joe could not get a clear view of the man's face. But as he turned and walked away, there was something very familiar in his gait.

Returning, Joe refilled his glass, sat down and for the space of about fifteen minutes relaxed and refused to think about anything. At the end of which time Sanderson came back, looking refreshed but still weary.

'I made it a quick one,' he said, lighting a cigarette and sitting down on the arm of the chair opposite. 'I don't imagine you want to sprawl around here all the evening. I wouldn't have asked you to come, only I tried 'phoning you a couple of times, and I'm not keen on telephone conversations, anyway. It's like this, Trayne. I don't know if I'm developing nerves in my old age, but there seems to be a man tailing me wherever I go.'

Joe asked cautiously, 'What sort of man?'

'Peculiar. I've only caught glimpses of him. He just pops up in odd places and disappears again. He's got a very blank, white sort of face, and goes around with his collar turned up as if he didn't want to be seen too closely. Last night, after I left you, I nearly caught up with him, but he gave me the slip round about Maida Vale. Do you know anything about him?'

'Sounds like the fellow who delivered the box to Thunder Mews in the first place,' Joe said. 'He called himself Green, then. He seems to be getting about quite a bit. You've seen him, and I've seen him . . . '

'Where?' Sanderson asked.

'Last night, on my way home. And while you were having your bath, there was someone remarkably like him on the other side of the road.'

'I saw him there, too.' Sanderson stared down at his slippered feet. 'He's been hanging around Handel Street on and off all day.'

'Why don't you nip down and have it out with him?'

'I did go down once. But I wasn't quick enough. He's got a way of disappearing before you can get to grips. He's got a car . . .'

'I know. A long, green tourer.' They looked at each other for a while in silence.

'I'm wondering if he's anything to do with Mendoza,' Sanderson said. He got up and began to pace restlessly about the room. 'I thought I'd managed to keep pretty well under cover, but he may have spotted me. Have you found out any more about this box affair? Not that it's any concern of mine . . .'

'There's been another murder,' Joe said.

'How do you mean, another murder?'

Joe gave him a fairly accurate account of his afternoon's adventures, and Sanderson dropped down into the chair opposite and regarded him with an expression between astonishment and vexation.

'You're the coolest thing on two legs I've seen for a long time,' he said at last. 'Despite all I said, you walk in on Mendoza, find him with a dead woman on his premises, and come and tell me about it as if you'd been out on a picnic. Are you trying to get yourself put away for life?'

'Now don't you start,' Joe protested. 'I may not seem like one big brain at the moment, but that crack on the head didn't do me any good.'

'If you ask me, you weren't too bright before. Why didn't you get on to me, or the police, when you found that box again?'

'I told you, I didn't get the chance. But next time . . .'

'There won't be a next time. I think you're wrong about Mendoza. In my opinion he's playing some double game of his own, and Green is probably in it with him. But I know that Bernard Solby was murdered . . .'

166

'Are you absolutely certain of that?' Joe queried.

'Positive. And I've got nearly enough evidence to prove that Mendoza and Dight were in it together. Tonight I'm going all out to finish it.'

'But why should he do it? He couldn't have known in advance that the man's pictures were worth anything, any more than Charles Solby could.'

'That wasn't the reason. And I can't tell you the real one, because when he knows, Charles Solby may not want to go any further in the matter. However, that doesn't affect me. I shall have done my part. But I'd be glad to know what you're going to do? I'm beginning to worry about you.'

Joe grinned and got to his feet. Picking up his coat, he said, 'You needn't. I'm going home to have a bath. The sight of you in that dressing-gown is filling me with envy. What's more, I don't have to do anything. I just wait for things to happen. Cheeroh, Sanderson. Sorry to have bothered you with my horror stories.'

'It was decent of you to tell me,' Sanderson said, accompanying him to the door. 'I appreciate that. Are you going to be in the rest of the evening?'

'I don't know. My movements are always erratic, and never more than now. But if you want to pop in or 'phone, just pop in or 'phone.'

'You're a funny devil,' Sanderson said. 'I'll give you a ring later, if I've got anything to tell you.'

The cool atmosphere of the house was welcome to Joe after the heat of Sanderson's room. But so great was the contrast when he reached the street, that he found himself shivering a little beneath the impact of the driving rain. There was no sign of any loitering figure now, and he walked rapidly back to Tottenham Court Road, where he engaged a taxi and drove straight home. The flat was empty when he arrived, and since Mrs Bushby did not work on Sundays, the traces of Johnny's recent occupation were all too obvious. There were cigarette ends lying about in odd places, empty cups and glasses, a couple of newspapers, and the kitchen sink was laden with used china. None too pleased, Joe tidied up a little, bathed, shaved, changed into fresh evening kit, prepared himself a trayload of food and settled down in the lounge to partake of it with a bottle of ale.

He glanced through both newspapers, but they contained nothing to interest him. He was about to telephone Melda, when Johnny returned. He came straight into the lounge, looking woebegone and ill at ease, and dropped down into the nearest chair.

'Isn't she here yet?' he asked.

Joe got slowly to his feet. 'Who? You're not going to tell me you've lost track of Wendy?'

'That's what I'm worried about.' Johnny lit a cigarette and looked very worried indeed. 'They said she left about an hour before I got there. She was coming to town to see us, so I thought she might be here already. You don't think anything's happened to her, do you?'

'Who told you all this?'

'MacNeil. Least, he said he knew she was coming to town, because she said so, although she didn't tell him what for. But she left a note for me in case I went down and she missed me. I sort of said I might, last night.'

'Let's see the note,' Joe said.

'It's sort of personal,' Johnny protested. 'I don't think she meant anyone else to read it.'

Joe sat down on the arm of his chair and regarded him fixedly.

'See here, Johnny. I was round at Mendoza's place today, and I found Lysbeth Ritchley lying dead in that blasted box in the basement. You wouldn't like anything of the kind to happen to Wendy, would you?'

'Lord save us and help us!' Johnny leaped to his feet, his eyes dilated with horror. 'That tears it right across. What's Wendy going to say to that? And her mother's all stewed up as it is. What did you do?'

'I didn't do anything, because Mendoza caught me napping and knocked me out. Then he and Dight whisked the body away in their inimitable manner. The box has gone, too. So for heaven's sake, keep your lid pulled down over this until we find out how we stand. Don't say a word to Wendy, when she turns up. *If* she turns up.'

'What d'you mean?' Johnny's voice had risen a note or two. 'She's got to turn up.'

'I hope so, for her sake. Because Mendoza showed me a note he found in Lysbeth's shoe. It was signed "Wendy", and asked Lysbeth to be outside some pub at Esher at 10 o'clock on Friday. If you remember, you put Wendy on a train for Salisbury on Friday evening, but she got off and came back to town and was at Waterloo round about nine. She'd have had plenty of time to keep that appointment, if she made it. The letter was typewritten, but I've got a tracing of the signature. So I'd like to see that note she left you.'

In silence, Johnny took from his overcoat pocket a half sheet of notepaper and passed it across to him. The writing was in ink, a bold, childish hand, and ran:

'Dear Johnny . . . This is to tell you that I'm catching the next train to London. I've got to see you and Mr Trayne urgently. I'm worried terribly. I'm leaving you this in case you come down in the meantime, so if I don't see you, you'll know why, if you see what I mean . . . Love, Wendy.'

Joe brought out the piece of mica on which he had traced the first signature, and placed one over the other. They fitted exactly, except for the tailpiece of the last letter. Joe handed both to Johnny, with the query, 'What do you make of that?'

Johnny compared the two, his brow furrowed in concentration. 'I'd say,' he declared at length, 'that someone forged the kid's signature. On this note she wrote me, the "y" ends sort of low down, but on this other one it goes on as if it ought to be joined to something. And I'll tell you what. That Green merchant had her signature, didn't he? On that thing she signed when he brought home the box. Only on that she'd have put her full name, wouldn't she? That's it, then. If she signed her full name, the "y" *would* be joined to something.'

'Possibly,' Joe grinned. 'You're prejudiced, Johnny, but I was thinking something of the kind myself. If Green wanted to get Lysbeth out to a convenient spot, he'd stand a better chance sending a letter which apparently came from her sister. The wording of it didn't sound quite like Wendy's style, either, so far as I remember. Can she use a typewriter?'

'Yes . . . no . . . well, I believe she did say she learned to type at some school. But she wouldn't be carrying a typewriter around with her, would she?'

'God knows. Let's hope she turns up in a minute and we can ask her a few straight questions. Just now I feel as if I'm at sea in a boat I've made myself. Grab a drink and I'll tell you about Mendoza. He was probably lying as regards that note, anyway.'

Johnny fetched a glass and two further bottles of beer. But he listened with only half attention to Joe's narrative, glancing at his wrist-watch from time to time. He jumped nervously when the telephone rang, and said, 'That'll be her.' But having picked up the receiver and listened for a second or two, his expression changed from eagerness to disappointment. 'It's for you,' he remarked, handing over the instrument. 'Can't think why they bothered inventing the telephone. It kept me awake half the night, with some nut ringing through to ask if you were here.'

His hand over the mouthpiece, Joe said, 'You didn't tell me. Who was it?'

'He wouldn't say, and I didn't care.'

Joe put the receiver to his ear, and said into the transmitter, 'Joe Trayne here.'

A voice came across the wire, speaking as if from a long distance. 'Name of Dight. Want to see me?'

'Why not?' Joe said, keeping surprise out of his tone. 'Always glad to see a friend. Drop in and have a drink if you're passing.'

'Can't come to you. Better come to me. Got things to tell you. Anything you want to know?'

'Where are you?' Joe queried softly.

'Place called "Trees", Water Lane, Weybridge. Big house, end of lane. I'm here alone. Will I see you?'

'Within the hour,' Joe said. 'Suit you?'

'It'll suit me. But no police, or you'll get nothing out of it.'

Whereupon the telephone went dead, and Joe replaced the receiver. Johnny asked, 'What's all that about? You're not going out, are you?'

'I am. And you're coming with me. Unless you prefer to mope around here. That was Dight, speaking from a house in Weybridge. He's alone, he says, and has got things to tell me. It didn't sound quite like his voice, so there may be a catch in it. On the other hand, it could have been a bad line. Anyway, it's worth a try.'

Johnny hesitated. 'But what about Wendy? She might turn up, and we can't leave her to sit on the doorstep.'

'We'll take a chance and leave the back door open. If anyone likes to move the furniture out, good luck to them.'

'I don't like it,' Johnny said.

'All right, I'll go alone.' Joe went into the bedroom, donned a heavy proofed overcoat, refilled his cigarette case and put a fresh battery in his electric torch. Returning, he said, 'Better still, I'll pick up Sanderson. I owe it to him to let him in on this if it's any good. And if it's not, well, it's nobody's fault.'

Eyeing him obliquely, Johnny asked, 'Will you be driving?'

'Why not? I don't know if Sanderson's got a car, so I'd better take mine.'

'I'll come,' Johnny said. 'You never know, this Dight says he's alone, but there might be a whole gang of 'em down there.' He brought out a stump of pencil and a piece of paper, scrawled a note to Wendy, and propped it up on the sideboard. 'I expect she'll find her way in all right. Oughtn't we to have a gun, or something?'

Joe laughed. 'Not for me. Such as they are, I prefer to depend on my wits. But you might bring half a bottle of Scotch. I've a feeling we're going to need it.'

Johnny had left the car parked in Johnsons Passage. Rain was teeming down as they went out the back way, leaving the kitchen door and the wall entrance unlocked. They took their places in the vehicle, and Johnny asked, starting the engine, 'Where does this Sanderson hang out?'

Joe told him, and they drove in silence to Handel Street. It was dark now, and the door of No. 29 was closed. Leaving Johnny at the wheel, Joe rang the bell several times before the door was opened by an elderly woman, wearing a chintz overall and an expression of grave respectability.

'Mr Sanderson?' she said, in answer to his enquiry. 'I'm afraid you've just missed him. He went out about five minutes ago.'

172

'He didn't leave any message, I suppose?'

'No, but he said he would not be long, if anyone called. Would you care to wait?'

'Can't, unfortunately. But you might ask him to give me a ring in a couple of hours' time, if he's back. Joe Trayne. He's got my number.'

'Very good,' she said, and politely watched him turn away and climb back into the car, before she closed the door upon the bleakness of the night.

'So much for that,' Joe remarked. 'Sanderson won't like me butting in again, but at least he'll know I tried to let him in on the ground floor. Full speed ahead, Johnny, first stop Water Lane, Weybridge.'

'It's not him I'm bothered about,' Johnny said, as he started off again. 'It's Wendy. And Wally. What would he say if he could see you now, after all I promised him? Specially if he knew you'd had a whack on the head already.'

'All the more reason for going to see Dight. I'm not sure if I owe that one to him or Mendoza, but someone's going to get a smack in the eye if they don't behave themselves.' He lit a cigarette and handed one to Johnny. 'Another thing, if they've got a place out of town, it's quite on the cards that's where they took Lysbeth this afternoon. They didn't go very far, because there wasn't much time.'

Johnny stared gloomily ahead at the rain-washed roadway, and tooted impatience at a taxi which did not appear to recognize the existence of any other traffic on the road. Thanks to the heavy rain, there was not the usual number of pedestrians about, with the result that they were able to make fair progress through town, and once outside its boundaries, Johnny gave expression to his pent-up feelings by letting out the car to the maximum speed compatible with safety.

'D'you know Weybridge at all?' he asked, as they were approaching the outskirts.

'Not at all,' Joe said, peering out through the driving rain at the swinging sign of a public house illuminated by their headlights as they rounded a bend. 'Pity it's gone closing time. We might have nipped in there and asked the way.'

'I'll nip in here,' Johnny said, sliding the car up to the kerb outside a brightly lighted café. 'They'll know.' He got out and made a dash for the steaming, sultry interior. Joe lit a cigarette and waited. The rapid driving had cleared his head, and he was aware of a certain sense of exhilaration. He was smiling a little when Johnny returned to say, 'About another half mile up the road. Turn right, turn left, turn somersaults. Hell of a way most of 'em have of directing anyone. If we find this dump on a night like this it'll be because I always go opposite to the way they tell me. What are you grinning at?'

'I feel happy,' Joe said.

'Gawd!' Johnny shook his head violently as they sped away. 'I wonder if they knew what they were doing when they reared you?'

They turned off presently down a winding road, and came at last to what was appropriately named Water Lane. Inches deep in mud and puddles, the car bumped its way forward with Johnny muttering odd remarks under his breath.

'I see what they mean,' he said, peering hopelessly through the windscreen. 'I'll be surprised if this house we're heading for doesn't turn out to be Noah's Ark.'

Joe was leaning out his side, trying to get some impression of the surroundings. The houses in this area appeared to be situated in their own grounds, and hedged in by high foliage. At the end of the lane Johnny brought the car to a standstill. In the light of the headlamps they saw large white gates, and a blur of trees and bushes.

'This'll be it,' Joe said. 'Let's have a drink before we go any farther.' He reached for the half bottle of whisky which he had tucked into the pocket nearest him, helped himself, and passed it to Johnny. Then he climbed out, approached the gates, and finding the name 'Trees' boldly painted thereon, he opened them and made a rapid dive back to his seat in the car. Johnny returned the whisky bottle, wiped his mouth with the back of his hand, and they proceeded to move cautiously forward along a drive overhung with trees and unkempt shrubbery, until there came to view a long, low brick house, without any sign of light or life to welcome them.

'Drive straight up?' Johnny asked.

'Certainly,' Joe said. 'Unless you can think of any way of walking from here to there without getting waterlogged.'

'I'm wet and worried already,' Johnny remarked, but drove up to the house and parked the car in front of the six steps leading to the porch. 'I'm wishing more than ever we had a gun or something,' he added, in an undertone, as they mounted the steps, and Joe rang the bell. 'I don't like the look of this at all.'

'What did you expect? An electric sign saying, "Welcome, boys, this one's on me"?' Joe pressed the bell again, and went on pressing for some time. 'To hell with it,' he said at last. 'I'm going round the back.'

'I thought you didn't want to get wet,' Johnny said, following him as he ran down the steps and turned sharp right along a gravel path, switching on his torch to light the way.

'I don't. But if Dight's there and intends to come to the door, he's had enough time to do it, and if he's not or he doesn't, then I'm going in just the same.'

At the back of the house was a verandah, overlooking a sloping lawn. Joe walked cautiously along until he came to french windows, which he tested and found locked. He knocked loudly for some minutes, and gaining no response, he stepped back a pace and eyed the window measuringly.

'What are you going to do?' Johnny asked.

'This,' Joe said, and lifting one leg, he rammed his foot through the window with his full weight behind it, shattering glass in all directions. Removing the surplus with a gloved hand, he unfastened the lock, pushed open the window and stepped inside.

'I feel there's a law against this,' Johnny whispered, following closely.

'Maybe there is. But Mendoza offered me five hundred quid, didn't he? I didn't take it, so if he has to stand a few incidental expenses such as putting new windows in, he can't grumble.' Joe had found the electric light switch and turned it on. The room was furnished in comfortable middle-class style, quite unremarkable and quite empty save for themselves.

After a careful inspection to confirm his first impression, Joe opened the door leading on to the main passage, switched on further lights, and stood looking and listening. The house had an unearthly silence about it, the kind of silence that engulfs the listener, until he hears noises in his head.

'I don't like it,' Johnny said again. 'It's a trap, that's what it is.'

'Either that, or another murder,' Joe agreed. 'But we may as well have a look round, now we're here.'

They did. Conscientiously, and with some further protest on Johnny's part, they explored all the rooms on both floors, all cupboards, wardrobes, drawers and other means of concealment, without bringing to light anything startling. There were a few receipted gas, electric light and telephone accounts addressed to R. Sebastian, Esq., but there was no sign of such a name at that address appearing in the directory which stood beside the telephone in the lounge.

'Probably hasn't had the house long enough, whoever he is,' Joe remarked. 'Let's take a look at the cellar. I'd have tried it first but it seemed too obvious.'

'Too obvious for what?'

'For hiding a dead body. According to Mendoza, he stuck that box and Lysbeth away somewhere so they wouldn't turn up again. He didn't have much time to do it, and it was broad daylight. If this house is his, or Dight's, they could quite comfortably have driven down here with that trailer . . . '

He broke off, listening. But there was only the sound of the wind that had sprung up, and rain lashing against the windows.

'If you must, you must,' Johnny said, and with many a glance over his shoulder, followed close upon Joe's heels as they went down the stairs that led from the back premises to the cellar. The door at the bottom stood open, swinging on creaky hinges. Joe kicked it wide, and swivelled his torch until he found the light switch. The subsequent illumination confirmed a little of what he had surmised.

It was not a large cellar, and had not been very much used in the past, to judge by the dustiness of the flagstone flooring and the lumber that cluttered its space. But some use had recently been found for it, for in the centre, six of the largest flagstones had been removed, and piled one on top of the other, leaving a considerable gap. Propped against one wall were two pickaxes and a pile of other workman-like tools, and the surrounding floor was covered in a mixture of dust and damp cement, bearing traces of many footprints.

'What the hell . . . ?' Johnny muttered, cautiously peering over as Joe crouched down and directed the beam of his torch into the gap. It was empty, and though it did not go down more than three feet, it had an evil, dank smell about it.

'Looks as if it might be a covered-in well,' Joe observed, running a hand along the edge of the flagstones. 'I'd say this is where Mendoza socked away the box, all right, with Lysbeth inside it. Not a bad idea, if he cemented it in properly. But why dig it up again?'

'Why ask me?' Johnny said, hastily stepping back. 'Lot of barmies, that's what I say. And if there's much more of it, I'm going along to a home and ask 'em to put me away. I'd feel safer.'

But Joe was not listening. He was busy examining the footmarks, among which was one comparable in size to that he had seen in the apartment of Melda Linklater. Straightening up, he said, 'Let's get back to town. I want to have another word with Mendoza.'

'You'll find yourself having a word with him in the next world,' Johnny grumbled, 'the way you two are going.' He was first up the stairs, leaving Joe to switch off the light and to follow, more slowly. In the passage above they both paused, as there came to them the urgent sound of the telephone ringing.

'That might be interesting,' Joe said, and made a dive for the lounge, where he picked up the instrument and muttered something incomprehensible into it, in a voice as unlike his own as possible. The voice that answered him was easily recognizable as that of Mendoza.

'That you, Dight?' Joe muttered again, and Mendoza went on, 'I think you'd better stay where you are for a bit. Things don't look too good this end. Everything all right with you?'

Joe hesitated. He could not hope to go on passing himself off as Dight, without Mendoza getting suspicious. He was also reluctant to end so promising a conversation. He decided in favour of the method direct.

'Everything's gorgeous,' he said, in his normal tone, and derived some satisfaction from the ejaculation of annoyance that came from the other end. 'I won't be coy and ask you to guess who I am. This is Trayne, speaking from Weybridge where I'm enjoying the hospitality of one R. Sebastian. How are you?'

Mendoza swore for several seconds. Then he said, 'What the blazes are you playing at, Trayne? And where's Dight?'

'Afraid you'll have to work that out for yourself. I take it he should have been here, but you can take it that he's not any longer. And neither is your treasure chest. But it wasn't much of a place to hide it, in my opinion.'

'What the hell do you mean? If I thought Dight had been talking . . . '

'Never mind what you think, Mendoza. I'm only interested in what *I* think, and I'm thinking this. Dight'll turn up at your place some time soon, along with the chest, and he won't be in any condition to talk, I wouldn't be surprised.'

Mendoza said softly, 'I believe I've misjudged you, Trayne. You wouldn't have a hand in this, I suppose?'

'Suppositions bore me,' Joe said. 'I was coming round to see you, but you've told me all I want to know for the moment.'

He hung up, and stood looking down at a large, flat parcel lying on the table, to which he had not previously paid much attention. Bringing out his pen-knife, he cut the string and unwrapped it, to reveal two paintings by Solby, one a study of two ballet dancers, and the other the portrait of Melda Linklater which he had first seen in Mendoza's office. The latter he re-wrapped carefully, tucked under his arm, and said, 'Come on, Johnny boy. Let's see how fast you can get us back to town.'

Johnny, who had been eyeing him from the depths of an armchair, got to his feet. 'You're not pinching that, are you?' he asked anxiously.

'Just borrowing it. Mendoza can't object to that, can he? I don't much care if he does.'

'We'll land in clink yet,' Johnny prophesied. But he had cheered up considerably at the thought of returning home, and found no further cause to grumble even when they had to splash through the six-inch puddle that had formed between the front steps and where he had left the car.

'I'll sit in the back,' Joe said, climbing in. 'Something tells me you're going to break all records, and I don't want to be beside you while you do it.'

Johnny chuckled, as he turned the car and started down the drive. 'I wouldn't take any risks on a night like this,' he declared. Nevertheless, they were clear of the drive and Water Lane almost before Joe had time to settle down and light a cigarette, and once through Weybridge, the car moved as if it had developed wings.

Approaching Westminster by side streets which, according to Johnny, cut off at least half a mile, he was easing the car past two others parked on either side of a narrow turning, when Joe, coming out of a reverie, saw an oncoming vehicle loom up suddenly in front of them, and shouted, 'For God's sake! You're about to run down a hearse!'

Muttering, Johnny slowed down and drew in to the side to give precedence. The hearse, empty save for the driver, slid slowly by, and Johnny, leaning out to peer at him, said over his shoulder, 'What the devil's he staring at? I know I'm no glamour boy, but he looks as if he was born dead.'

Joe, turning sharply, caught a glimpse of a deathly pale face, a hat pulled down to overshadow the eyes, a raincoat with the collar turned up, white hands upon the steering wheel. Then the vehicle slipped away into the darkness. Leaning over, he bellowed in Johnny's ear, 'Get after that thing, will you? I want to talk to the driver.'

'I can't turn here . . . '

'Run her back in reverse then. I've got to talk to that one.'

'What for?' Johnny asked, his head turned as automatically he acceded to Joe's request. 'You can't pick a quarrel with a hearse.'

'Can't I? That's the man who's been haunting me lately, and I'll take a bet he's up to no good now.'

'I don't like it,' Johnny said, swivelling the car round at the bend in time to see the hearse moving away at a fine speed to the left.

'Rev her up,' Joe urged. 'He can't get far on that.'

'He's having a damn' good try though.' His pride touched, Johnny stepped on the accelerator, and they sped off in pursuit. 'I thought there was a speed limit for those things? What does he think he is?'

'That's what I want to know.' Joe flung away his half smoked cigarette and leaned his arms upon the back of Johnny's seat. Two other cars on the road ahead of them gave way, and they drew nearer to the tail-light of their quarry. A pantechnicon momentarily hid their view, but overtaking, they were in time to see the hearse turn sharp left. With a hasty signal to the traffic behind, Johnny did the same.

'Thought you were crazy,' he shouted. 'But there must be something in it, or he wouldn't go like that. He knows we're after him.'

They were nearly upon the vehicle in front when it turned left again, right and then left, and they spent some ten minutes in twisting and turning thus. Then emerging upon a broad, residential thoroughfare, Joe said, 'Now's your chance. Nip up alongside, will you?'

'What do we do then?' Johnny asked, urging the car forward.

'Never mind that. Just overtake him on the right.'

The distance between them quickly diminished, until they were moving side by side, with Johnny a little to the fore. The driver of the hearse sat grimly crouched over the wheel, getting the most out of his engine. He did not even turn his head. At that moment, Joe swung open the car door, crouched upon the running board, and gathering strength for the spring leaped the intervening distance. He heard Johnny's gasp of dismay as he landed neatly, gripping the edges of the hearse for support. He balanced himself, edged cautiously along an inch or two, making ready for attack. But even as he moved, the driver's right hand left the wheel and a heavy cloth was flung over his bent head. A sickly, sweet smell assailed his nostrils, stifling him, turning him dizzy. He lost his grip, swayed and felt himself falling . . .

Chapter XIII

Dimly Joe was aware of Johnny's voice saying, 'Are you really dead, or just fooling?' He opened his eyes to find himself lying at an awkward angle in the back of his own car. He shifted, in an effort to make himself more comfortable, and groaned involuntarily at the pains that seemed to shoot through him in every direction.

He said, 'I'm not sure, but I think part of me is still alive. Got a drink handy?'

'What d'you think I've been pouring down your throat these last ten minutes?' Johnny demanded, anxiety and relief giving an edge to his voice. 'There's not much left, so you may as well finish it.'

'Thanks.' Joe took the half empty bottle, drank a little, and stared up at Johnny where he crouched alongside. 'What did we do, hit a 'bus or something?'

'Me? I've never hit anything in my life. It was you. Of all the damn' fool things you had to take a flying leap at a hearse, and landed flat on your face in the road. If there'd been anything coming . . .'

'I remember now.' Joe frowned, gingerly feeling a gash in his forehead. 'Did he get away?'

'Of course he got away. I couldn't leave you lying there, could I? You might have broken your neck for all I knew. I nearly piled up the barrow the way I jammed on the brakes . . . then I got you inside quick as I could. Maybe I ought to have got a doctor, but I felt you all over and you didn't seem to have broken anything.'

Joe said, 'If you felt me all over with those ham hands of yours and I still haven't broken anything, I'm tougher than is natural.' He sat up carefully, massaged his arms and legs and the back of his neck, turned his head from side to side, stemmed the blood that flowed from a cut in his wrist with a clean handkerchief, took another drink from the bottle and handed it to Johnny. 'You take the rest. You don't look any too happy. Can you still drive, d'you think?'

'Of course I can drive.' Johnny finished the whisky and dropped the bottle on to the floor of the car. 'Where shall I take you, the nearest hospital?'

'We'll go home. The day I'm taken to hospital you can start ordering the flowers. Let's have a cigarette.' Reaching for his case, he discovered a jagged tear in his overcoat. His clothes were wet through, and his trousers caked with mud. Lighting a cigarette and handing one to Johnny, he added, 'Sorry about this. I might have brought you to an early grave.'

'I wish you'd talk of something besides graves and hearses,' Johnny complained. He scrambled over the seat, manoeuvred himself under the driving wheel, and started the engine. Listening attentively, he said, 'She doesn't sound right. I'll have to run over her when we get back.'

'Take it nice and slowly,' Joe urged, as they moved away. 'Or you'll have a dead man on your hands yet.'

'It's a funny thing,' Johnny said, half turning, 'but whenever there's a body around, I always seem to miss it by inches.'

184

'Well, you won't miss this one, because it'll be right behind you, if you don't keep your eyes on that road.'

Saying which, Joe leaned back, closed his eyes, and lapsed into a kind of stupor. He was only three-quarters conscious when the car drew up outside the front entrance of Hamilton House, and Johnny came round to open the door for him.

'Can I give you a hand?' he asked.

Shaking himself back to reality, Joe stumbled out, gripped Johnny's shoulder for a moment, then contrived to walk unaided as far as the flat. Johnny followed, quickly opened the door and switched on the lights.

'Get me a drink, there's a good lad,' Joe said, staggered into the lounge and collapsed upon the divan, where he lay wiping sweat from his forehead with the back of his hand. Johnny came in with a bottle of rum and two glasses. His glance went immediately to the sideboard, where his note to Wendy still stood, propped against an empty tumbler.

'She hasn't turned up yet,' he remarked, opening the bottle.

'No.' Joe lay flat on his back, staring up at the ceiling, and trying to ward off a wave of nausea. He accepted the drink Johnny handed him, swallowed half of it, and put the glass down on the floor. Johnny helped himself to a drink and a cigarette and dropped into the nearest chair. There followed a long silence. Rousing himself at last, Johnny said, 'You ought to get cleaned up a bit. You look an awful mess.'

'What have you been reading?' Joe scoffed. '"First Aid for Beginners"?' He was glad to find that he could still smile. The nausea was going now, and given a chance, he thought, his brain might function again sometime. The front door bell rang, and Johnny leaped to his feet.

'That *must* be her,' he said, and went out at a run. Joe heard his voice, and that of a woman, but even in his cloudy state it did not sound like Wendy. Johnny reappeared to say in a low voice, 'It's not her. It's Miss Linklater. Want to see her?'

'Good God, no! Not like this.' Joe sat up so suddenly as to start a curious singing noise in his head. 'Wait a minute while I get changed.'

But Melda Linklater had already appeared in the doorway of the lounge. She stood there, in a black velvet evening dress and cloak to match, with a hood that had fallen back, revealing her hair, shining and immaculate. Her face was expressive of consternation.

'Joe!' she exclaimed, coming farther into the room. 'What on earth have you been doing?'

'Had a little accident in the car,' he said. 'Nothing much.' He got unsteadily to his feet.

'But you've got blood all over your face . . .'

'I'll soon fix that. Give Miss Linklater a drink, Johnny, will you? Be with you in a second.'

He lurched out and into the bathroom, where he locked the door and inspected his face in the mirror above the wash basin. There was some foundation for Melda's concern. Mud and blood combined had made him a startling sight, and the handkerchief round his wrist had turned a sticky red. With some difficulty, for his left shoulder had developed a dull ache, he removed his top-coat, stripped to the waist, and washed in hot and cold water. Then he went quietly into the bedroom, and resting a little between his exertions, changed into fresh clothes. A clean handkerchief about his wrist and a piece of sticking plaster across his forehead completed his labours, and he returned to the lounge looking, if not feeling, considerably better. Melda was seated in an armchair, smoking a cigarette. Johnny was walking about the room, doing likewise and looking extremely ill at ease.

'Hallo,' Joe said, dropping down on to the divan and retrieving his glass from the floor. 'Why aren't you drinking?'

Melda surveyed him critically. 'I've been doing that at home. I was asking Mr Gaff why you didn't come along to my party?'

'And did he tell you?'

'No. In the matter of neat evasion, you and he are the perfect pair.'

'I'll go and take a look at the car,' Johnny said. 'She was acting funny all the way home. See you later.'

'You might bring in that parcel I left in the back,' Joe called after him as he made for the door. 'You know, the one I picked up this evening.'

'I will,' Johnny promised, and went out, closing the door after him.

Melda observed, 'I don't think he likes me very much.'

'Johnny's all right,' Joe said. 'But you scare him.'

'Why is that? I don't scare you?'

'No.' He laughed. 'No woman scares me, except my house-keeper. How was the party?'

'Very good. Everyone arrived, including my two uncles. They're still there. I slipped away while no one was looking.'

'You shouldn't have done that,' he said, frowning. 'I told you . . . '

'I know.' Her face was suddenly very serious. 'But I rang through here a few times, and when I didn't get a reply, I thought something might have happened to you.'

'Such as what?'

'Oh, anything.' She crushed out her cigarette, rose to her feet and began to wander about the room. 'I kept thinking that you might disappear, and no one ever see you again.'

'Would that matter to you particularly?'

'I don't know. How can one tell, until a thing like that happens?'

'Your nerves are still bad,' he said. 'You ought to have gone down to the country.'

'It's not that. But you don't seem to have any sense of danger. And I was right, in a way. Something did happen.'

'It was an accident. The car door was open, and I fell on my face.'

Smiling a little, she said, 'You lie very well. You must have had a lot of practice.'

'But not quite enough. All right, suppose something did happen to me? I can take a knock or two.' A sensation of faintness had seized him again, and the contents of the room seemed to sway before his eyes. He rested his head between his hands for a moment.

'Why don't you go to bed?' she suggested.

He shook his head impatiently, and lay back on the divan.

'I can think of more interesting things to do,' he said.

She sighed. 'You're terribly obstinate. Isn't there something I can do for you now I'm here?'

'Well . . . ' He brought out his notecase, selected the slip of paper bearing Sanderson's address and telephone number, and held it out to her. 'You might put through a call to this bloke, and ask him to pop round and see me.'

'Now?'

'As soon as he can. There's a housekeeper you can leave a message with, if he's not there. Am I being a bore?'

'What man isn't, at some time or other?' she said, and went across to the telephone. He lit a cigarette and closed his eyes. He heard her dial the number, heard her talk to someone for a few minutes. Sanderson, it seemed, was not at home. She left the message, hung up, and came across to him. Laying her hand on his forehead, she asked, 'Anything else?'

188

He looked up at her. 'Shouldn't do that,' he said. 'I'm liable to come to life very suddenly. You'd better ring through to your uncles and tell them to come and collect you.'

Her eyes twinkled. 'They wouldn't like it. I didn't tell them where I was going. They're rather old-fashioned.'

'So am I. I'll be asking you to marry me if you stay around much longer.'

'I wouldn't take advantage of a man in your condition,' she said, and turned away, as Johnny entered, carrying the package containing the picture they had brought from Weybridge.

'There it is,' he said, putting it down on the table. 'Can't stop now. In the middle of a job. Shout if you want me.' His hands and face smeared with oil, his eyes alight with enthusiasm, he dashed out again.

'I'd forgotten about that,' Joe said. 'I was going to bring it round to show you.'

'What is it?' she asked, eyeing it curiously.

'Open it and see.'

She did so, and stood back, holding it at arm's length and regarding her own portrait with startled eyes.

'Where did you get it?' she queried at last.

'From a house in Weybridge. Something to do with Mendoza. I saw it originally at his place in Maida Vale.'

'I won't ask what you were doing there. I don't suppose you'd tell me, if I did.' She propped the picture on the floor against the table, and walked away to survey it at a greater distance. 'But why did you bring it to show me?'

'I wanted to know if it is genuine.'

She raised her eyebrows. 'Why ever not? It's signed, isn't it?'

'Apparently. But I've a suspicion Mendoza found a method of making a few pictures go a very long way.'

'That's easily settled.' She lifted the picture again, carried it over to the pedestal lamp and held it so that the light fell full upon it. Her brows drawn together, she tilted it sideways, and scrutinized it with extreme care. 'You're right,' she said presently. 'This is a fake. But it's a very good one.'

'How can you tell?'

She put down the picture and moved away. 'There was a certain mark Solby used to put in the bottom right-hand corner, just beneath his signature. Not in his earlier work, but all that he did round about the time he painted this portrait. It was partly my idea, and he only did it as a kind of joke. He was talking one day about faking pictures, and how easy it was for anyone of average painting ability and a flair for copying to produce something good enough to foist upon people who didn't know the original work. And I suggested he ought to protect himself in some way. I was quite serious about it, because I never doubted his genius, but since he was unknown then to anyone but his friends, and enemies, he thought it extremely funny.'

'But he always used it after that?'

'Yes. I'm particularly certain of it with this picture, because naturally I was there when he finished it.'

'What sort of a mark was it?'

'A kind of squiggle. You wouldn't notice it in the ordinary way.'

'And no one knows this but you?'

'I don't think so. It wasn't the sort of thing he would be likely to tell anyone, and I have never discussed him or his work, for the reasons I gave you.'

'In that case, you'd be the only person who could testify that this picture isn't genuine.'

'I wouldn't say that. It took me in at first glance, but on looking closer at it, the brushwork isn't particularly good. An expert could probably spot the difference between that and Solby's painting.'

'But it would be good enough to catch a mug with more money than knowledge? Someone like me, for instance?'

She smiled. 'Probably. But it was you who suggested it was a fake.'

'Only because I've met Mendoza, and my impression of him was that he'd cheat his own shadow. But he's got a nice, smooth manner that would go over with some people. He knew a young man named Carlo Betz. According to the press, when he was in jail Carlo was known as "The Artist". See any connection?'

'You think that between them they're faking Solby's pictures and selling them several times over?'

'I think they were. But Carlo's dead now. He was murdered a few days ago.'

'Murdered?' Her eyes opened very wide. 'Who by? Mendoza?'

'That's what it looks like. But I think it's a bit more involved than that.'

'Well, why doesn't someone do something about it?' she demanded, suddenly exasperated. 'It's damnable that Mendoza should be faking Solby's pictures and getting away with it. As if he couldn't make enough out of the genuine ones he had. The few times I've seen him I thought he looked a crook, but this . . . I'm going to report it.'

'The unforgivable sin,' Joe said. 'Here have I been trying to interest you in all kinds of novelties, such as burglary, murder and myself, but it takes a phoney picture to arouse you to action.'

'You wouldn't understand.' She paced about the room, her hands nervously flinging back the folds of her cloak, her face flushed and her eyes alight with anger. 'I saw him work, I saw the struggle he went through. And now this wretch, this disgusting

Mendoza, snatches greedily at everything Solby should have had, and more. He thinks, because Solby is dead, no one can do anything about it. But I can . . . '

'Come here a minute,' Joe interrupted. She hesitated, then came across to him, and he reached out a hand and drew her down beside him. He continued, 'I know roughly how you feel. You want to go out and poke Mendoza straight in the eye. All right. But you're getting worked up for nothing. He's got a lot to account for, and he'll be nailed pretty soon, one way or another. Meanwhile, he may have it in for *you*. Suppose he's heard about this secret identification mark of Solby's, without knowing exactly what it is? He might find it convenient to get you out of the way.'

'I don't care about that,' Melda retorted. 'He's got to be stopped.'

'He has been, temporarily, I imagine, unless he's found a substitute for Carlo. But he may still have a lot of stuff he wants to unload upon unsuspecting clients. In which case you might still be a nuisance to him.'

'But you don't suggest I should sit back and let him get on with it? Someone ought to know.'

'Someone does. I know, and I believe Sanderson knows, and the police, too, I wouldn't be surprised. Or, if they don't, they soon will. But it's not going to help, your getting mad at this stage. Suppose you report that picture? Where did you get it? From me. And I got it from a house in Weybridge. But I don't even know if that house can be linked up with Mendoza. I saw some accounts there addressed to R. Sebastian. Ever know anyone of that name?'

'No,' she said. 'But didn't you tell me you first saw the picture at Mendoza's place in Maida Vale?'

'I did. But there's only my word for that. And with nothing more definite to go on, he might slip out of it.'

'I suppose so.' She eyed him more calmly. 'I'll wait a little, then.' The telephone rang. 'Shall I answer that?' she asked. 'You don't want to talk to anyone, do you?'

'Not if I can help it. That's probably my partner, Wally. Tell him I'm in bed, and you're my nurse.'

She went across and picked up the receiver. After listening in silence for a moment or two, she said, 'Who is that, please? Oh . . . well, he can't talk to you just now, but he wants you to come round and see him.' She listened again. Joe rose cautiously and moved to join her.

'If that's Sanderson, I'll talk to him,' he said, and took the receiver from her. 'Hallo, Sanderson, Trayne here. Can you nip round for a minute?'

'Sorry,' Sanderson's voice came to him. 'I just got your message, but I can't get away for a while. Anything wrong?'

'Everything. It's difficult to explain over the 'phone. But like I said earlier, I think someone else is due to die pretty soon, if they're not dead already.'

'Now you listen to me,' Sanderson said sharply. 'This business has gone too far for either you or me or both of us to handle. I'm on my way to the Yard now, as a matter of fact, to turn it over to the police, and believe me, our friends will find themselves on the wrong side of the bars before they're much older.'

'Which friends?' Joe asked. 'I've got a nice little story about one of them that you'll be interested to hear.'

'All of them. Now don't you do anything to put your foot in it again. What are you doing, by the way?'

'Just spending a quiet evening at home.'

'Well, you go on doing that, and I'll call you back as soon as I can. Cheerio.' Sanderson rang off, and on a wave of irritability Joe slammed down the receiver.

'Of all the . . . ' he began, but found that he was talking to himself, for Melda was no longer in the room. He walked out and met her coming from the direction of the kitchen, a glass of water in her hand.

'You don't mind my helping myself?' she queried. 'I'm feeling thirsty.'

'I don't mind, if you don't. Personally, I can't stand the stuff.' He observed, then, with contrition, that she was looking pale and ill. He took her by the arm and led her back to the lounge, where she sank down into a chair as if glad to do so. Taking the glass from her as she finished drinking, he went on, 'Now I'm going to see you home.'

'No.' With sudden resolution, she got up again. 'I drove myself here, and I'm quite capable of driving back.'

'You don't look capable of anything,' he said.

'Neither do you. And if we're going to waste our time worrying about each other, we won't get anywhere.'

'If my car's not working, Johnny can drive yours, I expect,' he said. 'And I'll come along just in case.'

He walked out to the front door. Following, she said, with an obvious attempt at lightness, 'I don't think I trust Johnny. Look what he did to you.'

'That was my fault.' He opened the front door and shouted, 'Johnny! Can you spare a minute?'

Johnny came in, looking more oil-smeared than ever, wiping his hands on his handkerchief. 'What's up?' he wanted to know.

'Nothing at the moment. How's the car?'

'She's all right now. Why? You're not going out again, are you?'

'I want to take Miss Linklater home. You could drive her car, couldn't you?'

'That one out front? Of course. I can drive anything. But not

194

with you. There's something about you tonight that makes me nervous. You go to bed, and I'll take the lady home.'

Melda shrugged. 'If you can persuade him to go to bed,' she said, 'I'll come along quietly.'

Johnny said with a grin, 'Must have a bit of a wash first.' He moved towards the kitchen.

'Be careful of the chest out there,' Melda called after him. 'I nearly fell over it.'

Joe took a step forward and Johnny paused. They exchanged glances. 'What chest?' they said in unison.

'The one in the kitchen. An enormous thing. I couldn't think what it was doing there.'

With one accord Joe and Johnny made a dash for the kitchen. Johnny flung open the door, switched on the light, and they stood in the doorway, staring frozenly. In the centre of the room stood the thing they least wanted to see, Wendy's box, sombre, formidable, its carved sides and the closed lid ingrained with dust and cement.

They looked at each other again. Then remembering Melda, Joe turned quickly, only to find that she had gone.

Chapter XIV

Forgetting his injuries, Joe went quickly out of the flat and as far as the front door of the house. There was only one car parked in the street beyond, and that was his own. He was just in time to see the rear light of another turning out of St Giles' Place. Johnny, who had joined him, said, 'There she goes, and she can drive, too. Want me to go after her?'

'There's not much point in it,' Joe said wearily. He returned to the flat, and Johnny automatically followed. Shutting the door again, he went on, 'I think she's all right for the moment. I'll ring through presently and make sure. But we've got other things to do.'

Johnny, his young face looking haggard, jerked his head in the direction of the kitchen, and asked, 'That's it, I suppose?'

'That's it, all right. And I've a pretty good idea what's inside. But we'll have to open it.'

'Must we?'

'You get yourself a drink,' Joe advised him. 'It's my flat, and my responsibility, and this time there's going to be no slip-up.' He returned to the kitchen, very deliberately approached the box and raised the lid. As he had surmised, the body of Dight lay within and the manner of his death made no demands upon the imagination. His head was a mass of blood, the hair matted with it where it had flowed from a wound in the back of his skull. He lay sideways, and his face in profile looked ghastly. Johnny, entering just then, peered over Joe's shoulder, and asked in a shocked whisper, 'Did they all look like that?'

'No.' Joe turned away and mechanically lighted a cigarette. 'This is new. Things are speeding up a little.'

Johnny finished his whisky at a gulp and put down the glass with a shaking hand. 'I wish Wendy'd show up,' he groaned. 'This is killing me by inches.'

Joe leaned against the wall, where he could no longer see the contents of the box. 'That, I imagine, is how the others died,' he said. 'By inches. Remember when I jumped the hearse, that deaths-head of a driver flung a cloth or something over my face?'

'Is that what he did? I didn't notice, I was trying to see the road and him and the car and you all at once.'

'That's what he did. It must have fallen somewhere in the road when I went overboard. It was doped, a filthy, sickly smell. A few whiffs of that, and out you go. He had it all handy, didn't he, so it wouldn't be the first time he'd used it. The way I see it, he did the same to Carlo. And to Lysbeth, when she went to keep that phoney appointment. Then he locked each of them in turn into that box, and let them die slowly. Suffocated. Poisoned by lack of air.'

'God!' Johnny had turned a shade paler. 'Why would he do a thing like that? I mean, murder's bad enough, a quick bash on the head like this one, that's nasty, but the other . . . He must be stark, raving mad.'

'And now,' Joe said, 'he seems to be in a hurry. Suffocation's too slow. He's got other victims marked down and he knows he hasn't much time. So he bashes Dight to make sure he's not still alive when we find him.'

'But why pick on us?' The first shock over, Johnny was getting indignant.

'One of his peculiarities, I'd say. The body of one victim delivered to the next on his list. Carlo to Lysbeth, Lysbeth to Dight and Mendoza, Dight to me. It looks as if he might be planning to deliver my mortal remains to someone in the near future.'

'Or mine. I live here, too, don't I?' Johnny was almost inarticulate. 'Here, what are we waiting for? Standing around gassing when we ought to be getting the police.'

'All in good time,' Joe said. 'You don't mind if I do a little thinking, do you? I haven't done much in the last hour. I'm just coming to.' He returned to the box and inspected Dight at closer quarters. 'I'm no expert, but I'd say he's been dead too long to have put that call through from "Trees". That, I take it, was a trick to get us out of the way for an hour or two.'

'And like mugs we went out and left the back door open,' Johnny said bitterly.

He moved across to lock and bolt it with extreme care.

'This looks interesting,' Joe said. He had glimpsed something lying half hidden by Dight's body. With a feeling of revulsion he reached in and brought it to light, a British passport, containing an easily recognizable photograph, and an indication that the owner was Richard Sebastian Dight. 'Richard Sebastian,' he read aloud, and held it out for Johnny's inspection. 'That was the name in which Dight took the house. Rented it, probably.'

'And he was grabbed off before we got there,' Johnny said. 'And brought up here, box and all. What happened to Lysbeth, d'you suppose?'

'God knows. Dumped somewhere.' Joe dropped the passport

back into the box and closed the lid. 'Poor old Dicky Dight. I'd better get moving, if I'm not going to look the same in twenty-four hours.'

'You going to call the police?' Johnny asked anxiously.

'I am. At last I've got something definite, a body on my own premises, and this time something's going to be done. I'm sick of having them whisked away almost in front of my eyes. This one's going straight down to the mortuary, with a copper to guide it on its way. And that's not all. By fair means or foul, I'm going to get Mendoza along here. It's time he answered a few simple questions. Dight was his pal, so it's only right and proper he should be on the spot to do business with the law.' Saying which, he moved towards the door.

'Are we going to leave this here?' Johnny asked, following.

'Why not? Police regulations, and no one's likely to pinch it while we're on the spot, are they?'

'I suppose not. But I don't like it,' Johnny said. He accompanied Joe into the lounge, poured drinks for them both and watched while Joe dialled Mendoza's telephone number. Joe sipped his rum, and waited, listening to the ringing tone, registering a fervent hope that Mendoza was home. He reached for a cigarette, lighted it, and heard Mendoza's voice at last, unusually aggressive.

'Hallo, who's that?'

'Trayne here,' Joe said. 'I'm back home and full of surprises. Guess who's with me?'

'What the hell do I care?' Mendoza growled. 'If you've got nothing better to do than to waste your time . . . '

'On the contrary, my time's been very usefully employed. I find Dicky Dight an interesting companion.'

'Dight?' Mendoza's voice was sharp. 'You're bluffing.'

'How does it sound to you if I say I've got a long and very full statement from Richard Sebastian Dight, 43 years of age, British subject by birth, born in Richmond, England, and that it contains the whole truth and nothing but the truth concerning certain of your recent activities?'

There was a long silence. Then Mendoza said, 'If Dight's there, I'll talk to him.'

'Sorry, but he's not in a talking mood, not now. If you want to see him, you'd better come over, and quickly.'

'What exactly are you getting at?' Mendoza demanded. 'What's all this to you?'

'Nothing. But I think it might be worth quite a bit to you.'

'I see. So it's money you want. I might have known. Five hundred wasn't enough for a man of your tastes, eh?'

'You can put it that way, if you like. Are you coming over?'

After another pause, Mendoza said grimly, 'All right, Trayne. I'll be with you. But this isn't the end of it. I'm a nasty fellow when I'm crossed, remember that.'

'I've seen evidence of it,' Joe said. 'How long will you be?'

Mendoza answered, 'Shut up for a minute. I'm listening.' Then in a lowered tone, 'Are you there, Trayne? See here, I'm supposed to be alone, but there's someone moving about this house. I can hear them.'

'Who's bluffing now?' Joe scoffed. 'If you think . . . '

'It's true, I tell you.' Either Mendoza was an accomplished actor, or he was in a sheer panic.

'Now, look,' Joe said. 'I've been tricked before, but not tonight. Either you come over here . . . '

There came a strangled groan from the other end. Mendoza cried out, 'No! . . . Oh, God! . . . No!' Then the line went dead. Sweating, Joe hung up and got to his feet.

'Stark, gibbering, hell-damned madness all round and no hope in sight,' he exclaimed. 'That was Mendoza, yelling out for help, and this is me, going to the rescue, or falling head first into a death trap, I don't know which. Anyway, Johnny, this is what you do. Get right on to the police and shout "Murder!" at them as loud as you can. Tell them everything you know, and if that doesn't impress them, add a few frills. And when they've taken in Dicky Dight, send them over to unravel Mendoza and me, because something tells me this is not going to be a school treat.'

'What d'you have to go for?' Johnny protested, excitement turning his face vermilion. 'They'll grab you and put you in a box . . . '

'They can't, because you've got it. You stick to it, until the police come, and everything'll be fine. But if I wait until they arrive and finish asking me questions, someone else might die in the meantime.'

'Mendoza? What d'you care if he dies?' Johnny said, following him to the front door.

'It's not Mendoza I'm thinking about. He can rot, for all I worry. But he's the only line I've got to go upon. He may know that Dight's dead, and this is just a trick to get me over there so he can sift my story about the statement. I let him think he could buy me off, but if I know anything about this boy, he'd rather knock me off and keep the change. I've got to take a chance on that. But at least I'll know something definite.'

'Or die in the attempt. If I were you, I wouldn't fall for any of his yarns. If I were you . . . '

'If you were me you'd do just what I'm doing,' Joe said. 'You go and get on that 'phone, boy. Don't let me down.'

He went out, slamming the door decisively. On the pavement in St Giles' Place he stood and looked about for a taxi. He was out of luck. A few cars passed by, but no taxi came to his repeated whistling. But his own car stood there, where Johnny had left it after his recent ministrations. Upon impulse Joe walked round to the other side and climbed in under the steering wheel. It was a long time since he had driven himself. The wheel felt strange to his touch, his hands awkward, and he was annoyed to find that they were by no means steady. He swore a little, lighted a cigarette, adjusted the bandage about his left wrist, and drove away.

The rainstorm had lifted, but heavy clouds still hung low, making the night dark and humid. A strange throbbing had started somewhere inside his head, and he found that it required all his concentration and a tremendous effort of willpower to make any speed across London. Traffic lights bothered him, and the antics of wandering pedestrians drove him almost into a frenzy. In a side street he stopped the car near a telephone box, and put a call through to Melda Linklater's flat. It was some time before he obtained a reply, and when he did a man's voice answered him, a deep voice, pleasant and courteous.

'I'm sorry she's not here at the moment,' the man said. He sounded, Joe thought, a little anxious.

'She's giving a party, isn't she?' Joe queried.

'Yes. But she went out a while ago, and she's not back yet. Can I give her any message? I'm her uncle.'

'And I'm the guest who didn't turn up. When she comes in, tell her I'll ring later, will you? And if she tries to go out again, bolt all the doors. It's the wrong sort of night for her to be out alone. Thanks very much and goodbye.'

He rang off, returned to the car, overcame a slight difficulty in starting it, and headed for Maida Vale. There was no point, he reflected, in getting jumpy about Melda. He had not allowed so very much time for her journey home. Anything might have delayed her. Nevertheless, he continued to be jumpy, and it was with relief that he turned into the comparative quiet of Cleeve Rise and parked the car some distance away from No. 13.

Mendoza's house was in darkness when he reached it. He had half expected that. It would be like Mendoza to turn out all the lights and sit quietly waiting to bash him on the head again. But that, Joe decided, was right out. His head had taken enough knocks for one day. He would try the back entrance, and if there was no back entrance, he would make one.

The house, he discovered, was situated four doors from a side turning, down which he unobtrusively made his way. Each house had a garden, backing on to other gardens, all firmly fenced in and with no means of entrance other than from the houses themselves. All of which would have presented no great difficulty to Joe, had he not sighted, at that moment, a police constable strolling toward him. He stood motionless, fumbling with his cigarette case and lighter. The policeman approached, paused, and eyed him thoughtfully.

'Is that your car up the road, sir?' he asked.

Joe looked over his shoulder to where a long low car was parked at the end of the turning.

'No, I don't drive,' he said, and added truthfully, 'Not as a general rule.'

'I see.' The constable's glance suggested that he saw a lot, including the bandage around Joe's wrist, the sticking plaster on his forehead, and his lack of either hat or overcoat. 'Only, that car is unlocked, and there've been a lot of thefts around here lately.'

'Careless lot, the public,' Joe agreed. He lighted a cigarette as slowly as possible and took a long time replacing the case and lighter. 'Naturally you've got to keep an eye on things.'

'We do, sir. But you'd be surprised what little thanks we get for it. I was along the Vale the other evening . . . ' He proceeded to give Joe minute details of an incident involving an open front door and an irate owner who had left it for the cat to come home, while Joe idly wondered how Mendoza would react if he walked boldly up the steps of his house arm-in-arm with a police officer. The latter said eventually, 'Well, I must be moving on. Still very warm, isn't it?'

'Very. But nice and fresh, after the rain.'

'Not too fresh, though. The ground needed it.'

'All that and more, I'd say.'

'We'll get it, I expect. Good night, sir.'

'Good night,' Joe said, with the innocent smile of the law-abiding ratepayer *en route* for home. He walked slowly along the road and did not turn until he was certain the constable had rounded the bend. Then he doubled back and vaulted the fence without any more delay. He would have liked to investigate the parked car, for its long, low aspect had aroused his curiosity. But it was a question of now or never. He dared not risk another bout of crosstalk.

The garden in which he found himself was deeply shadowed and not very wide, with a similar fence to mark its farther boundary. He negotiated that one, and so on until he reached the fourth. Mendoza's garden boasted two tall trees and a lot of unkempt grass, dripping with moisture that saturated his trouser legs as he went cautiously forward. There were no lights on this side of the house, either, and he did not care to use his torch. By a process of trial and error, his feet found the asphalt approach to the back door, where he paused.

His arms and legs were stiff and aching, his head throbbed painfully, and his injured wrist had started to bleed again. To add to physical discomfort, he knocked against a dustbin and grazed his right ankle, as that impediment went over with a crash. He left it where it lay, cursing himself for the disturbance. But no answering sounds came from the house, no sign that anyone had either heard or cared.

Throwing caution to the winds, he brought out his torch and switched it on. The back door and all ground-floor windows proved to be locked. It occurred to him then that the dustbin had been standing in an odd position, just beneath what presumably was the pantry ventilator. But where once had been wire netting, now only a space remained, not a very large space, but enough for a spare individual to squeeze through. His own proportions, Joe judged, would hardly qualify, but the surrounding framework was old and rotten, and a little labour upon it with his jack-knife gave him an extra inch or two all round. Retrieving the dustbin, he mounted, thrust his lighted torch on to a shelf within, projected head and shoulders after, and became hopelessly stuck for a few seconds.

'Now,' he thought inconsequently, 'is the time for someone to bash me, if they're going to.'

But there was still no sound or movement, and vastly encouraged, he resumed his struggles, to emerge triumphant into the interior of a large pantry, its shelves lined with stores of various kinds. A row of bottles attracted his attention, and selecting a fine old liqueur whisky, he opened it and sampled the contents with the pleasure of a thirsty and much-tried man. At this stage, one drink more or less on Mendoza did not seem to matter very much.

The pantry door he found to be unlocked. It opened on to the kitchen, a large bare room, similar to any other kitchen of its kind. Another door led to the passage with which he was already familiar. Everywhere was still in darkness, still silent, a silence that he was beginning to find irksome, in that it compelled him to muffle the sound of his own movements, over which he no longer had his customary control.

Sweating, he leaned against the passage wall for a moment, sending the beam of his torch slowly up and down the empty stairway. His head felt as if someone were drawing red-hot wires through it. He should not have driven the car. He could take a knock or two, but driving did something to his nervous system that he preferred not to think about. Nevertheless, he thought about it, standing there in complete darkness with only a small circle of light to show him the blankness of his surroundings.

As if it had been yesterday, he visualized that night when he had sat contentedly at the wheel of his car, with the two women he had cared for most in the world seated behind him. The long, winding road, the play of the headlights, a cigarette between his lips, the sound of the wind rushing by. Then the hairpin bend, the oncoming car swaying as it bore down upon him. The crash, the sickening sound of splintering glass, a scream . . .

He ran a hand through his hair and found it damp. He shook his head several times in an effort to efface memory, and brought the beam of his torch down to the ground. He was alone in what appeared to be an empty house. There were things to be done . . . Edging his way along the wall toward Mendoza's office, he wondered whether Wally might be right, after all. Perhaps the crack his head had taken in that car smash had not done him any good. Wally had never said so, but Joe knew, just the same. It was funny, he thought, reaching the door of the office, how you could never really imagine yourself as peculiar. Whatever you did, it was all right, because you were doing it, although similar conduct in anyone else might invite censure on your part. What was he doing, prowling round someone else's house in the dark, climbing fences, through ventilators? Was that the conduct of a normal man?

He felt for the door handle, turned and pushed. The door opened easily, revealing, within the torch's small circle of light, a scene of remarkable confusion. Chairs were overturned, the desk askew, the telephone wire cut, the curtains drawn but dragged down on one side as if someone had caught at them in falling. Mechanically, Joe's hand fumbled for the light switch, found it, and pressed it down. Nothing happened. He stepped into the room and turned his torch this way and that. Apart from the obvious signs of conflict, there was nothing to suggest the present whereabouts of Mendoza. A trap? Possibly, he thought, but if so, a very elaborate one. He could not imagine Mendoza going to the trouble of wrecking his own office. Something quick, something more economical, would be more in his line.

Joe walked back into the passage and paused, listening. There was no sound, nothing to indicate that he was not alone in the house. Yet someone lived and breathed there, he was certain of it, and the certainty made him reckless. A quick survey of the entrance to the basement sufficed to tell him that there, at least, all precautions had been taken to keep out intruders. The door at the top of the basement stairs was firmly fastened and padlocked. The front door was locked, too, and double-bolted. He had already seen the kitchen.

Keeping his torch steady, he mounted the stairs as quietly as possible. On the first landing, he paused. Silence again, broken only by the sound of a car passing in the street beyond. He gave only a cursory glance into the rooms on that floor. Something urged him upwards, beyond the second floor to the attic. Up the stairs leading thence he felt his way and found, as he had hoped, the padlock removed, the door unlocked. He pushed it open, entered, and tired of this perpetual wandering in darkness, again reached for the light switch. But no light was forthcoming to his touch. Either the lights all over the house had fused, or someone had turned them off at the main.

He kicked the door to, and looked about him, within the

limitations of torchlight. A large room, clean, with an air of being much in use. The long skylight would give it plenty of illumination by day. The perfect workroom for an artist, and to give substance to the suggestion, artists' materials lay everywhere, paints and canvas, easels, brushes, pencils, T-squares. Here, Joe thought, Carlo Betz might have worked, arriving by night and working by day. There were no finished paintings, but upon an easel just beneath the skylight stood a partially painted canvas.

He moved nearer, turned his light full upon it. As far as he could judge, it had started out in life as the portrait of a man. Now it was ripped to ribbons, the canvas hanging in strips, bedraggled and forlorn. A few minutes' work with a sharp knife might produce just such a result. Holding his torch in one hand, Joe tried, not very successfully, to piece it together with the other. A magnificent head of dark hair, a broad forehead, penetrating but kindly eyes. The rest of the face was only roughed in, and barely discernible. Nevertheless, the image registered somewhere within his mind. If he could only think clearly . . . if he had time . . . He turned away, listening. It might have been a sound just outside the door, or merely a figment of his imagination. He moved cautiously to the door, flung it wide, focused his torch and stepped out.

He could see nothing, yet knew he was not alone. The landing was empty. He went to the head of the stairs, peered over, and went slowly down. On the landing below he paused. The atmosphere of the house was suddenly stifling. His throat felt dry and burning, his head one searing pain. Nausea seized him, and he stood swaying at the top of the staircase, gripping the banister for support.

Somewhere, as if from a long way off, he heard a soft chuckle of laughter, insane, hardly human. Then the dark well of the staircase seemed to come up and engulf him. His hand left its hold, his body went limp, and he fell headlong into space.

Chapter XV

Left to himself after Joe's departure, Johnny carefully shut and locked the kitchen door, put the key in his pocket and returned to the lounge, where he finished his drink at a gulp and reached for the telephone. At that exact moment it began to ring. With mixed feelings he picked up the instrument, announced the number, and heard a man's voice say, 'Is Mr Trayne there?'

'No,' Johnny said. 'Who is it?'

'Isn't he ever there? I've 'phoned several times lately.'

'Sometimes he is and sometimes he isn't. You're just unlucky.'

'Is Miss Linklater there? I'll speak to her if she is.'

'What makes you think she is?' Johnny queried, alert with suspicion.

'She's a friend of Mr Trayne, isn't she?'

'I couldn't say. He's got a lot of friends. I don't know one from the other.'

'So you don't know whether she's there or not?'

Nettled by the sarcasm in his tone, Johnny said sharply, 'She's not, though what the hell it's to do with you . . . '

'Are you sure?'

'I ought to know when I'm alone, didn't I? What d'you think I am . . . green or something?'

There came a chuckle from the other end. 'No, I am,' the man said, and hung up, just as the front door bell began to ring impatiently.

'Barmy,' Johnny remarked, replacing the receiver, and stood hesitating. Ought he to get on to the police or answer the front door? Joe's instructions had not provided for this contingency. The ringing continued, and to add to its urgency, someone began to hammer on the door at the same time. He went quietly out to the entrance hall, and called, 'Who's there?'

'Melda Linklater,' a woman's voice answered him. 'Please hurry . . . it's terribly urgent.'

He opened the door a chink, saw her standing there, and admitted her with some reluctance. But he had little option, for she pushed past him saying, 'Where's Joe? I want to speak to him.'

'He's not here,' Johnny said, closing the door and unobtrusively putting the catch down. 'He went out. You just missed him.'

She stood there uncertainly, brushing back a strand of hair that had fallen over her forehead. She looked very pale, her whole manner in complete contrast to her usual serenity, as she burst out, 'But he can't have gone out. He wasn't in a fit state . . . Why did you let him go?'

'Ever tried to stop a car going down hill without any brakes?' Johnny asked, exasperated. 'He wanted to go out, and he went.'

'But where? Did he go to my place? I'll 'phone through and see if he's there.'

'You'll be wasting your time, Miss Linklater. He didn't go to your place. But I'm expecting to hear from him, so you go home, and I'll call you . . . ' He paused, as the telephone started to ring again.

'Perhaps that's him now,' Melda said, and made a movement toward the lounge. But Johnny got there first, grabbed the telephone and bellowed 'Hallo' into the transmitter. A male voice said, 'Mr Trayne, please,' a different voice this time, curt and decisive.

'Sorry,' Johnny said wearily. 'He's not here. Who wants him?'

'Scotland Yard, C.I.D. I particularly want to talk to Mr Trayne. Know where I can find him?'

Johnny thought quickly. This was the moment when he ought to shout 'Murder!' down the telephone and follow it up with all the trimmings. But with Melda Linklater listening it was not so simple. She could not know what was in the box when she saw it in the kitchen, otherwise she would not have been so unconcerned about it. And Joe had said nothing regarding the taking of a third party into their confidence. Choosing the lesser of two evils, he said, 'You might try 13, Cleeve Rise, Maida Vale. And . . . '

'Thanks, I will,' came from the other end. 'And your name, please?'

'Johnny Gaff . . . I live here . . . But look . . . '

'Good. Then if I send a couple of men round, Mr Gaff, I take it you'll be there?'

'You bet I will,' Johnny said fervently. 'And you can send 'em as quick as you like.'

'I'll do that. And I'd like to emphasize that this is a serious matter, or I wouldn't be troubling you. Goodbye.'

Johnny hung up, ran both hands over his heated face, and met Melda's enquiring glance with every sign of discomfort. 'Friends of Joe's,' he said. 'Crazy, all of them.'

'So he went to Mendoza's.' She pulled her cloak closer about her shoulders and walked to the door. 'It's about that picture, isn't it? He shouldn't have gone alone.'

Sensing a reproof, Johnny said, 'I couldn't stop him. And he wanted me to stay here and look after things. Are you going home?' Both relieved and anxious, he followed her out of the room.

'No, I'm going to find him.' She paused at the kitchen door, and added, 'I'll go this way. There's a back entrance, isn't there? I left my car parked in Johnsons Passage.' She tried the handle. 'This door is locked. What's the reason for that?'

'Is it?' Johnny's surprise was just a little overdone. 'Better go out the front, then.'

'It wasn't locked when I was here before. And where is the key?'

'Joe must have taken it,' Johnny said. 'He's funny like that, very fussy. Ever since someone broke in.'

'So if you want to go into the kitchen you have to wait until he comes back?'

'I reckon so.'

'I sometimes wonder,' she said, 'whether men ever tell the truth about anything.' She went through, opened the front door, and looked back at him as if about to say something else.

Peering anxiously past her into the outer hall, Johnny said, 'Could we have that door closed if we're settling into a chat? There's a nasty draught . . . '

'You're not afraid of something, are you?' she asked, eyeing him narrowly.

'Me? Do I look like it?'

'Yes,' she said, and went out, leaving him to close the door after her, which he did, and quickly, putting down the catch and sliding the bolt into position. Then he brought out the key of the kitchen door, unlocked it, and peered round, half expecting to see the room empty. But the box still stood here, solid and sinister. He viewed it with mixed emotions. Since the police were on their way, it was as well to have something definite to show them. But now a new fear came to haunt him. Suppose they thought he had done it? There was nothing, so far as he could see, to suggest an alternative. Joe knew he was innocent of such practices, but Joe was not there to substantiate his story. And what a story it sounded, now he came to think of it. The police could hardly be blamed if they held him as an object of suspicion. He had a horrible vision of himself behind bars, Joe spirited away, Wendy failing to arrive, and Miss Linklater saying coldly that she had seen him acting in a very peculiar fashion.

With this picture in mind, he wandered back to the lounge, poured himself a drink, and derived no comfort from it. He smoked a cigarette, and listened with growing uneasiness to his watch ticking the minutes away. If they were coming, they ought to be here soon. But why were they coming? He had not had the chance to ask them anything. If that Linklater woman had not been on the spot, he could have asked them why they were 'phoning him, instead of *vice versa*. Did they know about Dight? Perhaps Joe had rung through to them on his way. But in that case, they ought to have been here long ago. The more he thought about it, the less comfortable he felt. It looked as if they had it in for Joe over something. Perhaps he should have told them he was out of town. Joe hadn't taken anything like that into account.

He started suddenly, thinking he heard something, though what, he was not at all sure. But it came to him very forcibly that they had not searched the apartment after finding Dight's body. Someone might be lurking, ready to spring out on him at any moment. He began to sweat at the thought. He went out to the entrance hall, selected a heavy-topped stick as a weapon, and made a complete tour of the flat, peering under the bed, into all the cupboards and the wardrobe, and anywhere that could possibly serve as a hiding place.

Relieved to find that he was, indeed, alone, he returned to the lounge to smoke several cigarettes in succession, keeping the stick close at hand, and a wary eye on the doors and windows, anticipating that any minute they might open slowly. Or the box. While he was sitting here, someone might be quietly forcing the lock of the back door, reaching stealthily in and snatching the box away. What would the police say, if he told them a story like that? Worse still, what would Joe say?

Gathering together the remnants of his spirits, he went out to the kitchen, dragged forward a chair with his foot and sat down, a glass of rum in one hand and a cigarette in the other. Sitting thus, with the box well in view, nothing much could happen. Or could it? He placed another chair with the top under the handle of the back door, and returned to his seat.

It seemed to him that hours passed. His eyes grew weary with watching and waiting. Was it his imagination, or had the box moved a little? And the lid ... that did not look quite securely fastened. Suppose it were to lift suddenly, and Dight rise up and stare at him, his head all covered in blood? He shuddered, got up, and sat down heavily upon the box. That would settle it. No, it wouldn't ... he could not sit there, knowing a dead man lay beneath. And those other two, who had been locked up and left to suffocate slowly ... He'd have to get out of this or go potty. He would ring the police, and tell them for God's sake to hurry.

He almost ran back into the lounge, lifted the telephone receiver and dialled. He hardly waited to hear what they had to say the other end, before he blurted out, 'This is Flat 1, Hamilton House, Westminster. You said you were coming round, but you haven't got here yet. There's a dead man in the kitchen, murdered, blood all over the place, and he's getting on my nerves ...'
His head jerked round as the front door bell rang with abrupt

insistence. 'All right, all right,' he shouted into the telephone. 'That's your people now . . . thanks very much.' He banged down the receiver and charged out to the front door, pulling himself up in time to call out, 'Who's that?'

'Police officers,' came the reply, and with relief he unfastened the door and flung it wide. He did not see what hit him, and gave only the faintest groan as he crumpled up and fell to the floor.

Chapter XVI

Joe was conscious of movement, of the sound of a car's engine drumming in his ears. It was still dark, but intermittent flashes of light passed across his closed eyes. He was lying flat on his back, yet was unaware of any particular discomfort, his limbs lethargic and strangely without feeling, his mind dull and feeble in its efforts to struggle back to normal.

Mechanically, he tried to piece together the situation. He would be travelling along a road at a fair speed, a country road to judge by the bumpiness of it. He was in a large car, or it would not take him full length. It could be an ambulance, though why he had no idea. He had a vague recollection of having driven somewhere . . . there might have been an accident, but it seemed a very long time ago. His mind went blank again for a while, and then with a tremendous effort he opened his eyes.

Road lights continued to flash by at intervals, the vibration of the engine still sounded in his ears. Lacking the power to move, his eyes heavy as if the lids were weighted, he glanced indifferently about him. It was not an ambulance, but a large car, with doors at the back, against which his feet rested. The back seats, if there ever were any, must have been removed, to allow of so much space, or perhaps it had been built that way. He wondered idly who was driving, and why, and what was the big, solid object standing beside him. He had seen something like it before, at some time, but could not remember where. He was tired, and it seemed years since he had slept . . . He drifted into unconsciousness.

He was lying on a bed when he came to himself again. His body had more feeling now. He could appreciate that it was a comfortable bed, and he was glad of it. But undermining physical comfort was a certain mental disquiet. There was, he felt, something he ought to do, something imperative. He could not afford to sleep any longer.

He jerked himself awake and stared up at the ceiling, observing that it was made of wooden slats and painted blue. The unfamiliarity of it probed deeper into his consciousness, and he sat up slowly. An unfamiliar room, small, the walls similar to the ceiling, the whole lit by a shaded oil lamp on a painted table beside the bed. Oil lamps were a novelty to him. He was hardly aware that they existed outside museums. His suit, he noticed, was dusty and torn in places. His head felt curiously light, as in delirium, and the huge shadows cast by the lamp, obliterating the farther objects in the room, enhanced his sense of unreality.

Dimly he could see curtains, and where there were curtains there must be a window. Gathering his returning strength, he swung his feet to the ground, hauled himself up by the old-fashioned bedpost, and reeled across the room. The window was closed, but his fumbling hands found the catch, thrust up the bottom half, to let in wafts of sweet-smelling, damp night air. He leaned far out, just in time to be violently sick. Recovering a little, he stood there, breathing deeply.

It was very dark, but a faint light, coming from somewhere in the distance, showed a ghostly silhouette of trees a few hundred yards to the right, and the gleam of water only a short drop below. Dark, treacly, moving water. He withdrew his head, and leaned against the wall uncertainly. The wall, it seemed to him, had a tendency to move. So did the floor, as he stumbled back and collapsed upon the bed, resting his head in his hands, trying to think. Everywhere was very quiet, except for a faint chirruping sound, like crickets.

'I'm going mad,' he said, and the sound of his own voice caused him to start. He stared at the bloodstained handkerchief about his wrist, and wrenched it away from where it had stuck to the wound. The sudden pain was pleasurable after his recent numbness. Blood began to flow, and he rebandaged it roughly. Memory was returning. He had fallen and cut his wrist ... Johnny had driven him home. He had left Johnny in some kind of trouble. Melda, too. He had got to get out of wherever he was, and in his right mind.

Upon impulse, he lifted the shade and glass from the lamp and held his left hand in the naked flame, until the searing pain brought sweat to his forehead and caused him to groan aloud. He stood up, wiping lamp black from his hand on to his trouser leg. He replaced the shade and glass, felt through his pockets with his right hand and found his cigarette case and lighter. He lit a cigarette, returned case and lighter to his pocket, concentrating upon his movements, enjoying the co-ordination of them. His left hand burned almost intolerably, but it was good to feel again.

He walked slowly across the room. He was still weak, but the mists were beginning to clear from his brain. And then turning, he saw it, where it stood beside one wall, in deepest shadow. Steadying himself against the painted furniture as he passed, he moved nearer, and its wooden sides and closed lid became reality to his touch. It should not be there. He remembered now, he had left it at his flat, with the body of Dight inside it, and Johnny in charge of it. Whose body was in it this time?

He turned cold at the thought, and tried to raise the lid, but it was securely locked, and the key missing. He looked quickly round the contents of the room, but nothing suggested itself as a weapon of attack. Flinging the end of his cigarette out through the window, he went to the only door and found that it opened easily enough.

With the utmost caution, he stepped outside, to discover a long and rather narrow passage, the floor of bare polished boards, illuminated by an oil lamp that hung from the ceiling. Immediately facing him was a closed door, with a small curtained window on either side. To the left, at the end of the passage, was another door, partially open, round which a dim light filtered. Carefully he began to move toward it.

Again that slightly swaying movement of the floor and walls, but now his mind was sufficiently clear to know it was not his imagination. A houseboat somewhere on the river was the obvious solution. He reached the open door and paused. No sound from within. He could see a tall gilt lamp standing on a low table, an armchair in sharp silhouette against its light. He pushed the door open and entered.

The room was large, well furnished, well used but uninhabited, so far as he could see. There were curtained windows all the way round, a curtained alcove in one corner, and three steps at the far end leading up to painted wooden doors. An anthracite stove was built in against the left-hand wall. It was unlighted, but the long iron poker hanging beside it caught Joe's attention. Confiscating it, he made a rapid tour of the room, but found nothing further to disquiet him. Upon a table in the centre stood a bottle of brandy, three-quarters full, and one glass. A Sunday newspaper was spread out alongside, and a chair drawn up as if someone had been lately reading. The curtained alcove was empty. The doors at the top of the steps were fastened with a padlock, which lacked a key.

He retreated, leaving the door to the passage half open as he had found it. So far he appeared to be in sole possession. Breathing heavily, and driving back the vestiges of giddiness that still assailed him, he returned to the room he had left, closed the door, carried the lamp across and set it down on the floor beside the box. The pain had subsided a little from his left hand, but it was badly blistered. He bound it with the cuff ripped from his shirt sleeve, and gripping the poker, commenced operations, pausing now and then to wipe his fevered forehead and to listen for the slightest hint of interruption.

The lock was well made, but the poker had a thin edge which, forced beneath the lid, acted as a lever, and desperation gave vigour to Joe's otherwise impaired strength. As the lock gave beneath his furious onslaught, there came from within the box a faint sound, as of someone stirring, the scrape of a shoe against wood. His whole inside seemed to turn over, and the creaking of the lid as he lifted it rasped his nerves.

Raising the lamp high, he looked down into the upturned face of Mendoza, a face tinged grey and fearful in expression, the eyes staring, the lips bloodless. But he was alive. His hands clawed frantically at the sides of his prison, his legs moved as if seeking an outlet. Setting down the lamp, Joe leaned over and heaved half Mendoza's bulk across one shoulder. The weight of him was terrific, and not made easier by the agitated movement of his limbs. Bending almost double, Joe hauled him out, staggered across the room and deposited him upon the bed.

'For the love of God, stop struggling, man!' Joe urged, disentangling himself. 'It won't help to choke me.'

But Mendoza lay limp and uncomprehending, breathing with a terrible effort, his hands making convulsive movements upon the coverlet. Joe went swiftly to the door, opened it, and stood listening. Still no sign of life save the chirping of the crickets, and the sound of a rising wind. He went out, fetched the brandy from the untenanted room at the end of the passage, and returned to administer it in small doses to Mendoza.

Seated on the edge of the bed, his own body a mass of aches and pains too numerous to be judged on separate merits, Joe watched him anxiously. He did not much care whether Mendoza lived or died, but he would prefer that he should not choose to die just then. There were still things he wanted to know. He was beginning to recall recent vague impressions, a journey in a car, with himself lying at the back, and it must have been the box beside him. The box with Mendoza in it, probably. He was immensely relieved that it had not been Johnny. But what had happened to Johnny? And to the body of Dight? And there was Melda . . .

Impelled to action, he did what he could in the way of first aid for Mendoza, and went out again, to discover, to the right of the passage, a miniature kitchen with a tiny oil lamp standing on the dresser. Here all fitments were calculated to the last inch, in nautical fashion. There were two windows, designed as portholes, two steps up to a white-painted door, locked from the outside, a sink but no tap.

His tongue and throat felt dry and gritty. He craved water as he had never done in his life before. Beneath the sink he found it, in a bucket to which was attached a length of rope. The water looked clean enough, and he drank large quantities of it, dipping his head into the remainder and rubbing it with a towel he found handy. He felt better then, more alive, more human. A quick dive through the window and a swim to the mainland seemed to be indicated, assuming that the houseboat was situated sufficiently far out for swimming to be necessary.

Returning to the room he had lately left, he found Mendoza lying with closed eyes, his face more natural in colour, groans and unintelligible mutterings coming from his lips. Pausing beside the bed, Joe said, 'Are you coming to life or not?' Dancing attendance on Mendoza was all very well, if there were anything to be gained by it. But it could be a very dead loss. He eased more brandy down the sick man's throat.

The latter opened his eyes, stared at Joe without recognition, and muttered, 'The lousy swine! ... The stinking ...' His voice trailed away, then gathering strength, went on with feverish speed, 'He can't do it, not to me. He can't kill me. Mad, yes ... but not me. Poor old Dick ... shouldn't have left him ... it's done now. But it's blood ... I can smell blood!' His voice rose and fell on an agonized note. He mumbled a string of obscene oaths, and was silent. Joe shrugged his shoulders and was turning away, when Mendoza cried out, 'The bloody fake! And he called himself an artist. All fake ... Oh, God, my heart!' He clutched a hand to his side and sweat rolled down his distorted face.

'Blast!' Joe said softly, and stood still as the houseboat moved. But this time it was a decisive, rocking motion, not just a gentle swaying against the buffeting wind. He went across to the window, and standing well to the side, peered out into the darkness. Somewhere to the left a light was approaching, a circle of torch-light, faintly illuminating a gangplank, a pair of feet walking along it, and the shimmering water surrounding it. They were large feet, in rubber overshoes, moving silently, slow but sure, and their movement caused the houseboat to shift in its moorings.

It could not be so very far from the mainland, Joe reflected. Not that it mattered, at this juncture. But it was an interesting point, since he was not very well versed in the matter of river craft. He backed away, saw that Mendoza had sunk into a silent stupor,

222

and went out, quietly shutting the door behind him. Turning his head right, he felt, rather than heard, someone coming round the house, nearing the back entrance to the kitchen. Quickly he retreated to the lighted room at the end of the passage, and stood just behind the door, waiting.

He heard the kitchen door being unlocked, opened and closed again. There came the sound of a match scraping against a box, and someone softly whistling the first bars of a familiar air. It was not the best rendering Joe had heard, but easily recognizable as *Lament for the Dead.* The whistling came nearer, straight along the passage, to stop abruptly just outside the half open living-room door. From his position behind it, Joe glanced sideways, and mentally cursed himself for not having replaced the brandy bottle on the centre table. Its absence might be noticed at once by anyone expecting to see it there.

Following a nightmarish silence, the door was suddenly pushed wide. To avoid its impact, Joe moved quickly, and they stood, a few yards apart, he in his dishevelled suit, the other a shadowy figure in a light waterproof coat, a muffler, and a hat with the brim concealing his eyes and the best part of his face from the glow of the lamplight.

Then as Joe, momentarily off balance, steadied himself, a sinuous white hand shot out and seized his bandaged one with uncanny strength in its grip. Red-hot pain flared up, causing him to stumble, and in a split second his arm felt as if it had been jerked from its socket as his body went hurling through the air. He landed on his back, his head an inch or so from the stove. Dazedly he saw now the face of his attacker, deathly pallid, the mouth set in an expression of malignant concentration. It was sufficient to revive his last remaining strength. As the figure came at him, hands outstretched, seeking his throat, he rolled over sideways and got to his feet. The man whirled about, but not quickly enough, for Joe had already stepped back a pace, and bringing up his fist, landed a punch to the jaw that sent him staggering. Another, and he went to the ground, causing a vibration through the whole structure.

Breathing deeply, Joe stood looking down at him, where he lay half in shadow. His hat had fallen off, revealing a head of dark brown hair, a high, intellectual forehead. But the jaw sagged a little, giving to the face in repose a hint of irresolution, almost of idiocy. A smoking cigarette lay on the carpet a few feet away where it had fallen during the brief conflict. Joe picked it up, and stubbing it out in the nearest ashtray, observed that it was hand-made and exuded a curious odour. Stooping again, Joe hauled the owner to his feet and pushed him into an armchair, where he made a rapid search of his pockets, to discover nothing more enlightening than a fountain pen and pencil, a wallet stuffed with banknotes, some loose change, a cigarette case half full and a box of matches.

Ascertaining that his late adversary was still unconscious, he returned to the room where he had left Mendoza. The latter raised himself on one elbow, as Joe entered, and blinking bloodshot eyes, muttered, 'What the hell . . . what the hell . . . ?'

'All hell'll be let loose in a minute, if you don't pipe down,' Joe said. For the second time he commandeered the brandy bottle, helped himself to what he considered a well-earned drink, scowled at Mendoza and went out again. The man in the armchair had opened his eyes, and was staring vacantly straight in front of him. Thrusting back his head, Joe poured a small quantity of brandy down his throat, whereupon he choked, and leaning forward, heaved and spat it out upon the carpet. Joe slammed down the bottle and seated himself on the edge of the table.

'Have it your own way,' he remarked. 'But one more trick out of you, and I'm going to drop you overboard. You're Charles Solby, aren't you?'

The man did not answer. He sank back into the chair, his chin buried in the collar of his coat. His face now was a mass of twitching nerves, and his eyes held a peculiar expression, a kind of sullen bewilderment, as they returned Joe's stare. Fumbling, his hands went to his pockets, produced cigarette case and matches. Still watching Joe, he took out a cigarette and put it between his lips. But to light it was an effort beyond him, and the matchbox slipped from his shaking fingers.

Joe retrieved it, struck a light and held it out. His own hands, he was glad to see, were perfectly steady now, although the left one was still painful. 'Allow me, Mr Green,' he said. 'I take it you prefer that name?'

For several minutes the man inhaled smoke deeply. His face became normal, his hands ceased to pluck at the arms of the chair. He said then, 'I prefer no name at all. I've a job to do, and when it's finished I shall slip back into obscurity.' His voice was soft and cultured.

Joe raised an eyebrow. 'But I'm one of the jobs you didn't do, and that's where you made a big mistake,' he said.

'I agree. I made the mistake of procrastination. But the stuff I gave you should have held you until I was ready. You must have an abnormal constitution. I didn't allow for that. But there's still time.' He held the cigarette in his mouth as he talked and only the thinnest spiral of smoke ascended from it.

Observing the rapidity with which he was regaining confidence, Joe said, 'Another mistake. You're full of them tonight.' And he leaned over and took away the cigarette and the case that had fallen down the side of the chair. Instantly the man's face became distorted with a paroxysm between wrath and anguish. His hands clenched and he made a feeble movement to rise.

'Give those back to me,' he said between his teeth.

'No.' Joe put the case in his pocket, pinched out the cigarette and flung it over his shoulder. 'They're doped, aren't they? You've a certain spurious strength, backed by dope, that gets you out of tight places. But you won't get out of this one. You've about as much chance with me at the moment as a flea has against an elephant.' He pushed him back into the chair. 'Now, look. I've got the dope, and you can have that little lot back when you've told me what I want to know. At the risk of being monotonous, you're Charles Solby, aren't you?'

The man had gone limp. His face was a white mask of self-pity and frustration. He no longer looked at Joe, his glance straying despairingly about the room. He tried several times to speak, and finally said in an expressionless voice, 'And if I am? What then?'

'Then you've got a hell of a lot to answer for. Charles Solby was last heard of in Paris. He was a doctor and a psychiatrist, and the story goes he took to dope after his brother's death. So it seems he couldn't do much to cure himself. And by the look of you, I'd say you haven't tried. You came over here to commit murder, didn't you?' He paused, but obtaining no answer, continued, 'Well, didn't you? Mendoza was faking your brother's pictures. Carlo Betz worked for him, and his girl friend, too, in some way. They're both dead, and you killed them. You doped them and locked them in a box and let them die slowly. And Dight died this afternoon, only quicker. Is that right, or isn't it?'

Charles Solby ran his hands through his hair, ruffling it into wild disorder, and emitted a thin chuckle of hysterical laughter. He was rapidly going to pieces. Shuddering, he said in a low voice, 'They're all dead, yes. All the lot of them. Mendoza's gone by now. He murdered my brother. *Murdered* him, d'you hear that? But we've had our revenge. A long time and a lot of trouble, but worth it. Slow torture. Perhaps you can't imagine it.' His face twisted in a

226

sneer. 'You're a healthy type, strong in life, vitality. You'd take a lot of killing. You couldn't hope to picture what goes on in the human mind when it sinks to the lowest depths. I ought to have killed you quickly, put you out of the way for a start . . . But I didn't know what a nuisance you were going to be.'

'You know now,' Joe said. 'That night I was at Lysbeth's place, after you'd delivered the box the first time. You were following me around in that car of yours, weren't you?'

'I was there, yes.' He was silent for a moment, his head sunk on his chest. Then raising both fists in the air, he cried out, 'In the name of God, give me a cigarette!'

With a painful effort, he got to his feet and came at Joe, his hands clawing with spasmodic fury. But a single push was sufficient to send him to the ground, where he lay, breathing in sobbing gasps. Bending over him, Joe said, 'There's something else I want to know . . . '

But Charles Solby had half risen again, and was staring toward the door. Joe, his back turned to it, did not move, suspecting a trick, until he heard Mendoza's voice, saying thickly, 'I'll blast the lights out of them!'

Joe spun round then, and saw Mendoza, propping his weakened frame against the jamb of the door, his lips curled back in an unhealthy smile. He swayed as he stood there, and in his right hand he held a revolver.

Joe said, 'Go back to bed, and don't be a blasted fool. You're a sick man.'

'Sick, am I?' Mendoza waved the gun in the direction of the man on the floor. 'But I can still shoot. Tried to drive me mad. But a madman can shoot and get away with it. It's your turn to die . . . '

Glaring, immovable, Charles Solby whispered, 'He ought to be dead. How did he get out?'

Mendoza laughed. '*He's* got me out, my old friend, Joe Trayne. So you and he can die together, and no one any the wiser. You shouldn't try and kill me. I'm too smart for you. Mendoza always comes out on top. Bristling with ideas and the weapons to carry them out, that's the kind of man I am. You didn't find this one, did you?' He waved the revolver again, and Joe edged sideways along the table. Another half yard and he would be within jumping distance. 'Any more than you found the note Lysbeth put in her shoe. Lousy amateurs. You were a match for her and Carlo and Dight, but not for me. You got Dight, didn't you?'

'I got Dight,' Charles Solby said hoarsely. 'And I'm going to get you.'

On a wave of desperate energy, he rose to his feet and sprang forward. Mendoza fired twice. There came a strange, choking sound from his victim, before he fell to the ground and lay still. Joe, who had moved a couple of seconds too late, reached Mendoza's side and wrested the weapon from him. Swearing, Mendoza struggled for a moment, clutching a hand to his heart, and leaned against the wall, his face grey. He muttered, 'Not me . . . they couldn't kill me . . . ' Slowly his outspread hands slithered down the wall, as his knees gave way, bringing his heavy body to the floor. He gave Joe one last hostile look, and then crumpled up, face downwards. Joe turned him over, put a hand over his heart, and left him to inspect Charles Solby, beneath whose body blood was beginning to ooze. Joe straightened up, wiping his hands on his handkerchief. Two dead men, and a houseboat the neighbourhood of which he did not even know.

He sat down on the nearest chair and lighted one of his own cigarettes. He felt very tired.

Chapter XVII

The distant sound of a motor-boat approaching roused Joe from the state of lethargy into which he had fallen. His mind had gone back, and was trying to figure out what had happened to Johnny. Jerked back to the present, he looked about him, frowning. The room was in no state to receive visitors. He rose, walked across to Mendoza and heaved him head first across one shoulder. Staggering, he made his way out and into the bedroom, where he dropped his burden upon the bed and straightened up, sweating all over. In life, Mendoza had been weighty enough. In death he was formidable. Turning the lamp low, Joe went out, closed and locked the door, and put the key in his pocket. The engine of the motor-boat was slowing down as it came nearer, and there was not very much time.

Returning to the living-room, he lifted the body of Charles Solby, an easier weight, and carried it across to deposit it within the curtained alcove. It was necessary to re-arrange the curtains a little, to cover the feet. Then he sponged all obvious marks from his suit, and placed a rug over the bloodstained floor. Charles Solby's cigarette ends he collected and tucked away in one of his pockets, together with Mendoza's gun.

He paused, listening. The engine had stopped. There followed a few minutes' silence, and then the house rocked as someone came aboard outside the kitchen entrance. Without haste, Joe procured a clean glass from the sideboard, poured himself a measure of brandy, and drank it. He heard someone enter the kitchen. He refilled his glass and sipped appreciatively, enjoying the flavour of it, and the consoling warmth as it slipped down.

Decided footsteps approached along the passage. He had left the living-room door half open, and raised his head as it was flung wide. Eric Sanderson stood there, clad in a long black ulster, beneath which showed corduroy breeches, tucked into gumboots. He, too, looked tired, and showed every evidence of surprise at sight of Joe.

'I might have known,' he said, somewhat bitterly. 'I thought I told you to keep out of this?'

Joe smiled. 'So you did. You even warned me I might come to a violent end. I may do yet, but I'm not complaining. It'll be worth it for one last talk with you, Mr Bernard Solby.'

Sanderson thrust his hands deep into his pockets and inclined his head to one side.

'You're delirious,' he said. 'Has someone been knocking you about again?'

'Just a little.' Joe did not move, but his eyes were watchful. 'This time they knocked some sense into me. That picture in Mendoza's attic, the one you ripped to ribbons . . . it was only half finished and a copy at that, but it was a pretty good likeness. What was the original called, "Self Portrait by Bernard Solby?"'

'I'm sorry . . . ' the other began, but Joe went on quickly, 'Don't apologize. You have my whole-hearted admiration, stringing me along the way you did. But it wasn't quite fair. You've aged a lot in ten years. You'll be about thirty-five now, but anyone might take you for nearer fifty. Sit down and have a glass of your own brandy. It's pretty good.' He paused, as the houseboat moved again. They heard someone fumbling at the back entrance. Joe said casually, 'That'll be your brother, Charles, won't it? I believe he's well in this with you. Or are you expecting someone else?'

His companion did not reply, being engaged in lighting a cigarette. There came a swift patter of footsteps along the passage, and upon the threshold stood Melda Linklater, her black evening dress and cloak mudstained and torn in places, her hair dishevelled. Her glance passed over Joe and came to rest upon the man standing just inside the room. He returned her look, standing frozenly, the lighted cigarette in his hand forgotten.

Solby!' she said, reaching out her hands toward him in a pathetic gesture. She swayed, and automatically both men moved to assist her to the nearest armchair. 'No, no, I'm all right, thank you,' she protested, as Joe plied her with brandy. 'It's nothing . . . ' Her voice trailed away and she covered her eyes with one hand.

Above her bent head the two men exchanged a measuring glance. Joe shrugged his shoulders and moved away to sit down on the other side of the table. Bernard Solby, painter, supposed suicide, the man whose body they had never found, continued to stand, staring down at her, brooding, mechanically drawing on his cigarette. He said at last, patting her shoulder, 'Sorry, little one. I should have been more careful.'

He picked up the brandy bottle, sat down on the edge of a chair from which position he could see them both, and drank deeply. 'Thanks for leaving me some,' he remarked, replacing the bottle not far from his elbow. 'It's a wonder you're still sober.' Joe lit a cigarette and remained silent, as he went on, 'Trayne, you're all kinds of a fool. And Melda, you're not being your old tactful self. How the devil did you find me here?'

She surveyed him gravely, her hands clasped in her lap. She said, 'I recognized your voice, when you telephoned Joe's place this evening.'

He frowned. 'I was afraid you might. I knew you immediately.' He shot a glance full of hostility in Joe's direction. 'What then?'

'I drove over to your address in Handel Street. It was on the slip of paper Joe gave me to telephone you the first time, when I left a message for you to ring him back. It all seemed impossible, and you said your name was Sanderson, but I'd had a feeling for some time . . . anyway, I had to be sure. I'd just pulled up on the other side of the road when you came out. It was dark, and I could not see you very well, but it looked like you . . . your walk . . . everything.' Her eyes had a strange brightness, and she spoke as if recounting a dream. 'You drove away in a car and I followed you to Cleeve Rise. You parked the car in a side turning and went into a house opposite Mendoza's. You came out again with another man. I was standing in a doorway and I saw you clearly, but not the other one . . .'

'That was Charlie,' Solby said. 'My brother. You never met him, did you? He's a grand fellow, the grandest fellow in the world. You don't know what he's done for me. I owe him my life, and more.' He drank again, both hands clasped about the bottle as if it were precious to him. 'He'll be here presently. Can't think what's happened to him. He only went to put the car away, and it's not far to the garage, just up the towing path.'

'Hit the bottle and passed out?' Joe suggested, with studied carelessness.

'He doesn't drink. I'm the drinker of the family.' He finished the remainder of the brandy, pushed back his chair, and walked across to the sideboard to procure another. Melda glanced quickly at Joe, her eyes tear-filled. He gave her a reassuring smile, while keeping his attention on Solby. The latter returned, opened the fresh bottle and sat down again. 'Want any?' he asked, looking from one to the other of them. Melda shook her head. Joe said, pushing his glass across, 'Thanks. I feel you owe me a few drinks.'

'Perhaps I do. And that's not all I owe you. But I'll be paying you back some time, don't worry.' He filled Joe's glass, and tilted the bottle to his lips. 'Can't be bothered with a glass when I'm being myself. And God! . . . what a relief that is! Charlie doesn't mind. He's a great fellow. A genius. He'd have made his name if he hadn't spent the last ten years looking after me. And what a neat sense of humour. It was his idea, taking a room opposite Mendoza's place. He called himself Green, I don't quite know why. Something to do with the green car, association of ideas, I expect. Not that it mattered. All we needed was somewhere we could keep an eye on Mendoza, and no questions asked. We did, too. He never made a move we didn't know about, nothing important, anyway.' He paused, staring into space with a curiously fixed expression.

Melda leaned her elbows on the table, her chin in one hand. She said softly, 'But *why*, Solby? If your brother saved your life, why did you and he pretend you were dead all these years? Even I thought you were dead. They drove me nearly mad with questions about you, and I wouldn't tell them anything, because I thought you were dead. And Mendoza . . . I know he's been faking your pictures, but you could have prevented that.'

Solby came to life suddenly, crashing one fist upon the table, his face flushed, his eyes wide and fanatical. He shouted, 'I'll tell you why. Mendoza murdered me. As surely as I live and breathe now, he murdered me ten years ago, shot me full of morphine, and with the help of that little fiend Dight, nailed me into a box and buried me. He may have thought I was dead at the time, but knowing Mendoza, I don't think he'd have cared much either way. As far as he was concerned, I was dead, finished, written off. Melda . . . ' He leaned forward and his voice dropped almost to a whisper. 'Do you remember that evening when I was supposed to meet you in Paris? You were returning from the country . . . But I didn't meet you, did I? Because I met Mendoza earlier, and I never remembered any more until I came to and found that I was *buried alive*. I, who used to shudder at the thought of being buried after death.' Beads of sweat stood out on his forehead and his face was contorted with emotion. 'It was what Charlie called one of my phobias. You remember, Melda? You used to sympathize with me, humour me, when life seemed unbearable, and I was afraid to die in case someone buried me. And then . . . *that*. You can guess what I went through, a little?'

She reached out a hand and touched his arm. 'Don't think about it,' she said.

'Think about it?' He laughed on a hysterical note. 'I dream about it. I dreamed of it for years . . . nightmare, horrible. I used to wake up sweating and crying out for help. Charlie was with me. He was always there. It was he who rescued me. He never trusted Mendoza. But he was only just in time. He got me out and away, but he had to work like ten men to bring me back to life. He had a nursing home in Provence. He took me there under another name. I was out of my mind . . . a gibbering idiot. He worked on me, got me back to health and strength. I still painted . . . the products of a wandering mind . . . coffins, I could paint nothing but coffins, with hideous backgrounds. I kept them but I wouldn't dare show them even to you. They say I'm a genius, don't they? And a genius is usually a little mad. But you don't want to overdo it. I'm better now, but not well enough to paint. That's why I say Mendoza murdered me, the only part of me that was any good.'

'Why didn't your brother go to the police?' Joe asked. 'They usually take a serious view of attempted murder. In this country, at any rate.'

Solby eyed him stonily. 'You take a pretty close interest in my affairs, don't you?' he said, and helped himself to another drink. Then he sat silent, his head bent, as if listening for something.

Joe drank his brandy, and lit a cigarette. Melda said, 'Me, too, please,' and he pushed the case across to her. Solby raised his head and watched Joe supply her with a light. His eyes were narrowed and thoughtful. Melda continued, 'I always thought Mendoza was crooked, from the little I saw of him. But murder? I can't understand why he should go as far as that. You were in debt to him, I know, but how would it help, killing you?'

Solby sighed. 'You're still very young. Ten years older, ten years more experienced, a great artist, but still very young. Because we meant a lot to each other, you wouldn't expect me to do anything crooked, would you? But even a genius has to have money, and I needed plenty. Debts? I was sick of them. I was sick of taking money from my brother, my friends, anyone who would lend it to me. Mendoza and his kind I didn't care about. He could whistle for his, for all I bothered. But it was he who showed me how I could make money, in the days when I couldn't sell a picture for the price of a meal. He was always a faker, you know. And with organization and my painting ability . . . well, I once told you it was easy, didn't I? I knew, because I'd done it. But it didn't work out so well. Mendoza paid me a little, a fraction of what he was making. I didn't mind that so much, because I was only doing tenth-rate stuff, nothing that I'd consider art. Then he wanted me to try my hand at faking pictures I knew and admired. We fell out very quickly over that . . . you know my temper. I suppose I scared him, and he thought I'd be better out of the way.' He paused, made further inroads upon the brandy, and burst out, 'For the love of God, don't look at me like that! I wouldn't have told you, I couldn't expect you to understand. But you asked for it, and there it is.'

She said, with concentrated feeling, 'I do understand. I think I could understand and forgive anything in someone I thought worth while. But you hadn't enough faith in me to give me the chance. If I'd known you were ill, I'd have come to you at once, helped you to start again. You could have trusted me . . . '

Solby laughed bitterly. 'What had I to offer you? A broken down painter, whose merits might not have been discovered yet if he hadn't disappeared so mysteriously. A drink addict, with a diseased mind. I get fits even now, when if I didn't drink . . . My health's not so bad, on the whole. Charlie and I were always tough as nails. Drink . . . dope . . . we've survived the lot so far. But I've aged terribly. My God! What else could anyone expect? My sight half gone . . . spectacles, my hair turned grey in a year . . . Not that it hasn't been useful.' He flashed a sardonic grin in Joe's direction. 'It's a wonder you recognized me, Melda.'

'I should always recognize you.'

'As woman to man, or one artist to another? The latter, I think. But either way, I wouldn't wish myself on a young and attractive woman, not any woman, let alone you.'

She leaned back, exhaling cigarette smoke toward the ceiling. Her face wore its remotest expression, composed and thoughtful.

'Yet you came into my room on Saturday night. It was you, wasn't it?'

'Yes, it was me. I wanted to see you close at hand, just once. Stupidly sentimental, but even the toughest of us have moments of weakness. I'd seen you at concerts, I'd watched you drive home, I even followed you a couple of times. I had a box at the Titanic Hall on Saturday afternoon. I heard you play . . . it was hell, in a

236

way, and yet I enjoyed it. I even imagined myself paying a surprise visit to your dressing room. But this one got there ahead of me.' He waved a hand towards Joe, and smiled with a touch of malice when he saw her flush faintly. 'But it didn't matter, I shouldn't have come to you, in any case. I'd have been afraid of upsetting you too much.'

'You did, that night,' she said. 'When I woke up, and you were standing there. I felt it was you, but when I put on the light and you'd gone, I thought it was just part of my dream.' She closed her eyes for a moment.

'I'm sorry.' Gently he took the end of the cigarette from her fingers and dropped it into the ashtray. 'I should have had more sense. It was just an impulse. My brother came with me into the empty house next door. Poor old Charlie. He didn't want me to go, but when I insisted, he would come with me. I didn't mean to wake you. But then you cried out in your sleep. I hadn't time to get through the window again so I made a dash for the door. I heard you telephoning Trayne. You picked a man of action, didn't you?' His smile was a mask, covering hidden emotions. 'A Squad car couldn't have arrived sooner. It didn't suit my plans to be found in your apartment, so I got out through the lounge and back along the verandah. Charlie was in an awful sweat. He doesn't trust me for long alone. I'd just dived back to the car, with Charlie hot on my trail, when up dashed your hero.'

Joe said, 'And I suppose you laughed like hell all the way home, thinking how you'd spent the evening with me, passing yourself off as a private detective?'

Solby shrugged his shoulders. 'I don't remember. I got drunk. I believe I 'phoned you a few times that night, but you weren't home. I only made your acquaintance in the first place out of curiosity. I wanted to find out just what your game was, you seemed to be everywhere at once, and without any reason, so far as I could see. Then I began to see a reason, which was a pity, because I rather liked you.'

'But you don't any more.'

'Shall we say, not as much as I did?'

Joe brought out his notecase, produced the photograph of Melda which he had originally found in his flat, and slid it across the table. 'Yours, I think,' he said.

Solby picked it up, glanced at it, and thrust it quickly away in his pocket. 'Where did you find that?' he asked.

'In my apartment. I don't know what you were looking for . . .'

'Nothing in particular. I was just curious about you, as I said.'

Melda looked searchingly from one to the other. 'What is behind all this, Solby?' she asked, her tone suddenly practical. 'Why did you come to England? To see Mendoza? Was that what you did tonight?'

With an obvious effort, for the effects of the brandy were beginning to tell, he swivelled his attention back to her. 'You saw me, didn't you?' he countered.

'Only for a moment. I didn't wait to see what you were going to do. I was afraid . . . Oh, I don't know *what* I was afraid of, but it all seemed so odd.'

'You thought I might be a little mad?'

'No . . . no, not that. If anyone was mad, I thought it must be me. But I wanted advice, and I knew Joe was interested one way or another. I drove back to his place, and Johnny was acting queerly. He said Joe was out, and then someone 'phoned and he said he'd gone to Mendoza's. I was afraid I'd miss him if I went back, so I sat in the car which I'd parked down by the side entrance and waited. I was still there when you, and your brother I suppose it was, backed your car into the passage and went off again. I followed you down here. It was all like a nightmare. I didn't know it was your brother, but I knew you'd been mixed up with Mendoza. I couldn't think what you might be doing . . . ' She was plainly agitated, turning from Solby to Joe and back again. 'I went back along the road until I found a telephone box and tried to ring Joe. I thought he might be home by then. But I couldn't get through. It took me ages to find this place again. Even now I don't know exactly where it is, or what you're both doing here.'

'I'm waiting for Charlie,' Solby said. 'I never make a move without him. And I'm in a particularly difficult position just now. Two against one, even though one of you is a woman who used to care for me. But women are hellish unpredictable, especially . . . '

'Suppose we send Melda home?' Joe interrupted. 'That'll leave just the two of us, and we can both wait for Charlie.'

Solby narrowed his eyes in suspicion. 'You're very sure of yourself, aren't you?'

'Certainly. One has to be sure of something in this life, and I usually start with myself.'

Solby said, 'No, it's not good enough. I'd like to keep Melda out of this, I've tried to all along. But I can't have her running off to the police . . . '

'I don't think she will. Or she'd have done so before, wouldn't she? In any case, she doesn't know anything to tell them.'

'She might get them curious. No, thanks. Melda stays here.'

'I say not,' Joe said.

Melda pushed back her chair and got to her feet, dispelling the moment of tension. She said coldly, 'Forgive me for interrupting your private conversation, but I'm not going until I know what brought you here. What is all this mystery, Solby? You're alive . . . you're almost well. Myself apart, why can't you take up a normal life again, forget Mendoza, have nothing more to do with him?'

Solby began to laugh, insanely. He went on for a very long time. Melda sat down again, gripping the arms of her chair. Recovering at last, he helped himself to another drink, and his flushed face settled into an expression of sheer venom.

'I'll never forget him,' he said. 'If he died three times, it would be too good for a rat like that. For years I dreamed of him dying slowly, horribly, as I nearly died. I didn't want love, help, sympathy. I wanted revenge. I decided I was going to do to Mendoza what he did to me. He and Dight. I came over here as Eric Sanderson. Eric was a friend of mine at one time, ran a detective agency in Paris. He died some years ago. It wasn't very difficult, identifying myself with him. We had plenty of money. Charles came with me, but as himself. He only took the name of Green this side. We ran Mendoza to earth, and then we found, among other things, that he was faking *my* pictures. That did it. We decided they'd all got to go, everyone in it with him. It was my idea, and a damned good one, delivering the bodies in a box. That way I figured Mendoza *would* die three times, in imagination. He was tough, it took a lot to frighten him, but we had him terrified in the end.'

He sat staring ahead of him again, apparently oblivious of his audience. Melda watched him, her eyes wide with an expression between horror and disbelief. He went on,

'We started with Carlo Betz, Mendoza's substitute for me. We got a lot of amusement out of that. We planned to send the body of Betz to his girl friend, Lysbeth, who was employed on the selling side of the business. So Charlie went to a sale to buy a box we'd seen, just right for the job. There was a girl there, bidding for it. He recognized her. She was staying with Lysbeth Ritchley. That appealed to Charlie's sense of humour. He let her outbid him, and then arranged to deliver it for her. She was only a kid, the kind who still believes in Santa Claus. He gave her a card from the carriers we'd been going to use. All we had to do then was to collect the box, run it down here, lock Betz into it, and leave him to die in his own time. We got two men with a horse and waggon to deliver it. They grumbled a bit at the weight, but we paid them pretty steeply, and Charlie went with them. He kept it safely locked until it was in the parlour, then he unlocked it and left a lovely surprise for friend Lysbeth. It was hard on the other one, but I expect she got over it. She was dopy enough not to know a corpse if she saw one, Charlie said.'

Joe rose quietly and went round to Melda's side of the table. 'You'd better go,' he said in her ear. 'I'll look after this.'

Her brows drawn together, she shook her head decisively. He sat down on the edge of the table, just behind her chair. Solby went on talking, taking no notice of them.

'Lysbeth was easy. We guessed they'd be at their wits' end to get rid of Carlo. They couldn't go to the police, without a lot of awkward investigations being made. Mendoza wouldn't like that. So he and Dight ran the body out of town. But not the box, and that suited us all right. We knew the other girl had moved out. We were keeping watch on the place that night and we saw her go. But we had her signature on a delivery note, and Charlie forged it on the letter we sent Lysbeth, making an appointment at Esher. It was the last appointment she ever kept. We got her, and we got back the box they'd left in the garage. As Charlie said, why bother to find another? We left her car for anyone to find, and when she'd had time to die, we took her to Mendoza's place. We made sure he and Dight weren't there. We sent them a phoney telephone message that kept them out half the night and part of the next day.

'I'll give the swine this much, though. They'd got nerve. We saw them take that box away on a trailer. We followed, to the house

Dight had rented at Weybridge, where they buried it. Mendoza left him, to keep an eye on things, I suppose, but he wasn't sharp enough. We got the box back again and finished off Dight into the bargain. A pity he had to die so quickly, but there wasn't a lot of time. We had to dump Lysbeth in the river, for the same reason. She'd served her purpose, and we couldn't handle too much at once. For one thing, we had to handle *you*.'

He raised his head and looked at Joe. The latter, thrusting his hands into his pockets, felt his fingers encounter Mendoza's gun. He returned Solby's stare, toying with the idea of removing Melda from harm's way forcibly, if necessary. But that would give Solby the opportunity he needed. Biding his time, he said, 'So you put a call through to me, in the name of Dight, and left his body at my place while Johnny and I went down to Weybridge on a wild goose chase.'

Solby nodded, and broke again into convulsive laughter, until tears came to his eyes. Removing his spectacles to wipe them away, he said, 'Charlie pinched a hearse! He's not lacking in nerve, either. We've laughed over that since, it all went so smoothly. You made it smoother still by leaving the back door unlocked. We had no trouble there, but I left Charlie to finish the job as I'd other things to do. He told me what a close shave he had, nearly running into you on the road.'

Melda turned to glance at Joe. He queried, 'According to your plans, shouldn't I be dead by now?'

Solby smiled, in the slow way he had. 'Not necessarily. Dropping Dight in on you was a kind of joke. Thought it might shake you up a bit, teach you to mind your own business. You'd been getting in our way a little too much. Even so, I wasn't very keen on finishing you altogether. If you'd taken the hint in the first place . . . but I can see now I should have listened to Charlie. He said you wouldn't give up until you were dead, and he usually knows what he's talking

242

about. Anyway, there it was. I couldn't be bothered with you. I wanted Mendoza.'

Melda asked, in a strained voice, 'Is he dead, too?'

'I shouldn't think so . . . yet.' Wholly absorbed now, impervious to her agitation, Solby got up and began to pace about the room. Joe, keeping a wary eye upon him, observed that his gait was far from steady.

'He's not here?' Melda persisted.

'Of course he's here. Why not here? The box is here, too. Want to see it?' He surveyed them with a hint of cunning.

'Nonsense,' Joe put in. 'It was at my flat, and Johnny was there. I told him to get the police.'

Solby laughed. 'You told him to get the police,' he echoed. 'And what do you think I was doing? Sitting down and letting you mess up my plans for Mendoza? You ought to know better than that . . . ' He paused. He was, Joe thought, probably trying to work out whether he did know better than that, deciding against it, deciding to play for time, for he went on, 'I'll tell you what I was doing. Charlie and I broke into Mendoza's house the back way. He got through a ventilator, being a bit on the thin side, and let me in. We locked the door again so we wouldn't be disturbed. And then . . . we went after Mendoza. He was in his office, talking on the telephone, talking to you. We were outside the door and heard him, just before we went in. It did me good to see his face. If ever a man was scared . . . Can you picture it? He thought I'd been dead and mouldering in my grave for years. He'd been kidding himself that it was all coincidence, his pals popping off like they did. And suddenly, there I was. He put up a fight for it, but Charlie's got a quick way with him. He's pretty good over the psychological angle, too. He reckoned you'd have heard enough over the 'phone, Trayne, to bring you along like a shot. But to make sure, he got

243

through to your place, and your young friend was good enough to say he was alone.'

Joe said, with dangerous affability, 'You weren't so far gone as to kill Johnny, I hope?'

'Nothing of the kind. I've no quarrel with him. He wouldn't have been in this if it weren't for you. But I had to make certain he didn't do anything hasty, like calling in the police, and I wanted to be sure of you. So I 'phoned again, and told him I was Scotland Yard. I did it rather well, very upstage. I asked for you, and he told me to try Mendoza's place. Couldn't have been better. I said I'd send a couple of men round, and that was that. I did, too. Me and Charlie, after you'd fallen head on into our hands. You really asked for that, you know. Careering about the place in such a state . . .'

Suppressing a string of ungentlemanly phrases, Joe said, 'Are you going to tell me what happened to Johnny?'

'Nothing much.' Solby was quick to reassure him. 'We simply knocked him out and left him with Dight for company. We needed that box, empty, just once again.'

'For what?' Melda whispered.

'For Mendoza, and this one.' He jerked his hand in Joe's direction. 'We'd decided, by then, that he'd got to go. That bothers you, doesn't it?'

'Not particularly.' She appeared calm, choosing her words with care. 'Only I'd rather you didn't kill anyone else, Solby. That's what worries me.'

'Because you think I'm mad.' He laughed. 'That's very funny. I *know* I'm mad, at times, and it doesn't worry me. I can see it in your eyes, trying to humour me, trying to think of a way out. But there isn't any way out, because you haven't a plan. I have. I know what I'm going to do. I went up the river just now to find a nice quiet spot where our box can go to its final resting place. Mendoza's in it now. We didn't give him long to think things over, but he's had plenty of time since. And Charlie says it'll take another one comfortably. We like our guests to be comfortable. He made your friend Joe very comfortable in our best bedroom. But something went wrong. I must ask Charlie about that. He'll be annoyed.'

He became motionless, standing with his hands clasped behind him, staring down at the rug near his feet. Traces of blood were beginning to show through, blood from the floor underneath. He kicked the rug to one side, knelt down, ran his hand over it, and looked up at Joe, his lips drawing back from his teeth. Joe was mechanically lighting a cigarette. Replacing the case in his pocket, he said, with forced casualness, 'Now what's the matter?'

'I don't like blood,' Solby said quietly, 'when I can't account for it.' He glanced about the room, and his eyes focused upon the alcove, the disarrangement of the curtains. He walked across, pulled them back, and stared down upon the hunched-up body of his brother. Turning, he said, 'For that alone, I'd kill you, Joe Trayne.'

'I don't think you will.' Joe was on his feet, Mendoza's gun in his right hand. 'I'm not in the mood to die.' But something had happened to his vision. Solby looked distorted, larger than life size. Sounds about him had become intensified, his right hand was inclined to tremble. In the other he held the lighted cigarette, from which, he now noticed, came a curious aroma. He recalled lighting it, mechanically taking it from the case he had brought from his pocket. But his own case lay on the table where he had left it. This was one of Charles Solby's cigarettes from the case he had confiscated. He let it drop from his fingers, stamped it out, made an effort to steady himself.

He heard Melda say, 'Joe! You can't do it.' Solby gave vent to a prolonged burst of laughter. His right hand, groping, seized upon the oil lamp and flung it straight across the intervening space between them. It caught Joe's arm, sending the gun flying. Shattered glass tinkled, flames leaped up, there was a pungent smell of kerosene. Joe moved, but not with his usual precision. Solby was across the room upon the instant and out of the door, which he slammed and locked behind him. He shouted, 'Burn and be damned to you!' as his stumbling footsteps receded along the passage.

Joe turned from the locked door, to see Melda trying to beat out the flames with her velvet cloak. She dropped the cloak as he dragged her back, and the fire caught at it greedily and proceeded to its destruction.

'That's finished that,' he said. 'And you'll finish yourself, if you don't watch out.' Helped by the oil, the flames were spreading rapidly. He made a serious assault upon them with the rug, but blinding smoke caught at his throat, choking him. All the windows were closed. He tried to open one on the side of the house nearest the river bank, but the lock was rusty, and refused to budge. He picked up a lamp and smashed the glass to smithereens. 'We'd better get out this way,' he said to Melda, who had followed, and was gratefully breathing the incoming air. 'This place'll go up like matchwood.'

Her hand was at her heart, as if it pained her. 'But Mendoza . . . ' she said. 'And Solby?'

'Mendoza's dead. I got him out of the box, but after he'd shot Charles Solby, he collapsed and died.' He was removing jagged pieces of glass, throwing them over his shoulder. The heat was now intense, and even with ventilation, the smoke caused them to cough. 'As for Solby, he's probably taken to the only boat. Can you swim?'

'Not very well.' She leaned against the wall, putting a hand to her smarting eyes.

'I'll take care of that, if necessary. But the water's shallow this side, I wouldn't be surprised.' The windows were low, with narrow ledges. On the other side was a wooden structure, about a foot in width, running the length of the house. Just below, the water gleamed with the reflection of the fire. He lifted Melda on to the window ledge. 'All right?' he queried. 'Not going to faint or anything?'

'No. Are you?'

He grinned, as he put a hand under her elbow and helped her through the aperture. 'If you can't be polite, be careful,' he said. But his injunction was too late. As he climbed on to the window ledge and was about to follow, the wooden structure on the other side, old and rotten in places, gave way, and she disappeared with a splash into the river. He squeezed through, and eased himself into the murky depths, to find that the water was barely waist high. But Melda was nowhere to be seen.

Feet crunching on the river bed, he plunged below, felt about frantically, found her and brought her to the surface. Her face had the pallor of unconsciousness, and blood flowed from a wound where she had struck her forehead. Her long evening dress heavy with water, his own clothes clinging wetly on him, he began to carry her toward the dock.

Turning his head, he saw Bernard Solby, in the room where he had left Mendoza, standing with an oil lamp poised in one hand. Only for a moment, before he hurled it to the ground, and smoke and flames obscured him from view. His mad laughter echoed eerily as Joe waded on. Lights had sprung up on the river bank immediately opposite, and people were moving about there, voices shouting. A group of three, a woman and two men, ran to assist him as he came up out of the water.

The woman said, 'Is she hurt? You'd better bring her into my house, just at the top there. We saw the fire ... my husband 'phoned for the Brigade, they'll be along in a minute. Shall I get a doctor?'

'Thanks,' Joe said. 'Which way?'

She went ahead to show him, and he followed, his arms feeling numb, his head curiously light. They went into a brightly lighted house on the other side of the towing path. He heard the sound of a fire engine as he laid Melda upon a settee in the living-room. The woman who had accompanied him brought sal volatile and other restoratives, while telling Joe, in detail, her exact emotions on seeing the flames, how she had aroused her husband, and her reaction to fires in general.

Melda stirred, opened her eyes, and murmured, 'Solby?'

Forcing a smile, Joe said, 'I'm going to see. You rest. You'll be all right.'

'You ought to rest yourself,' the woman protested, following him to the front door. 'You look done in.'

'I nearly was,' Joe said. 'Thanks for looking after her. I'll be back in a minute.'

Outside was a scene of great activity, the sky lit with a red glare, the trees dark against it, figures moving, more voices, three cars drawn up on the towing path. The fire had gained ascendancy, helped by a stiff breeze, and the play of water from the firemen's apparatus made little headway. Joe, moving at a run, was pulled up by a figure that blocked his path. Johnny's voice said, 'God help us! So they didn't get you?'

'Nor you.' Relieved, Joe clapped him on the shoulder. 'I was worried. What happened after they'd snatched that box?' He resumed his stride toward the river bank.

Stumbling along beside him, Johnny said, 'I came to and found myself with that horrible little Dight, and the coppers pounding on the front door. It really was them that time. I got a phoney call just after you left, supposed to be Scotland Yard, but I got fed up waiting for them. So I sent through an SOS on my own account and yelled "Murder!" like you said . . . well, something like you said. They were coming round in any case, so they told me. They knew a whole lot about these rum goings on, and they've been keeping their peepers on this place . . . Just look at it now! Burns like paper.'

'What about Wendy?' Joe asked, coming to a standstill as they reached a high ridge on the bank commanding a view right across the river.

'Oh, she's all right. She turned up while the police were there . . . they're looking after her. You know what she did?'

'Don't tell me,' Joe said. 'I can guess. She got on the wrong train.'

'You've got second sight. That's just what she did, found herself right off the map somewhere.' Shading his eyes with one hand, he added, 'They'll never save that thing now. There's no one on it, is there?'

'Two dead bodies. And possibly a third, by this time.'

'I don't like the sound of that.' Johnny shivered, and glanced over his shoulder to where a group of people stood watching the activities of police and fire brigade. 'There's a super copper from the Yard wants to see you. He's asking questions. I just dodged away from him to give you the tip, in case you might be some-where about. You want to be careful what you say and how you say it. He's got a lot of chin and not much sense of humour.'

'I'll try,' Joe said wearily. 'But I'm beginning to think I'm not the careful type.'

Johnny clutched his arm. 'God! Look at that!' he exclaimed in an awestricken whisper. Amid the flames, a figure had emerged, standing on the flat roof of the crumbling houseboat. It remained there for a moment, tall and gaunt, silhouetted against the light. Then the whole structure gave way, sending broken planks and burning embers hissing into the surrounding water. An involuntary groan came from the spectators as the figure disappeared among the debris.

'And that,' Joe observed, pointing. The wreckage had begun to disintegrate, the glare to subside, and the Death Box, half burned, half submerged, was floating with the stream.